Marheh of the Silberay, Book 2.

Apprentice Still

By

Rosalind Kentwell

L'Optimisme

Melbourne

ISBN 978-0-9874868-2-0:

DEDICATION

Specially for Mum and Dad

.

ACKNOWLEDGMENTS

Thanks as always to my writing friends, Elwin, Elenor and Noni.
Helen Bulley Barnes of Varuna provided new insights into the techniques
of writing.
Also special thanks to Sally and Dorothy for proof reading help.

.

Day Bringer

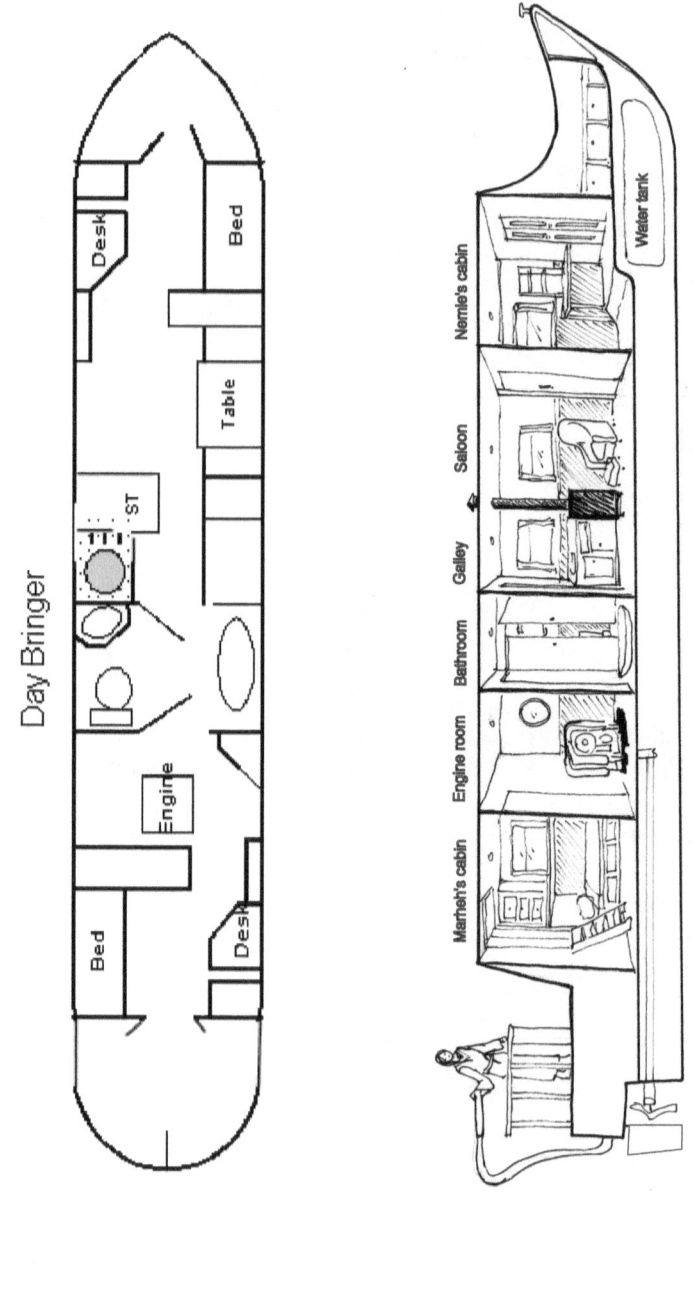

Top view labels: Desk, Bed, Table, ST, Engine, Bed, Desk

Side view labels: Marnie's cabin, Engine room, Bathroom, Galley, Saloon, Nemie's cabin, Water tank

"Rules and regulations! If we were really pursuing the aims we believe in would we need them? It seems the answer is yes."

Sila's Journal: the early years

Chapter One

"Marheh Carron, we find you guilty of using your mental ability for the purpose of exploitation."

There was a small gasp from somewhere in the room and Marheh's face drained of colour.

"Stand while sentence is pronounced."

Obediently she stood, straight and still. Only Nemle, her mentor, knew her well enough to recognise the tension in her clenched hands.

"The proscribed penalty is that you be grounded and *Day Bringer* lifted out of the water for ten years."

Marheh stared down the emptiness of ten years imprisoned on land.

"However, in view of your youth, I am authorised to offer you the choice of a beating and a two year extension of your apprenticeship."

Silence.

She stood motionless, determined to reveal nothing, but she dared not meet Nemle's anxious gaze. Those nearest saw her close her eyes for a moment, saw her swallow with difficulty. Everyone in the room heard her clear soft voice when she said "I choose to be beaten."

There was an exhalation, as if the room had been holding its breath.

"Very well."

The voice paused. A page was turned in a large book.

"Sentence will be carried out in this room on Tuesday next at 10.00 am."

The owner of the voice left the room and a babble of sound rose from the spectators, but Marheh still stood motionless as if any action would break her fragile control. At last Nemle went to her, took her by the hand and led her away to *Day Bringer*.

The Harbour was looking particularly beautiful in the spring sunshine. Light played on the water and the shining brass of the Silberay boats gathered there. The trees that bordered the moorings were veiled in new green. A gentle breeze touched the water, the trees and Marheh herself, but she was isolated from it all, encased in a hard shell that prevented feeling.

It was not until they reached the haven of *Day Bringer*'s cosy saloon that her control broke and she began to shake so much that it seemed easier to drop to the floor than force her legs to carry her further. Nemle crouched beside her holding her in her arms while she sobbed.

At last, when her trembling had ceased she looked at Nemle.

"I won't let them force me from the water road, no matter what it costs."

Nemle's arms tightened around her.

"But you don't have to do it this way. Accept the grounding. That will give us time to find the truth. Tuesday is only three days away."

"And if we don't find out, if the sentence is not overturned? Ten years could be the rest of your life and if we are off the water we will never learn who hates me so much."

Nemle closed her eyes, opened them again. There was nothing to say. Marheh sighed and snuggled into her arms.

"Hold me a bit longer Mama Nemle," she whispered. "Then I'll be brave."

Nemle held her and kissed her and helped her to wash her tear-stained face so that when a businesslike rap on the roof demanded entrance she was in control of herself again. Their visitor was the man who would carry out her sentence. He was matter-of-fact, even cheerful, like a doctor with a pleasant bedside manner. He carried folded garments of white cotton and a small piece of blue rubber, half moon shaped. He put the things on the table and waited for Nemle and Marheh to sit.

"You will present yourself at 9.45 wearing these clothes only. They fasten at the back," he said. "You may have this to bite on."

Marheh looked at the blue rubber in horrified fascination.

"Nemle will prepare you by fastening your wrists and ankles to the frame that will be constructed. She will then uncover you. You will receive fifty strokes of the cane in the space of an hour."

Marheh shivered and Nemle heard a tiny whimper from deep in her throat.

"Now you need to come outside so I can measure you for the frame."

Obediently Marheh followed him out to the back deck. She stood on tiptoe with her arms stretched above her head when instructed. She waited while he made this measurement and that. Nemle stood on the back step watching with anxious eyes. When he was done he rolled up his tape measure and nodded to her.

"I'll see you on Tuesday," he said. Then, as he was stepping off the deck he turned back to add. "Best if you don't have breakfast and be sure to empty your bowels and bladder."

Nemle thought Marheh would faint she became so white. She sprang up the steps and supported her into the back cabin, held her through spasms of uncontrollable shaking. She was still trembling when they felt *Day Bringer* move as someone heavy came on board. Nemle looked up angrily, afraid of some new refinement of mental torment, but relaxed when she realised it was Marheh's Uncle Jik. He came down the steps and took in the scene in the cabin.

"Wrap her in a blanket and I'll carry her through to the saloon," he said. "I saw that pantomime on the back deck."

Hastily Nemle pulled a blanket from Marheh's bunk and wrapped it around her. Jik gathered her in his arms and carried her into the saloon as if she was a baby. He put her onto Nemle's lap in the big chair. Nemle cuddled her until she was calm while Jik perched beside them on the footstool.

"I'm sorry," she said at last. "I didn't know … how it would be."

Nemle still held her, but now she tried to get up.

"I'm too heavy for you Nemle," she said.

"You stay here daughter, just let me hold you."

Jik reached out to take one of her hands in his. Marheh held it tightly.

"I didn't do what they said, Jik, truly."

"I know you didn't."

"You won't tell them at home, will you?"

He shook his head. "Not that they would doubt you, but it would hurt them."

Marheh nodded. "That's what I thought."

"Marheh," Jik said. "You know there will be people watching don't you?"

"I guessed there might," she said, cuddling in to Nemle again.

"Will it make it better or worse if your Uncle Jik who loves you is there?"

Marheh clutched his hands.

"Oh, better. I can be brave for you and Nemle."

You are the old, our wisdom our strength,
As you pass let our love wrap you well
Let it nourish and warm as you journey ahead
To enrich all the stories we tell.
Songs of the Silberay

Chapter Two

Marheh had known she had enemies. She and Nemle had been involved in a confrontation with Yareblis in the first months of her apprenticeship. Now it seemed there was an enemy within the Silberay. It hurt almost more than the prospect ahead of her.

"My own people," she said, looking at Nemle with tragic eyes. "Who I've chosen to spend my life with."

Nemle held her.

"I feel as if I've been blind," she said

She put Marheh away from her and moved impatiently around the saloon.

"This is about power, but the Silberay have never been about power. How could things change so much when I wasn't looking?"

Marheh stood at the window. The Harbour looked as it always did on a fine spring afternoon.

"It's like a stick that gets stuck in the water," she said, trying to work it out. "There it is and the water flows around it. If you notice it at all it's to enjoy the pattern it makes. Then another stick comes and gets trapped against the first. Then there's another and another and before you know it the water is breaking the banks trying to get past."

She turned back to Nemle.

"No one cares about one stick," she said.

The first inkling that Marheh had become a target should have been at the Gathering two years ago, Nemle thought, but neither of them had realised that the trouble then was anything more than the passion and curiosity of youth rubbing against caution and conservatism.

Like all whose vocation was to be Silberay, Marheh made her life choice at twenty. She became apprenticed to seventy year old Nemle, to live with her on the boat *Day Bringer* and travel the water road learning from her and serving her. Nemle had quickly discovered that Marheh was exceptionally talented at the Silberay disciplines of mind and soul and it became an imperative for her to teach Marheh how to control and develop her natural ability. Now, although she hesitated to say so, she could not help wondering whether someone wanted to stop Marheh from reaching her full potential.

Gatherings were held only every second year, in the first weeks of spring, and were a time of discussion and reflection, of sharing difficulties and joys and, for the apprentices, an opportunity for formal instruction.

Two years ago was Marheh's third Gathering. She was twenty-four, idealistic, passionate, adventurous, inclined to be arrogant and impulsive. It had been a hard winter and the journey to Silberay Harbour and the Gathering had been challenging, but as the boats began to converge, conquering the bitter weather became a source of pride. Marheh had wanted to push on in all weathers hoping for a good mooring at the harbour, hoping to be amongst the first to arrive. Nemle had laughed and let her have her way only making sure there was a hot drink and a warm fire when she came in from the tiller, blue and shivering.

"You know there is room for us all at the harbour," Nemle teased as Marheh's teeth chattered against the mug she held with both hands. "You don't actually need to do this."

"Yes I do." Marheh was determined. "We are going to get a mooring in the old part, where it's quiet, but not too far from the meeting room."

Nemle shook her head and watched to see that Marheh's competitive spirit did not lead her to inconsiderate behaviour, but she kept her speed legal, slowed when passing moored boats and achieved her aim by early rising and stamina.

The old part of the harbour was the nicest, the trees were established, the jetties were wider and seemed more stable and by arriving early they not only got a good place, but an extra day to enjoy it. Marheh was out with the brass polish first thing, making sure that *Day Bringer* was at her very best. As they sat together over lunch Nemle ventured a word of advice.

"This is a Gathering, not a competition," she said carefully. "We're not putting on a special effort to be on show."

Marheh flushed.

"But *Day Bringer* has to look her best," she protested.

"Of course she does, but she has to look her best every day and I don't often see you quite so enthusiastic with the brass cloth."

Marheh made a face acknowledging the truth of Nemle's words.

"But I can do it today, can't I?"

Later, as more boats arrived, Marheh went striding around the harbour looking for her own particular friends, the two apprentices who made their choice the same time as she did, her Uncle Jik on *Autumn Wind* and *Storm Cloud* where Kel and Sul lived. Nemle was happy to stay by the fire for the most part, but she did make her way to the main meeting room early in the day to see what had been planned for the Gathering and consider what contribution she might make. There were Mentor discussions scheduled that she should attend although she was always reticent about her experiences. She had never confessed that she had burned her copy of *Guidelines for Mentoring the Young Apprentice* within the first six months of trying to apply its precepts to her relationship with Marheh.

Marheh came back to help prepare the evening meal full of enthusiasm and news.

"Jik's just arrived. He's been boating all day so I invited him to come for supper. That's alright isn't it? I got an extra chop from the store."

She grinned.

"He sent you commiserations and hoped you'd been giving me plenty of spankings."

Nemle smiled at her.

"And Sul?" she asked.

Marheh shook her head.

"Not here yet, but Tippa said they passed them moored up a couple of days ago, so they must be on their way."

Nemle moved to set the table as Marheh peeled potatoes and carrots.

"The big welcome breakfast is tomorrow morning so they'll want to be here for that."

Marheh nodded.

"And then classes for us in the afternoon and singing and stories by the fire after supper."

There was a knock on the roof and *Day Bringer* rocked gently as someone stepped on board. Nemle called a welcome and Jik made his way through to the saloon. He was a big man and seemed to fill the narrow space, his head scarcely an inch from the ceiling.

"I've left my coat in the engine room," he said, coming closer to the fire. "This is good of you."

"You're very welcome," Nemle said. "I remember well what it is like to feel too tired to cook after a day at the tiller."

She indicated the one big armchair by the fire.

"Sit down. Marheh's got dinner under control, but it will be twenty minutes or so. Can I get you some sperit?"

He subsided gratefully into the chair and the saloon suddenly seemed less crowded. Marheh grinned at him from the galley.

"You'll never be able to have an apprentice," she said. "There won't be enough room for two of you on *Autumn Wind.*"

"I'll have to find a little scrawny one and starve him," Jik said.

He stretched lazily and reached for the mug of sperit Nemle had made him.

"This is good of you," he said again.

He rested the mug on the arm of the chair and closed his eyes. A few minutes later Nemle lifted the mug to safety on the bench.

When the meal was ready Nemle woke him gently and they squeezed around the small table, Marheh balancing on a folding stool, while the others used the fixed seating.

"So what's the news?" he asked when the first hunger was sated.

Marheh ran through what she had discovered so far.

"*Sunrise* needs a whole new floor, she got flooded in a lock. Tippa said it was touch and go whether she would sink. Tomorrow my classes start and we're going to take down an engine." Her eyes sparkled at the prospect. "*Storm Cloud* still hasn't arrived. I hope they're alright. Oh and there's a new tutor for Silberay law. His name is Hud. Do you know him?" She paused and looked from Nemle to Jik.

"Are you sure?" Jik said.

"That's what it said on the notice board."

"It seems odd," he said and Nemle nodded.

"The tutors are always taken from the older mentors, the ones whose apprentices are past the need for formal classes. Hud is not old enough to even have an apprentice."

Marheh shrugged. "Perhaps he has done lots of study or something." She wrinkled her nose. "I can think of better things to study though."

The next afternoon Marheh came back to *Day Bringer* very grubby and full of the joys of engine maintenance.

"It's just the three of us," she told Nemle. "Tippa and Pon and me, and we've practically taken the engine apart. I don't think Tippa likes it very much because we do get dirty, but I love it."

Nemle smiled at her.

"A wash before supper might be a good idea."

"I've put my name down for one of the bathrooms. Imagine a real bath."

Nemle laughed.

The bath on *Day Bringer* was a large tin basin with the sole advantage that it was portable enough to be moved from the bathroom to the hearth on very cold days. The half dozen bathrooms at the Harbour were always very popular during the Gathering. Marheh collected her towel and washing things and raced off for her bath and Nemle smiled and enjoyed her enthusiasm.

The days passed busily and Nemle's friends commented on Marheh's delight in all she was learning and doing.

The classes in Silberay law were not scheduled to start until the second week of the Gathering and were for all the younger apprentices, not just the three at Marheh's level. Silberay were of course expected to know and obey the laws of the land, but Sila, founder of the Silberay, had set down guiding principles for the appropriate use of the discipline of the mind. Then, more than a hundred years later, had come the Great Debate when guiding principles had hardened into laws because the growing number of Silberay disagreed about the use of the discipline of the mind.

Nemle had been a first year apprentice at the time and she had told Marheh all she could remember of that challenging time when some dozen Silberay had left to become Yareblis and turn Sila's dream on its head.

There were perhaps a dozen young men and women gathered in the smallest of the meeting rooms awaiting the arrival of their tutor. Marheh could not help being a little apprehensive about this class. She had been practising the discipline of the mind without really knowing what she was doing even before she became apprenticed and in the early days of her apprenticeship her skill was not developed enough to control her instinctive response to situations where she was angry or afraid. She knew she had not always acted according to the law, but Nemle knew and understood and was teaching her the techniques she needed. Marheh realised it was time she understood the law better and had even provided herself with a note book and pencil to make notes of what seemed important.

Hud came sweeping into the meeting room a few minutes after everyone else had arrived. He was not a particularly tall man, but carried himself with such an air of confidence that he seemed to fill the room. He was wearing tunic and trousers cut to the traditional Silberay pattern, but the material was much richer and more luxurious than any Marheh had seen before. The midnight blue fabric had a subtle sheen to it that gave the folds mysterious darks and glowing highlights. His belt gleamed silver against the deep blue tunic. Marheh wrinkled her nose disdainfully. He obviously never wore these clothes when boating and the belt would not have held a windlass.

Unaware of Marheh's disapproval he surveyed the class with an air of condescension that did nothing to dispel her first impression. Then he began to speak. Marheh got ready with her pencil. His voice was beautiful; colour, light and shade, sometimes soft and caressing, sometimes sharp and biting, sometimes deep and strong. The class was transfixed. For a few minutes Marheh listened with the rest, spellbound by the brilliance of his elocution, but she had her pencil in her hand and she was writing nothing. She tried to focus, to find the gold amongst the glitter that was spilling out before them, but for all the clever technique it seemed to her that he was saying nothing. She really tried, but all too soon her pencil drifted into little doodles, then she began to draw in earnest, and the mellifluous voice was just music in the background.

"It wasn't just me," she said later, trying to explain to Nemle why her note book was full of sketches. "Some people thought he was wonderful, but even they could not say what they had learned about Silberay law."

Nemle turned the pages of the notebook smiling a little at Marheh's clever drawings.

"Just be careful," she said. "I think he could be a bad person to cross."

Marheh nodded. "Maybe it will be better tomorrow."

She went next morning, hopeful, armed with her notebook and pencil and found that in some respects it was better. Certainly there was more content to the flow of words, but what dry, narrow, nit-picking content it seemed to be and delivered not in the colourful persuasive tones he had used to woo them the previous day, but dictated from an important looking tome full of handwritten lists.

"It's all the wrong shape for Silberay," Marheh said to Nemle again displaying her notebook, this time full of scribbled oddments. "There are so many little picky prohibitions it's surprising we ever do anything. It doesn't seem a bit like Sila's dream for us."

Nemle looked at her thoughtfully. "I suppose most of us older ones just go along with what we think is right and forget that every Gathering someone wants to add to the rule book."

"Well I think we should have another Great Debate and see if we can make things simpler."

Marheh was very much in earnest. Nemle remembered how she and Sul had shared with Marheh and Kel their memories of that long ago Gathering where rights and wrongs had been debated and affirmations made. Some of the Silberay left the water road to become Yareblis, denying the value of the discipline of the soul and challenging the way the discipline of the mind should be used. It had been important then to take a stand, but now, perhaps, it was time to re-think.

Nemle looked at Marheh.

"So you think we have let things slip since then."

Marheh flushed but returned Nemle's gaze bravely.

"I suppose I do a bit," she said. "Not you, but ..."

Nemle smiled at her.

"You're quite right. I ought to know what the book of rules has turned into and I don't and I doubt whether many of the other mentors do either. Perhaps that's why Hud is teaching you."

Marheh made a face.

"It doesn't seem like teaching, not proper teaching, just lecturing."

"Only one more class," Nemle said sympathetically. "Perhaps he will give you the opportunity for questions and discussion then."

"Perhaps," Marheh said doubtfully.

She went off to visit Tippa looking thoughtful and determined.

Nemle watched her go and resolved to ask her own question when the mentors met again that evening.

It was a comfortable, easy group she met with, all of them over seventy, confident of who they were and of their place in their world. Although there were twenty-three mentors at the moment only fifteen were there in the small lounge. Apprenticeship for the Silberay lasted twenty years and during the last five or six years the aging mentor was often physically dependent on the apprentice, who thus learned practical service along with the disciplines. These older mentors were usually respected and consulted for their wisdom, but did not necessarily join the mentor discussions.

Nemle looked around the room, most of the fifteen were her contemporaries, some her friends. Sul, six years older than she, had been a particular friend and guide. She wished that Loma had joined them, but at eighty-eight she suffered from arthritis in her hips and knees and was often in pain. Nemle pictured Hafa, her own mentor and wondered what she would advise. The oldest person present was eighty-five year old Yin and he drew them into silence. It was the only formality and once he broke the silence a few minutes later they were ready to listen and talk.

"Has anyone else been hearing about the classes for law?" Nemle asked. "Do we know why Hud is taking them?"

It was enough to spark a vigorous discussion.

"It should have been Loma but she felt she could not manage this time."

"Tippa thinks Hud is wonderful."

"Yin would have done a better job."

"There seem to be so many rules now. I don't know them all."

"Marheh spoke of a large book, full of lists."

"I can't help wondering whether I'm missing something."

"If we don't know all the rules does that mean we are breaking them?"

"Perhaps we should ask to see this rule book. How can we mentor properly if we don't know?"

"Perhaps it is time for us to take another real look and try to simplify," Nemle said at last.

There was a brief pause while the others thought about this.

"I think it is too late for this Gathering," Sul said. "But we need to think seriously between now and the next."

There were nods and murmurs of affirmation.

"And we need to see the rule book," Yin added.

"Before the Gathering is over," Nemle said firmly, and again there was agreement.

Next morning Marheh went off to her class with a determined look which Nemle observed with a degree of concern, wondering what she was planning. She was early and chose her seat carefully so she could watch all the others as they came in. She wished Kel was part of the class because she knew he would understand the reason for the question she planned to ask, but he had moved beyond the need for classes.

As he had on the previous mornings Hud swept in last, the big, ornately bound book of rules clasped to his chest. He laid it on the table and stood back from it dramatically. His peroration began as an elaborate defence of the book. Marheh wondered suddenly in the middle of it whether Nemle had raised the issue in her mentors' meeting. When it seemed that he might be coming towards the end of his diatribe Marheh raised her hand politely.

At first Hud ignored her, but she persisted, and once the students near her realised and began to cast covert glances in her direction he could no longer pretend not to have seen.

"Yes young woman," he said at last, his voice patronising.

Marheh was aware that he knew her name, but she responded politely. "My name is Marheh. I belong to *Day Bringer*. I wanted to ask why we need so many rules and whether the rules sometimes stop us from doing what we think is right?"

There was a moment of silence. Faces turned towards Marheh and then back to Hud.

"I presume you have been listening while you have been sitting in this room," he said.

"Yes sir," Marheh said.

"And you still need to ask that question?"

He raised his eyebrows and looked around the group asking them to share his surprise.

"Yes Sir," Marheh said again, controlling herself rigorously, knowing she must not let him provoke her into an unconsidered response.

"Am I to assume from your questions that you are of the opinion that there are too many rules and that these may stop us from acting rightly?"

"Yes Sir."

"Then perhaps you will give us all the benefit of your reasoning," he said. "With examples from your own experiences of course."

"Really?" Marheh asked, surprised and pleased to be given the opportunity.

"I insist," Hud said.

Someone giggled and Marheh flushed, unaware that none of her audience thought she had any experiences to draw on.

"We have a rule that we must not use the discipline of the mind to coerce or exploit," she said. "And that was one of the first rules, one of Sila's rules. I think that is like a guiding principle, but underneath that are all those little rules you told us about, like not entering a Silberay mind without asking and receiving permission, or not speaking mind to mind if you haven't spoken voice to voice first. But sometimes that is not possible. We have no "do" rules, only "don't" rules, but when we become apprenticed we choose the active pursuit of goodness and beauty."

She paused and looked around at her fellow apprentices.

"Nemle and I go for a week each year to help at Haven Cottage. People live there whose minds have been partly destroyed. We have to enter their minds to show them even simple things like how to go downstairs and eat breakfast. It seems to me we must be breaking some of the rules, but they would starve if we didn't."

She stopped abruptly, aware that she had allowed her feelings to overcome her discretion.

"You said to speak from my experience," she muttered.

Hud looked scornfully at her.

"From your experiences, not Nemle's," he said. "An apprentice at your level is hardly likely to be directing minds."

Marheh managed to bite back an angry response. How she would love to enter his mind and prove her ability by making him do something silly, but she refrained, closing her mouth and spending the rest of the lesson deciding what the something silly would be, supposing she were to allow herself to take that kind of revenge.

17

The class ended soon after, Hud sweeping out of the room in much the same way as he had entered. Tippa turned to Marheh as they stood to leave.

"You can't really do that mind stuff, can you?" she asked.

"Yes," Marheh said, not wanting to elaborate.

"I don't believe you."

"Give me permission to enter your mind and I'll prove it," Marheh said.

"No way!" Tippa moved back from her a little.

"Then you'll just have to take it on trust," Marheh said lightly, turning away a little to hide her hurt.

She was rather quiet for the rest of the day and Nemle received no report of the events in the class. She wondered a little, but did not ask, trusting Marheh would tell her when she was ready. Instead Nemle spoke of the Mentor meeting and how they had all felt challenged to investigate the rule book.

"We have asked to see it at tonight's meeting," she told Marheh as she put on her big coat ready to go.

Marheh's face lit up. "Good," she said emphatically.

Nemle smiled and came across to kiss her.

"You're looking a bit tired. Why don't you have an early night?"

"Mmm, I might." She looked down at the doodles in her notebook. "I'm not doing much good here."

"Last day celebrations tomorrow," Nemle said. "Practise the discipline of the soul for half an hour or so then get a good sleep, alright."

"Mmm," Marheh said again and stood up to give Nemle a hug before making her way to her cabin.

She was in the habit of obeying Nemle and although this last instruction was merely advice Marheh knew it was good advice. She lit her candle and lay quietly on her bunk until she felt *Day Bringer* move as Nemle left her. Then she began to build the image of a candle flame in her mind, carefully, painstakingly until she was lifted out of herself and into the space where her soul could sing.

Next morning she seemed to have recovered her good spirits and talked happily over breakfast about the forthcoming celebrations. These would include the presentation to the apprentices of their new tunics, a different colour to show their progress. This Gathering Marheh's tunic would be a deep claret colour, a great improvement she thought on the mid-grey she had been wearing.

The most important ceremony though was the Consigning. Two mentors had turned ninety and would leave their boats. Their apprentices would become full Silberay and take over the boats they had lived and trained on for the past twenty years. There was sadness and joy mingled, for the mentors seldom lived for long once they had relinquished the boat that had been home for seventy years, where they had learned, cared, struggled and lived. Yet they seemed content to let go, Nemle thought, remembering past ceremonies and wondering how she would feel when her time came. Only yesterday she had been as young as Marheh, now she was a mentor and the years in between had gone, sunrise to sunset and then the night.

She and Marheh spent most of the morning cramming every available space on *Day Bringer* with non-perishable foodstuffs; flour, cereals and pulses. They had filled the diesel tank early in the Gathering but the water tank needed continual topping up. They planned to make an early start next morning. Marheh was looking forward to being on the move again, especially as they would be travelling a section of the water road that was new to her. Just before lunch she went off to the store to pick up the order Nemle had made for the more perishable foodstuffs. It was always cheaper at the Harbour and the Harbour Master knew there would be large orders needed during the Gathering.

There was a short queue in the store. Marheh and Nemle were not the only ones preparing for an early departure. Marheh smiled and greeted the other customers, most of whom were apprentices. There was another grey tunic nearer the counter. Pon turned round to smile and waved a pair of new boots at her.

"New ones," Marheh said. "You are lucky, I had to have mine re-soled this time."

"You were pretty brave to tackle Hud," Pon said. "He didn't treat you very well."

Marheh shrugged. "I should have known he didn't want questions."

A blue tunic turned around. "You were showing off, of course he squashed you. Silberay don't show off."

"I asked a question," Marheh said angrily. "How is that showing off?"

"Pretending to have done all that mind stuff with Nemle," the blue tunic said severely.

Marheh studied her accuser. She was a young woman of twenty eight, blonde and blue-eyed, quite heavily built. Marheh did not know her well but remembered her kind but rather condescending manner from the previous Gathering when she had appointed herself guide and instructor to the younger apprentices.

"Lati," she said carefully. "It would have been wrong of me to pretend."

"Of course it would," Lati said. "I'm glad you recognise that."

"But you weren't pretending, were you?" Pon asked quietly.

Marheh smiled gratefully. "I wasn't actually."

"Pretending or lying if you like that better," Lati said. "You should be ashamed of yourself."

"What gives you the right to accuse me of lying?" Marheh said. "I never lie."

Lati shook her head sorrowfully, a response that angered Marheh more than speech would have done.

"I suppose you think I can't do it because you can't." She tossed her head. "If there were not so many stupid rules I'd prove it to you."

Pon put a hand on her arm but she shook him off impatiently.

"I don't need to lie," she announced.

By this time everyone in the store was aware of her anger. One of the older Silberay turned to look at her, caught her eye, spoke her name. She flushed and took a deep breath.

"Sorry," she muttered, controlling herself with difficulty.

Fortunately at that moment Lati's order was called and she involved herself in the transaction at the counter and departed with her bundles, giving Marheh one more sorrowful head shake as she went.

Marheh took another deep breath and let it out in a sigh. "Sorry," she said more calmly. "I shouldn't let her get to me."

Pon gave her a bit of a grin and departed with his new boots and Marheh looked at the floor and tried to be invisible. She was conscious that her outburst had resulted in general disapproval quite unrelated to the question of her probity. She was glad when she could collect her order and go home to *Day Bringer*. Nemle would probably be disappointed in her, she thought, knowing she must confess before the story reached her in magnified form.

Nemle listened gravely as she explained what had happened.

"Silly child," she said affectionately, when Marheh had finished. "Getting angry just rebounded on you, didn't it?"

Marheh nodded and Nemle gave her a hug. "I would have been angry too," she said. "Perhaps it's just as well I wasn't there."

"I wish you had been," Marheh said. "She would not have dared to call me a liar then."

They watched the Consigning together late that afternoon. Marheh, happy that Nemle understood, had forgotten the troubles of the morning. Nemle had not quite forgotten, but thought the difficulty would blow over before the next Gathering.

The Consigning ceremony took place in front of the dry docks and around the waters of the Harbour. The two boats that would be handed on had been thoroughly overhauled and the front cabin of each, that used by the Mentor, had been re-modelled to provide a work area appropriate to the needs of the two apprentices who were about to graduate.

The ninety odd Silberay stood in silence as the boats were refloated and bow hauled out of the dry dock to the empty loading dock. There the two retiring Mentors waited with their apprentices. Carefully the Mentors stepped on board and held out a hand to their apprentices, offering an invitation to join them. The Mentor started the engine, the apprentice went forward to take the front line and the two boats began a slow lap of the Harbour. The gathered Silberay began to sing. Marheh felt close to tears as the two old Silberay, standing straight and proud steered their boats for the last time. Nemle found she was watching Marheh as well as the boats. She was singing with attention, words and music rendered with thought and feeling. She had an expressive face and Nemle saw that she was deeply moved by the occasion.

As the boats drew up again at the loading dock the song ended. Apprentice and Mentor embraced. The Mentor carefully removed the tiller arm and handed it to the apprentice who bowed and took it in both hands. There were words too, spoken quietly between them then the Mentor stepped ashore to stand and watch as the apprentice refitted the tiller arm and made another lap of the Harbour. The Silberay began to sing again, a song of welcome for the newly graduated ones.

Marheh turned to Nemle, still singing, a single tear visible at the corner of one eye, her face revealing a complex mixture of feelings. Nemle hugged her as the song ended and the boats returned to be carefully moored before the former Mentor and the former apprentice greeted each other again and made their slow way towards the Harbour buildings where the oldest Silberay made their home. The gathered Silberay parted to allow them passage and clapped softly as they went.

As the crowd began to disperse Marheh sighed and turned again to Nemle.

"How can something be so sad and so happy at the same time?" she said.

Nemle smiled sympathetically but said nothing, knowing she did not expect an answer.

"One day it will be me," Marheh said, then looked quickly at Nemle.

"And me," Nemle said. "And one day it will be you and your apprentice, but we've both got a way to go yet."

"And now a party," Marheh said gleefully, her mood changing again. "And goodbye to my grey tunic."

Nemle laughed at her. "What a baby you are," she teased.

Marheh spun around, her long dark plait flying out behind her. "I'll wear the grey one to get the coal in and check the engine," she said. "It won't show the dirt."

Nemle laughed again. "Go on, run if you want to. I can see you can't wait to get there."

Marheh danced off laughing. Nemle followed more slowly, smiling at Marheh's enthusiasm.

The big meeting room was transformed. Chairs had been moved to the edges and two long tables were laden with food. In one corner, near the dais, a small group were making music. Violin, flute and guitar played folk tunes and Silberay songs. The room quickly filled with happy chatter as Silberay took the opportunity to speak to friends they may not see again until the next Gathering, two years away. There was a moment of quiet while the Harbour Master welcomed them and invited them to enjoy the food then the cheerful conviviality continued.

At last came the concluding ceremonies. Marheh brought Nemle her grey tunic to hold and went to stand in line with the other apprentices. First the two new apprentices received their gold coloured tunics and spoke the words of the Silberay choice and their mentors went forward to sign their indentures. The Apprentice Master welcomed them formally and the assembled company sang as they walked with their mentors across the dais and back into the group they had joined.

The ordinary apprentices came next, Marheh among them. Nemle positioned herself where she would see Marheh's face. Four apprentices came to stand before the Apprentice Master and have grey tunics pulled over their heads. To each the Apprentice Master spoke words of congratulation and encouragement. Nemle smiled to herself, remembering that Marheh had been enthusiastic about her grey tunic two years ago. Then came Tippa, Pon and Marheh. The deep claret colour was lovely Nemle thought, as first Tippa then Pon put on their tunics. It would suit Marheh too. At last it was Marheh's turn. She was very white and her eyes were alight with excitement. The tunic was pulled over her head. Suddenly the warmth and conviviality disappeared. For a second or two Marheh's face registered hurt, bewilderment, betrayal, then set into the blankness of stone. The longed for claret coloured tunic was disfigured by a large yellow P sewn on front and back. Nemle stared, not quite sure what she was seeing, then bit back a cry of protest.

"The P is for Probation Marheh," the Apprentice Master said. "One of your tutors does not feel you are ready for promotion."

"I see."

Marheh's little stiff voice wrenched Nemle's heart.

"It's not right," she said loudly.

There were mutters around her and Sul touched her arm.

"Later," he said quietly.

Nemle glared at him then accepted the sense of his advice. Marheh, holding herself rigid, walked carefully off the dais and the ceremony continued.

Nemle saw very little of it. All she could think of was Marheh. She watched her walk stiffly across to the edge of the room then lost sight of her as she began to make her way towards the back.

"How dare they," she thought angrily. "How dare they treat her like that."

The apprentices filed on and off and received their tunics, then the two newly graduated Silberay were given badges and certificates and finally the two retiring Mentors were honoured. Nemle, who normally had her temper under control, felt her anger growing through it all. The Harbour Master had barely completed his final greeting, the Apprentice Master had scarcely stepped down from the dais when Nemle was confronting him, but to her surprise she was not alone. Sul was beside her and she might have expected that, but several of the other mentors gathered around including the woman who taught engine maintenance and there, with his mentor, was Pon in his red tunic.

"If she doesn't get promoted then neither should I," he was saying earnestly to his mentor.

"You hear that?" Nemle said to the Apprentice Master, her small, stocky figure standing firmly in front of him. "What could she possibly have done that deserved public humiliation? What kind of people are Silberay to let it happen?"

The Apprentice Master looked anxiously at Nemle, his blue eyes worried. "Hud said she was lying, boasting about using mind control at Haven Cottage. I'm sorry Nemle," he finished regretfully. "But you know we couldn't let that pass."

"Hud said!" Nemle bit off the words. "Hud said! What would he know?"

Sul put a hand on her arm. "Marheh has no need to lie or boast when it comes to mind control," he said quietly. "She has been using the discipline of the mind very capably for a number of years."

"But she's only twenty four," the Apprentice Master said. "She is hardly old enough even to know what is possible."

"I don't think age has anything to do with it," Sul said. "She is very talented."

"And she wasn't boasting," Pon said.

The Mentors all turned to look at him and he reddened slightly but held his ground.

"She was asked to give examples from her own experience. I was there."

Nemle looked disgusted.

"You let that posturing lawyer manipulate you because Marheh asked a question he didn't like," she told the Apprentice Master. "You believed him and didn't even think to verify what he told you. Who is the liar would you say?"

She turned away.

"I need to find her," she told them. "You need to think of a way to give her back what you've just taken away."

She pushed through the group around the Apprentice Master and made her way to the door, heedless of the glances, curious, sympathetic, occasionally mildly disapproving, that came her way from those Silberay who had lingered in the meeting room.

It was almost dark outside. Nemle made her way along the jetties to *Day Bringer* where she hoped she would find Marheh. *Day Bringer* was showing no lights and for a moment she worried Marheh might have gone to hide somewhere else. She stepped on board and into the back cabin, Marheh's cabin, and there she was lying on her bunk on her back staring at nothing, only visible in the dim light because she had shed the new tunic and was wearing only her light coloured shirt. There was a small movement from the bunk and a small voice said. "Go away Nemle please."

Nemle did not answer, only moved quietly into the cabin, lighting Marheh's candle, drawing the curtains, picking up the claret coloured tunic from the floor and folding it. Then she sat down on the bottom step beside Marheh's bed. Marheh turned her head away.

"It won't go away Marheh," she said. "And neither will I. You have to deal with it."

There was a long silence.

"In front of everyone," Marheh said at last, still not looking at Nemle, speaking so quietly Nemle had to strain to hear.

"It was unkind and unjust," Nemle said matter-of-factly.

"I was so looking forward to getting my new tunic."

"Yes, I know."

Nemle had the tunic on her lap. She looked at the stitching around the yellow letters, saw that it would come away without much trouble.

"Now it's all spoiled."

"Only if you let it be. You knew when you asked your question that there might be repercussions."

"I didn't know it would hurt so much," Marheh said, looking at Nemle for the first time.

Nemle smiled at her, touched her cheek lightly with one finger.

"That's life," she said. "Things do hurt."

She stood up carefully.

"Now you will practise the discipline of the soul while I find some scissors. I think you will find there are souls wanting to sing with yours."

"The other women are happy with my
suggestion that we wear the same uniform as the
men and I like Lor's idea for the apprentices. It
seems to me to be important that we identify
ourselves in this way to those who cannot see
the water. I hope perhaps the time will come
when the uniform stands for something
worthwhile."

                              Sila's Journal : the early years

Chapter Three

They went off on their travels the next morning and Marheh, who had
vowed she would not wear the new tunic, recognised the sense of Nemle's
words and not only wore it, but tried to take pleasure in it.

The spring and summer passed without incident. Marheh helped Nemle
with the plants and herbs she collected and propagated and tried to learn
something about the remedies she made so she could at least answer
questions. Nemle encouraged Marheh to continue to practise with her clay
and even discovered a pottery that was willing to fire her little sculptures in
exchange for a day of her labour. It was the first time she had been able to
make real use of the skill she had developed before she was apprenticed to
Nemle, working in her father's pottery. Now she hoped perhaps even to
have a few little pieces to sell and contribute to their household funds.

In Nemle's mind Marheh's next trouble sprang from trouble of her own.
They were travelling towards the small market town of Marisford aiming to
arrive in time for market day. She had plenty of seedlings and a good stock
of her comfrey ointment as well as a range of medicinal herbs and Marheh
could add her little models to the stall she would set up at the market.

Towns, even small towns, could sometimes be hostile to Silberay and
Nemle was always cautious as they approached, but she had not thought to
take particular care visiting a village five days journey from Marisford. It

was perhaps ten years since she had been this way and she was not sure whether the little shop that had bought her plants was still there so she had left Marheh cooking dinner on *Day Bringer* and gone to investigate.

The village had certainly changed since her last visit. There were two new shops in the High Street and a whole field that used to belong to the farm closest to the village was now covered with newish semidetached cottages with little gardens in various stages of care and development. The old pub had been refurbished with window boxes and a newly painted sign. A small garden at the side held a couple of tables and overlooked the village pond. There was rather a lot of noise coming from inside the pub and it seemed to have attracted more than just the locals because there was a motor vehicle standing outside.

Nemle went closer to look at this unexpected sight, wondering where it had come from. She was just examining the rather attractive badge decorating the front of the radiator grill when three men pushed their way out of the pub talking loudly.

As she looked up one of them shouted at her. "What do you think you're doing?"

He was quite young, not much older than Marheh, Nemle thought and one of his companions was of similar age. She straightened and smiled.

"I was just taking a closer look at the motor. There are not many of them about."

The third man, some ten years older than the other two, stepped towards her.

"Not too many old women in trousers about either." He grabbed her upper arm too tightly for comfort. "Perhaps we should take a closer look."

He pulled her towards him so that she stumbled and fell against him.

"She's one of those travellers," one of the younger men said as Nemle regained her footing and considered the situation.

"Some kind of water witch," the other said.

The older man laughed and Nemle seized the moment to use her ability with the discipline of the mind. Without realizing that Nemle had instructed him, the man released his hold on her. She took a quiet step back, thinking to encourage them to forget they had ever seen her, but she was not quite quick enough.

"Perhaps she'd like a closer look at the water," cried one.

"Drown the witch," cried the other.

Before she could act the two younger men had grabbed her and rushed her into the pond.

It was neither large nor deep, but it was dirty and very cold. Nemle had sprawled full length when they pushed her and she could scarcely see for dirty water as she lifted her head and opened her eyes. She rolled over to squat on the bottom and take stock. First have them forget her. She turned them towards the road so subtly they had no idea they had not thought of it themselves. A few seconds later they were strolling to the car with no memory of what they had done.

No one had come out of the pub to investigate. Everything had happened very quickly and quietly. Cautiously she crawled to the edge of the pond and got to her feet, shivering a little. She was aware she needed to get back to *Day Bringer* as fast as she could and get out of her wet clothes. She climbed out and started off down the lane towards the water road keeping in the shadows as best she could. Her wet clothes seemed to get heavier and colder as she went and it was an effort to keep going. At least the way was down hill, she thought trying for humour, she could roll home if she had to.

Marheh was sitting reading when she felt Nemle's return. Everything was ready for dinner except the rice and she had a saucepan of water placed on the edge of the stove just waiting for Nemle's return. She put a marker in her book and got up expecting to see Nemle appear from the back at any minute. She heard her first however, calling her name, then she appeared in the entrance to the galley. Her face was streaked with mud, her usually neatly disciplined hair damp and straggly. Her clothes were wet and dirty.

"Nemle!" Marheh ran to her. "What happened? Let me help you."

She knelt at Nemle's feet and began to tackle her bootlaces.

"You're freezing."

Nemle let Marheh pull off her boots and socks.

"Get me some hot water, there's a good girl. I need to get out of these clothes and have a wash."

Marheh darted across to the stove for the kettle.

"Shall I bring the bath out by the fire?"

Nemle shook her head.

"Just pour the water in. I'll do the rest."

She pulled off her tunic and took the pins from her hair.

"Perhaps you could have my dressing gown ready for me."

Marheh ran to do her bidding as Nemle shut the bathroom door and began to divest herself of the rest of her clothes.

Marheh was not often in Nemle's cabin but she knew where to find her dressing gown hanging on the back of the door. She brought it out and put it by the fire to warm. Nemle had a hot water bottle too, she remembered, going back and looking around the neat little space. It was not much different from her own, but Nemle had a bed, not a bunk. It was higher and wider than hers and although there was storage beneath there were no cupboards above. Nemle's slippers were neatly placed beside the bed and she grabbed them, remembering the bare feet, square and workmanlike, revealed when boots and socks were removed. She would have to ask Nemle about the hot water bottle, Nemle would not like her to look for it amongst her things.

Despite all Marheh's attentions by next morning Nemle was ill, coughing and snuffling with a fluey cold.

"I think you should be in bed," Marheh told her. "Please Nemle, I'm sure you have a temperature too."

"We'll see," Nemle said. "I'll just sit here by the fire for a bit and let you look after me."

"I could look after you just as well if you were in bed," Marheh said. "And you could go back to sleep."

"We'll see," Nemle said again.

Marheh made her sperit and brought her a dose of her own cold remedy. She made up the fire and brought her a blanket and a bowl of porridge.

"Sit down for a minute and have your own breakfast," Nemle said. "I'm feeling better already."

So Marheh perched on the footstool beside her whilst she wolfed down a bowl of porridge, but she couldn't settle.

"Please go back to bed Nemle."

She looked at Nemle's flushed face and extra bright eyes, listened to her laboured breathing.

"Please Nemle."

Nemle saw her worried face, heard the pleading in her voice and allowed herself to be persuaded.

"There will still be time to reach Marisford for the market if we don't set off till tomorrow," she said.

Tomorrow however she was not much better so after going carefully over the map with her and making sure she would recognise the next mooring place she yielded to Marheh's pleading and not only went back to bed, but agreed that Marheh should take them onwards by herself.

"I'm just being an old fool," she said, suddenly giving in. "Of course you can do it. It's just that if you did need help I couldn't give it."

Marheh promised to be careful and took what she fondly imagined to be secret delight in doing things all by herself. She was not really doing anything new, but always before she had been conscious of Nemle's watchful eye, her concerned presence.

She sang softly to herself as she performed the engine checks and started the engine. She held the centre line, just to be sure *Day Bringer* did not drift out while she untied the back line, pulled out the back mooring pin and stowed them neatly. Then she released the front mooring and gave *Day Bringer* a gentle push out from the bank before moving back to step on board, still clasping the centre line. As *Day Bringer*'s bow swung slowly into the channel she coiled the centre line and placed it on the roof where she could reach it easily. She grabbed the tiller and opened the throttle a little, then a little more, and *Day Bringer* was moving comfortably in the channel. She smiled to herself and began her song again.

In the end Marheh took them all the way to Marisford as Nemle's cold continued to develop. She was sensible, stopping every couple of hours, not just to give herself a break, but also to check on Nemle and make sure she had everything she needed. The first couple of days Nemle spent in bed dosing herself with her own herbal remedies and sleeping a lot. Once she felt well enough to get up she still spent much of the day dozing by the fire.

At first Marheh's pleasure in her new responsibilities was marred by anxiety but as Nemle began to recover she began to enjoy herself.

Nemle watched with an inward smile as Marheh the Great began to emerge. Marheh's younger brothers had given her the name and there had been times when self-confidence had edged towards arrogance and earned her a reprimand. Now however Nemle was glad to see it, feeling that Marheh had at last recovered from the humiliation of the Gathering.

They reached the mooring at Marisford early in the afternoon the day before the market was to begin. Marheh moored up neatly and went inside to Nemle to report, trying hard not to look too pleased with herself.

"It's a nice mooring," she said.

Nemle nodded.

"I've brought in the tiller arm and turned the stern tube greaser."

Nemle's eyes twinkled.

"The ground is just right for the mooring pins, not muddy at all."

Nemle smiled. "And you want me to tell you what a good girl you are," she teased.

Marheh laughed at that. "Well I am, aren't I?"

"I hate to have to tell you," Nemle said, the teasing smile still in place. "But there is one more thing."

Marheh groaned theatrically.

"The barrow!"

"The barrow!" agreed Nemle.

There was nothing intrinsically wrong with the barrow. It was a neat, functional piece of equipment that was designed to be both market stall and transportation device, but because of the limitations of space on *Day*

Bringer it needed to be taken apart after use and stowed in pieces in all sorts of inaccessible corners. Before Marheh's apprenticeship, when Nemle was alone on *Day Bringer* she had had space for it in the forward cabin that was her workroom and she had used it much more frequently then. Now, with two to carry, it was often easier just to turn themselves into beasts of burden. For the market though they needed a place to display their wares so the barrow it had to be.

Marheh changed into her oldest clothes and grabbed a duster. The frame was in pieces under the back deck and nothing could be done without that. Also under the back deck was a spare tank for the toilet, three bags of coal, tins of paint to touch up *Day Bringer*'s hull, spare oil for the engine and a box of the tools they might need if the engine broke down. Marheh lifted the access hatch and plunged in, emerging eventually with coal dust on hands and face, an oily smear across her tunic and dirty knees as well as the pieces of frame. The rest of the pieces were much more accessible but it was nearly tea time before she had it all assembled and ready on the back deck.

"Done," she said to Nemle before disappearing again to wash.

Nemle had a mug of sperit and a slice of bread and butter ready for her when she came back and she fell on them gratefully.

"It could really do with a coat of paint," she told Nemle. "But we have left it too late for this market."

Nemle nodded and sipped at her own sperit. She was feeling much better, though not quite her usual self.

"Early to bed tonight," she said. "We'll leave everything ready to load at first light."

Next morning they were away just as the sun emerged from behind the hills that surrounded them. Marheh carried a pack filled with her little sculptures, carefully wrapped, as well as pushing the barrow loaded with jars and packets at the bottom and boxes of seedlings on top. Nemle's pack held more of her herbal remedies. They walked in silence appreciating the cool still autumn morning and saving their breath for the long climb to the edge of the town.

"It's always uphill from the water road," Marheh said, a little breathless.

She set down the barrow onto its legs and stretched.

"Always," Nemle agreed. "Are you alright with that?"

"Mm," Marheh nodded.

She was looking particularly beautiful this morning, Nemle thought. Her face was a little flushed with exertion, her brown eyes expectant. Fine tendrils of hair escaped from her dark plait and curled around her face. She looked trim and workmanlike in her best uniform. She gripped the handles of the barrow again and looked at Nemle.

"Ready?" she asked.

"If you are," Nemle said, and they set off again towards the High Street and the market square.

Once there they found the man in charge, handed over some money and were allocated a small space.

"With the also-rans," Nemle said, explaining to Marheh that the regulars had regular places and people like them had to make do with what was left.

Marheh nodded and began to open out the barrow to make their stall. Their display space was very limited, but they found room for half a dozen of Marheh's little sculptures as well as examples of Nemle's various remedies and one box of seedlings. The other boxes of seedlings they put on the ground and found storage in the barrow for everything else.

All around them stall holders were setting up, spreading out their wares, calling greetings to each other. Nemle was conscious that they needed to do well here if they were to manage comfortably over the winter. Marheh was a loving companion and a great help, but she had a youthful appetite and youthful energy that was hard on her clothes, and especially on her boots. What had provided amply for Nemle alone was very thinly stretched when it came to the two of them and this year the apprentice allowance, which was less each year as the apprentice progressed, was only one fifth of what it had been in Marheh's first year. It would be a help if Marheh's sculptures sold, Nemle thought, but she wondered whether market goers would be interested in something purely decorative, charming though they were.

"What do you think I should ask for my things?" Marheh asked her when the display was ready.

"You'll have to decide," Nemle told her. "Don't be too ambitious, but don't sell yourself short either. You can always adjust your prices next time if you get it wrong."

"I don't expect anyone will want them," Marheh said, suddenly losing confidence in her work.

"People will want them I'm sure," Nemle said. "But whether they buy them will depend on what kind of summer they have had. Some years people don't have much cash left for treats."

"It would be better if I could make useful things wouldn't it?"

"Your little figures are lovely," Nemle said. "Just the sort of thing a young man might buy for his mother, or his sweetheart."

She put her hand in her pocket and drew out a couple of coins.

"Why don't you go and have a look around, and see if you can find us something warming to eat. We're all set here now."

Marheh took the coins and put them carefully in her pocket before heading off. She so much hoped to sell some of her figures so she could contribute to the household expenses. The lack of her own money had been one of the hardest things to adjust to when she became apprenticed. She had begun working in her father's pottery as soon as she left school at fifteen and he had paid her an allowance from the beginning, but Silberay boats operated from a common purse and her apprentice allowance had been paid to Nemle.

Nemle was as generous as she could afford to be and Marheh knew she was trusted but it made her feel like a child always to be taking and asking. She turned over the coins in her pocket. Even a few shillings would make a difference, she thought, looking around at the goods displayed in the stalls she was walking past. Then she could buy Nemle a treat instead of always being treated.

The smell of cooking drew her towards a group of stalls where food was being prepared and she wandered amongst them trying to choose. It was very rare for them to eat food they had not prepared themselves. Would it be best to think breakfast and choose egg and bacon butties, or would Nemle like a steak and kidney pie better or even something sweet, she wondered. At last she decided and went back to Nemle carrying two egg and bacon butties and enough change to pay for a hot drink and a biscuit later.

As they ate their breakfast the market square began to fill with shoppers. Soon the stall holders were calling their wares, the customers were arguing the prices, saunterers with no intention of buying tossed their comments in to swell the sound and the quiet morning was gone.

Marheh and Nemle stood behind their stall as the crowd surged about. Once or twice someone stopped to look, but Marheh thought she and Nemle were the curiosity not the goods they had to sell.

Ten years was too long, Nemle thought rather despondently, there was no one who remembered her.

Once the first rush of bargain hunters was past however customers began to appear and they made some sales. Nemle's comfrey ointment was the most popular, but the borage tea had a steady following also. Marheh liked the thought of it "borage for courage" was the old saying, but she did not care for the taste.

Then, in the middle of the morning an old man came past, stopped, looked and greeted Nemle in the kind of gruff, scolding voice that attempted to conceal real pleasure.

"It's been too long woman, that's not the way to do business," he said, examining the trays of seedlings. "I've looked for you these five years past."

"It's been longer than that," Nemle said. "But I've to go where I'm needed."

"Why would you think you're not needed here?" he said. "I'll take all your seedlings, but you'll have to keep them for me. Can't carry them all at once."

"My apprentice will help you if you like," Nemle said. "Are you sure you want them all?"

"Apprentice eh!" the man said, examining Marheh with interest. "Strong and willing I hope."

Marheh wanted to laugh. She had heard ponies described in those words.

"You didn't have an apprentice when you were here before," he went on.

He was looking carefully at all that was displayed, first Nemle's medicines and dried herbs then at last Marheh's little sculptures.

"What's this then?" he asked, picking up a little piece and turning it over in his hands. "You didn't have this last time."

He did not wait for an answer, but studied it intently then smiled.

"Good that is. I've watched them just like this."

Marheh held her breath. It was a pair of badger cubs playing. She had spent hours watching and sketching in the spring and she thought she had captured them well.

"Reckon I might find a spot for them on the mantle piece. They'd be company."

Money changed hands. Marheh wrapped it carefully for him along with some liniment of Nemle's. Then she picked up a couple of trays of seedlings and followed him to the back of the pub where his horse and cart were waiting. The horse turned its head as they approached, but seemed to understand that this was not time for departure and involved itself again in the contents of its nosebag. The man put the seedlings on the floor of the cart and fished in his pocket, held out a halfpenny. Marheh flushed and shook her head.

"Why not?" he asked.

Marheh hesitated, not quite sure how to explain, then she smiled. "Free delivery," she said.

She made her way back to Nemle, hoping she could tell her something about the man, her first customer.

How tired she looked, Marheh thought as she approached the stall. Nemle was not fully recovered whatever she pretended. She detoured towards the food stalls and returned to Nemle bearing two steaming mugs and an Eccles cake.

"Why don't you go back to *Day Bringer* for the afternoon?" Marheh suggested when the mugs had been emptied and returned and the Eccles cake divided carefully and eaten to the last crumb.

Nemle protested a little, but Marheh persisted and at last she allowed herself to be persuaded, promising to come back when it was time to pack up.

Marheh shook her head. "There is no point in coming back. I can manage what is left even if we sell nothing more."

"It feels wrong to leave it all to you."

"Go," Marheh said, making shooing movements with her hands. "Go and lie down. I can manage."

Nemle smiled a little, gave Marheh a kiss and left to go back to *Day Bringer*.

Marheh watched as she made her way through the market. The uniform marked her out from the other shoppers though there was nothing ostentatious about it. Nemle chose to wear drab greens and browns, but her trousers and boots were unusual for a woman of her age. The way she moved was different too. Even though she was tired and ill she still had a freedom and sense of purpose that a woman half her age might have envied. Marheh noticed too how the other shoppers reacted to her uniform. Most just looked and then looked away, a few even changed course to avoid her, but one or two older people stopped her and reached out to her for a word or a smile.

People don't know who we are any more, Marheh thought, or if they do they don't want to understand.

She stared thoughtfully after Nemle even when she had disappeared from view and was only called back to herself by the demands of a customer.

"Come back, come back wherever you are!"

Marheh laughed and apologised and looked curiously at the man who was waiting. Average height, strongly built, thick curly dark hair with a few threads of grey, he stood smiling at her, a teasing look in his eye. He didn't fit with the market. The shoppers were mostly women or old men.

"How can I help you?" she asked.

The teasing look developed and she blushed and looked away, moving the items on display in a show of busyness.

"First of all you can sell me some of that comfrey ointment," he said. "I hear it is very good for bruises."

Marheh nodded. "Bruises or sprains," she said. "You massage it in."

"But it's my shoulder," he said. "I can't do it for myself."

"Your wife?" suggested Marheh.

He shook his head.

"Your mother?"

"I'm a poor orphan."

"I'm sure you'll find someone to help you," Marheh said, one hand over the jar of ointment, the other outstretched to take his money.

"I have," he said meaningfully. "A beautiful witch in a red jumper." The teasing look was back. "No massage, no sale," he said.

Marheh looked at him uncertainly for a moment then said firmly "No sale."

He made a disappointed face and leaned in towards her.

"Unkind. Won't Granny witch be cross if you're mean to me."

Marheh frowned. "I don't know what you are talking about," she said, wondering whether it would be breaking the law if she used her mind to send him away.

The man raised his hands and backed away. "Sorry, sorry, just teasing."

"Do you want the ointment or not?" Marheh asked, trying to be businesslike.

"Ointment please," he said.

His pretence at humility was not intended to deceive. He offered his money and the transaction was completed. Marheh's mouth remained under her control, but her eyes were amused. He pushed the package into the pocket of his jacket and continued to hover. Marheh ignored him pointedly. He began to finger the half dozen little sculptures that remained on the stall. Marheh watched out of the corner of her eye.

"It's no good you know," he said at last in conversational tone. "I won't go away."

Marheh did not reply. He picked up one of her sculptures and began tossing it from one hand to the other. At first Marheh attempted to ignore him but when he pretended to fumble a catch she could stand it no longer.

"Oh please be careful!"

"Got you!" he said replacing the piece on the stall with exaggerated care. "Why won't you talk to me?"

"Because you're being silly," Marheh said. "And I don't know you."

"Can't help being silly," the man said. "The sight of you knocked me for six."

Marheh's eyes widened. He held out his hand.

"My name is Daniel."

Marheh studied him for a moment, looked at the outstretched hand.

"I'm Mary," she said at last, not wanting him to have her soul name since he had not offered his. She reached out to shake his hand and found hers firmly grasped in both his.

"Well Mary," he said, giving her hand a little squeeze before letting it go. "Now will you talk to me?"

Marheh laughed. "Go away," she said. "I'm busy."

At that moment a customer appeared to add truth to her words.

"Alright," he said. "But I'll be back."

"Lor and I have thought long and hard about the nature of our friendship. Part of me longs for a child, his child, but how could I give only to one child when I believe I have something to give to the world."

Sila's Journal: the early years

Chapter Four

Marheh served her customer and several more over the course of the afternoon. All of the comfrey ointment was sold and quite a lot of Nemle's other products. Even Marheh's little sculptures had sold well. There were still plenty of quiet moments however and Marheh could not help thinking about the man Daniel and wondering whether he really would come back as he said. She was not quite sure what she felt about the possibility. She and Nemle led quiet, rather austere lives and because they were continually on the move there was little opportunity to develop close friendships. Marheh had three younger brothers who teased her, but this man's teasing was not like theirs. He made her feel uncomfortable but it was not altogether an unpleasant feeling, a bit like being on the edge of something unknown.

The afternoon dwindled towards evening. There were a few customers but those wanting comfrey ointment were disappointed and disinclined to browse for anything else. Still, Marheh was happy with the day. She had sold five little sculptures and had fifteen shillings to contribute to household expenses. She began to pack up. Everything would fit into the barrow now with room to spare. Deliberately she concentrated on her packing so she did not see Daniel join her as she folded over the hinged tray that formed a lid for the barrow, but somehow she was not surprised when she found him beside her. He pushed her gently aside and grasped the handles.

"Off to the pub are we?" he suggested.

"No we are not," Marheh said firmly, trying to reclaim the barrow.

"Granny witch would be cross I suppose," he said, beginning to push the barrow. "Will she turn you into a black beetle if you disobey?"

"You are silly," Marheh said, but she laughed and walked beside him along the High Street.

"Just temporarily of course. I'm sure you're much more useful than a black beetle and I know you're much more decorative. Does she put you in a match box when you're a black beetle?"

Marheh laughed again.

"So where are we going if not to the pub?" he asked after a short silence.

"I am going home," Marheh said. "I don't know where you are going." She stopped walking. "Thank you for pushing the barrow for me. I can manage now."

He gave her a look and kept walking so that she had to follow him. At least they were going in the right direction, she thought, wondering whether he was planning to escort her home or abscond with the barrow. If he tried to do that she would be justified in using her mind to stop him she decided.

They reached the edge of the town and Marheh stopped at the intersection of the High Street and the lane that led to the water road.

"I go this way," she said. "Please let me take it now. You've been very kind."

He stopped and turned the barrow towards the lane then looked at her with the teasing look.

"What about a thankyou kiss?" he suggested.

Marheh looked up at him and before she quite knew what was happening he had leaned down and placed his mouth gently on hers. A moment later he had turned and gone, striding away back up the High Street. Marheh watched him for a few seconds then she rubbed the back of her hand across her mouth and turned to take up the barrow.

It did not take long to get back to *Day Bringer*. The half empty barrow and the downhill slope made it much easier than the morning's uphill slog. In a way she would have liked longer to sort out her thoughts about what had happened before meeting Nemle's sharp eyes.

She parked the barrow beside *Day Bringer* and pranced on board with the afternoon's takings. Nemle was in the galley busy with dinner preparations.

"Here's my strong and willing apprentice," she said, smiling at Marheh who laughed with her.

She took the bag with the takings and upended it carefully onto the bench then she reached into her pocket and placed her fifteen shillings on top of the pile of coins.

"We're rich!" she said.

"Rich indeed," Nemle agreed. "Suppose we keep out ten shillings to be going on with and put the rest away."

Marheh nodded. "And then I'll empty the barrow and take it apart," she said.

She took the money and put it away in the box they kept hidden in a corner under the floor of the engine room. It had filled up quite nicely today, she thought, remembering how they had needed to scrape together every last penny during the spring just to buy milk and eggs. Then she changed out of her good tunic, grabbed a screwdriver and went to empty and disassemble the barrow.

Next morning Nemle suggested she had earned a lie in, but they were nevertheless away by mid-morning. Marheh took the tiller while Nemle sorted through her remaining stocks and decided what might be able to be replenished before winter curtailed her activities. Marheh found her thoughts kept wandering to the previous day's encounter. She had not told Nemle about Daniel. At one point during the evening she had almost joked about the black beetle, but changed her mind, not wanting to embark on the explanations that would be necessary.

She had grown up knowing she would be Silberay even though she could not become apprenticed until she was twenty and Silberay left the water road if they married so she had never thought much about the opposite sex except as brothers. In many ways she knew her life was quite circumscribed, but it needed to be so she could concentrate on practising the disciplines. Daniel had called her a witch, and Nemle. She still had an uncomfortable, edgy feeling when she thought about him. She could still remember the feel of his mouth on hers. She shivered unexpectedly and corrected her course, resolving to stop thinking about him and concentrate on her steering. "Or Nemle will turn me into a black beetle," she thought, wondering whether she would ever see him again, thinking perhaps it would be best if she didn't.

They moored up in time for a late lunch. Marheh was aware that she had not been steering as well as usual, but Nemle did not comment when she came up to take her turn, only suggested that Marheh might like to fit in an extra half hour at the discipline of the soul since she had missed the previous day.

"And then we'll take some time to practise the discipline of the mind together," she said. "I've been a bit lazy about working with you lately."

"You've been ill," Marheh said.

Nemle nodded. "But I'm better now."

She looked at Marheh, a hint of mischief in her smile.

"And I have had time to think up a few new challenges."

Marheh grinned, then involuntarily the black beetle popped into her head again and she laughed. But when she went below to do her practice her mood sobered. She did not want him appearing in her thoughts like this. He would interfere with her practice as well as her steering if she was not careful.

Her practice went badly as she had been afraid it might. Try as she would she could not reach the place where her soul made its song, spilling melody into dark spaces, sometimes touching other souls with joyful harmony. It was no good forcing it, she knew, but she was disappointed in herself. Singing the soul song was an important part of who she was. Silberay believed this practice was a benign influence in the world as well as on themselves as individuals. It was what made them different from the Yareblis.

She sighed and allowed herself to drift back from the candle flame she had been imagining that was her usual portal for entering the song. Maybe Nemle would let her go for a walk after lunch, before they settled to practise the discipline of the mind. She needed to stretch her legs. She wondered what new challenges Nemle had thought up. Thank goodness they had not yet made a rule about practice between apprentice and mentor.

A walk after lunch was approved even encouraged and Marheh set off happily, looking forward to exploring new territory. She had a map in her pack just in case, but did not expect to need it, having planned a route that followed the water road then curved around to pass through a small village on her way back to *Day Bringer*. She would fill her pack with wood for the fire if she could find any since the evenings were chilly now and keep an eye out for any wild food. If she found any brambles they could have crumble for dessert. She set off happily enjoying the exercise and the autumn sunshine, bright and warm but not hot as it could be in summer.

She had found enough dead wood to fill her pack by the time she reached the village although she guessed she was not the first to be scouring the roadsides for something to burn. It would be worse in the winter when they would be competing with the villagers for what wood there was and sometimes unpopular because of it. This seemed a nice little village though and she slowed her pace to admire the golden afternoon shining on warm sandstone and red tiles. There was one big house set back from the road in a garden of glowing autumn colour and lush green grass and on the opposite side of the road a series of small, thatched cottages with neat gardens. Then the road divided around a big tree and a small green. The church and the pub looked at each other across the green and then came a terrace of houses with one small shop at the further end. Outside the shop was a bench seat looking out over the field opposite and on the seat, looking very much at home, sat Daniel.

Marheh stopped, wondering whether she might find a back lane so she did not have to pass him, but before she had made any move to find out he turned around and looked at her. She felt herself blushing hotly and looked down at her feet which seemed to be moving forward without any conscious effort on her part. He was not controlling her mind though, she decided, making an effort to stop and collect herself. Then she continued towards him, feeling self-conscious under his lazy, smiling gaze.

"Hello beautiful witch," he said as she came near. "Did you spend the night in a matchbox for talking to me?"

"Don't be silly," Marheh said. "I'm allowed to talk to you, *if* I want to."

"Do you always do what Granny witch tells you?"

"Don't call her that, she's my mentor."

"Oh, I'm sorry," his eyes mocked her. "Do you always do what *your mentor* tells you?"

Marheh did not answer, not quite sure she wanted to tell him the truth, which was that although she tried to be obedient she was not always, especially in her thoughts.

"My mentor loves me," she said in the end, an answer that seemed relevant to her.

It silenced him for a minute at least and she began to walk on. In a moment he was walking beside her.

"You're going in the wrong direction," he said. "You know you're coming to the pub with me."

She continued to walk the way she was going. He strode ahead of her and turned to stop in her path and drop on one knee.

"Come to the pub with me, Mary mine," he said, holding out his hands.

"I'm not yours," she said, but she hesitated and somehow he had relieved her of her pack and she was following him back to the pub.

She and Nemle did not have money for pubs and it was sometime since she had been into one. She hesitated in the doorway then stepped down into the dim, smoky little room as Daniel urged her forward. There were not many customers, but she could feel them look at her as Daniel led her to a quiet corner and waited for her to sit down. Just for a moment she wished she was not wearing the uniform she was so proud of, wished she was indistinguishable from any other young woman in the village. She held her head up and tried not to mind the glances as Daniel went to the bar for their drinks. Then he came back.

He sat down beside her, but not too close and began to talk to her quite sensibly, asking about her walk, commenting on the fine autumn weather and cosy little pub where they sat. Marheh was very quiet at first, answering him briefly and wondering what she was doing drinking beer that she did not much care for with a man she barely knew, in a village she was about to leave. He was patient though and encouraging so she gained confidence and began to smile at his quips and laugh when he teased her. Then somehow she found herself half way through a second drink and realized how much time must have passed.

"I have to go," she said almost in a panic. "Nemle will be anxious."

"Black beetle time!"

"No, it isn't funny. She'll be afraid for me."

He nodded and finished his drink in one long swallow. "Come along then. Drink up and I'll walk with you a little way."

She pushed her glass across for him to finish.

"I'm sorry."

"I won't hold it against you as long as you tell me where to find you tomorrow."

"Oh!" She bent down and fumbled with her pack, wondering how to answer him. "Maybe it would be better if you didn't find me tomorrow," she said at last.

He took her pack from her.

I'll find you," he said. "Whether you help me or not."

She hesitated, then reached for the pocket in her pack and pulled out the map.

"I'm not sure I should be showing you this," she said, spreading it out on the table.

He looked at it curiously. It was a Silberay map, showing the water road.

Daniel could not see the water road. The Silberay had built it in a different dimension and it lay over the landscape unseen by many or glimpsed only as the hint of a ripple. Most people no longer believed in its existence.

Marheh traced the route from Marisford with one finger then pointed to where *Day Bringer* was moored and showed the direction they were heading.

"We move on most days," she said. "But not far."

She began to fold up the map again, carefully so she did not have to look at him when she spoke.

"I usually go for a walk in the afternoon," she said, feeling the heat in her cheeks as she blushed.

She pushed the map back into the pack and Daniel swung it onto his shoulder.

"Come on then," he said leading the way out.

They walked quickly through the village, Marheh setting the pace, knowing Nemle had reason to be angry, not just because she would be worried, but because dinner would be late and there would be no time for practising the discipline of the mind. Daniel tried to make conversation at first, but she could not respond and walked mostly in silence. When she could see the water Marheh stopped.

"You'd better not come any further," she said, reaching for her pack.

"Why not?"

"Down there is the water road."

"But you're *allowed* to talk to me," he quoted with heavy emphasis.

"Just give me my pack," she said, flaring up. "I have to go."

"In a minute," he said, swinging the pack to the ground and taking hold of her shoulders.

He turned her towards him, moved one hand up to cup her chin and leaned down to kiss her. He was gentle, but his mouth was insistent, demanding a response. At last he drew away and let her go. She fumbled with the pack, looked at him and turned and walked away.

"Remember me until tomorrow," he called after her.

She ran nearly all the way back to *Day Bringer* almost as if she was punishing herself for something. The movement, the thumping of her pack against her back, the hard breathing all served to push away thought and she did not want to think about the way Daniel was making her feel. She reached *Day Bringer* and flung herself on board then hurried through to the saloon. Nemle, alerted by her tempestuous arrival was beginning to get out of the big chair where she had been sitting but Marheh came hurrying to kneel by her side so she sank back again.

"Nemle, I'm so sorry," she blurted out. "I'm so sorry. I lost track of the time."

Nemle looked at her, flushed and dishevelled from running, breathing hard, the pack still on her back.

"I was beginning to be worried," she said slowly. "It isn't like you to be away so long."

"I'm so sorry," Marheh said again, struggling to control her breathing, taking one of Nemle's hands in hers so she did not have to meet her eyes. "I was enjoying myself and I forgot the time."

Nemle removed her hand from Marheh's and used it to push herself out of the chair. She did not think Marheh would lie to her, but she was very aware that there was something more than mere lateness that was being concealed by Marheh's elaborate distress. In fact, and Nemle frowned trying to place the memory, there was a faint smell of something different about her.

"That's very nice dear," she said, moving away and leaving Marheh still on her knees by the chair. "Try not to let it happen again."

Marheh stared after her. Nemle never spoke to her like that, like a kind but disinterested school teacher.

"Get up now Marheh," she went on. "Get rid of your pack and come and help me with dinner. I'm afraid we shan't have time for any practice this evening."

They moved on again every day that week. Each afternoon Marheh went for her usual walk and each afternoon Daniel was there, somewhere on her route. He would walk with her, help her pick up firewood, tease and flatter her and end up kissing her with increasing passion. She never allowed herself to be so late again, but her work suffered for she found her thoughts continually turning towards Daniel, what he said to her, how he made her feel, when she might see him again, what he might say or do. Nemle knew she had a secret and watched her with concerned and loving eyes when she thought Marheh would not realise. Four years ago when Marheh had first become her apprentice she might have questioned, scolded, but not now. Now she had to hope that Marheh was not in trouble and trust that she would tell her eventually.

Then came an afternoon when Daniel did not come. Marheh looked for him around every bend and approached *Day Bringer* more and more slowly as she came closer and he still had not appeared. He had not said he would not be there but then he had not said he would either. She boarded *Day Bringer* slowly, almost reluctantly and instead of going through to the saloon lingered in her cabin. She lay down on her bunk on her stomach, her face turned to the wall and tried to make sense of her feelings, but it was too easy just to remember his kisses and how he looked when he teased her and the tone of his voice and the excitement that rose inside her when he embraced her. She did not really want to face Nemle and pretend there was nothing wrong but she did not want to tell Nemle her secret either. Eventually she made herself get up and go through to the saloon, carrying her pack and busying herself emptying her collection of sticks into the wood basket so she did not have to meet Nemle's eyes when she greeted her.

Next afternoon he was waiting for her again. Marheh ran to meet him, her face alight and responded to his kisses with an intensity she had not shown before.

"So you missed me little witch," he said at last, taking her hand and leading her off the path and into a field towards a tumbledown farm building backed into a corner near the hedge. Her shining eyes were enough response and he laughed softly.

Nemle, increasingly worried about Marheh, had begun to spend her afternoons within the discipline of the soul instead of with her salves and seedlings. She was skilled and experienced in this practice and had used her soul song to surround Marheh with protection in the past, but then she had had some knowledge of what threatened. Now she could only offer the love within the song and hope it would be there to be called on if needed.

"So little witch?" Daniel said softly sometime later.

He had taken her into a dry corner of the farm building and sat down with her. Then he had encouraged her tunic over her head and unbuttoned her shirt to kiss and caress her small white breasts. Lips and tongue aroused her until she cried out with pleasure and thrust herself against him. Now he was propped on one elbow, watching her face and gently encouraging one pink nipple to harden again under thumb and forefinger.

"I love you Daniel," she said, soft as a sigh.

"Do you little witch," he said, kissing her breasts once more then sitting up to begin buttoning her shirt for her.

She watched him regretfully for a moment or two then said lazily. "Why do you keep calling me a witch?"

"Because you can disappear," he said. "Here one minute, gone the next."

"Don't be silly. Of course I can't disappear."

She reached up to take his head in her hands and guide his mouth onto hers. He kissed her lightly then gently detached himself.

"You do, you know," he said. "I've watched you walk down the road and turn into a field and suddenly you are not there any more."

"Well I live on the water road," she said, allowing him to pull her tunic over her head. "And you can't see it, but I don't disappear."

She thrust her arms into the sleeves then wrapped them around him as he pulled down the tunic and got to his feet, bringing her with him.

"If I can't see you then you disappear," he said. "Come along, black beetle time."

Nemle needed only a glance at her dishevelled hair, flushed face and glowing eyes and she understood at last the nature of Marheh's secret. No wonder she was distracted, unable to concentrate on the disciplines or anything else. She reached out a hand to her and drew her down to sit on the footstool beside her. Marheh looked up at her, a little guilty, a little defiant. Nemle chose her words carefully.

"You don't need to tell me anything if you don't want to Marheh," she said. "There is nothing wrong with loving someone, but perhaps you'd like to ask him to dinner."

Marheh's mouth dropped open. Nemle smiled and patted the hand she still held in hers.

"Oh Nemle," Marheh said at last. "You don't mind?"

"Of course I'll mind if it means losing my apprentice, but in the end that will be your decision."

"Losing your apprentice," Marheh said slowly, as if the realisation had only just struck her.

Nemle watched and saw Marheh shake off the knowledge almost as a dog shakes to rid itself of the rain.

"Would you like to tell me about him?" she asked, knowing that the need to choose one life or another was something Marheh did not want to face just yet."

"I do love him Nemle," Marheh said. "He makes me feel special."

Nemle waited.

"I met him at Marisford, at the market. He bought some comfrey ointment and teased me to massage it into his shoulder. I didn't though," she hastened to reassure Nemle. "I would now though," she added, almost to herself.

"But it's barely a fortnight since Marisford," Nemle said.

Marheh blushed. "He has met me every day on my walk," she said.

"Oh Marheh," Nemle shook her head. "No wonder you were late sometimes."

She opened her arms and Marheh leaned in to be hugged, happy to have things out in the open.

Having once begun to talk about him Marheh could not stop and Nemle listened carefully while she chattered on. She could not help feeling anxious about the suddenness and intensity of the friendship. Marheh was beautiful, passionate and loving, but how could this man find time to meet her every afternoon? How could he find her? He could not see the water road. Most disturbing of all from Nemle's point of view, he had not told Marheh his soul name.

"I don't think he knows it," Marheh said. "And though I told him mine he usually calls me Mary."

That evening for the first time since leaving Marisford Marheh got out her clay. She sat with it at the table and while Nemle was writing up the log she patted and pushed, moulded and carved until she had produced the figure of a man. He lay on one side, one booted foot crossed over the other, his head and upper body propped on one elbow. When she saw it Nemle understood it was a portrait of Daniel. Marheh held it carefully, almost tenderly as she showed it to Nemle.

"I do love him Nemle," she said again and the expression on her face made her seem so vulnerable Nemle longed to warn her though she said nothing.

Next morning as usual they moved on for a couple of hours. It seemed to Nemle to be just a pretence of normality for Marheh clearly could not pay attention enough to learn anything that required mental discipline. She was happy though, Nemle thought, watching her face as she stood steering while Marheh attacked the brass on the roof and sang under her breath.

After lunch she went dancing off to meet him with Nemle's invitation to bring him to dinner if he cared to come. She had been walking for nearly twenty minutes and she was just beginning to be afraid that he might not find her, when suddenly he was beside her.

"Oh Daniel," she said turning to him. "I didn't see you."

Her face was alight as she lifted it for his kiss. He stopped and pulled her to him a little more roughly than she was expecting. His kiss seemed rough too, his mouth hard on hers, his tongue almost a violation. When he let her go she pulled away a little and looked at him uncertainly.

"Daniel?" His name held a question.

"What is it Mary mine?"

"I told Nemle about you," she said reassured. "She said for me to invite you to dinner."

"On a boat I can't even see," he said, his voice mocking.

"That doesn't matter," Marheh said eagerly. "Nemle said she would show me how to guide you."

He gave a short laugh and grabbed her hand.

"Come on," he said, pulling her after him off the path and into a small patch of woodland.

She went with him willingly, longing for the excitement of his touch, wanting to show him how much she loved him.

She saw he had prepared for her coming. A rug lay on the ground in a tiny, sheltered clearing. She turned quickly to kiss him, then blushed and looked away. He took hold of her belt and pulled her close. After a while he picked her up and laid her down on the rug. She ached with love and longing and something more primitive that she did not understand. He seemed impatient today, but then so was she and made no protest when he unfastened her belt and pushed up her tunic and shirt to uncover her breasts, no gentle unbuttoning this time.

Marheh abandoned herself to Daniel's lovemaking, his hand on her breasts, her back, his mouth on hers, his mouth on her breasts, her hands in his hair until she felt as if she might explode with longing. When his hands began to unfasten her trousers it seemed only natural to arch upwards to help him. Then suddenly everything stopped. She opened her eyes. Daniel was kneeling over her looking at her with an unreadable expression on his face."

"Daniel?" she said, her voice husky.

He did not answer, but continued to look at her. He sat back on his heels and lifted his hands from her hips.

"Daniel?" she said again.

"I must be a better man than I thought," he said bitterly as if to himself.

Marheh struggled to sit up, imprisoned between his knees.

"What is it?"

She found she wanted to cry.

"I can't do it," he said, but he was not talking to her. Then he seemed to get angry. "What is a little innocent like you doing with enemies?"

She did not know how to reply.

"Cover yourself up," he said next, standing up and stepping back from her.

Struggling with tears she pulled down her shirt and tunic and stood up.

"I don't understand," she said trying to keep her voice steady.

He gripped her upper arms and pulled her towards him as if to shake her.

"You little fool," he said angrily. "You shouldn't be so trusting. Granny witch ought to give you the whipping of your life."

She was trembling so much she could not speak only look at him with piteous, uncomprehending eyes. He let go one hand and thrust it into his pocket.

"He paid me," he said, pulling out a gold sovereign. "Two of these and eight more to come if I could get into your knickers."

Marheh gave a cry of pain and tried to pull away from him, but he pulled her back.

"You listen to me."

In curt angry phrases he told her how a wealthy young man had heard him joking about her and Nemle in the pub at Marisford and offered him money to seduce her.

"Why?" She choked on the word.

"Who knows? Perhaps he wanted to teach you a lesson." He gave her a little shake then thrust her away from him. "Go on, get …"

She staggered and found her balance again still looking at him as if she could not quite believe what she was hearing. He lunged at her as if to strike her.

"Go on, go! Run to Granny witch, quick! Tell her I won't be coming to dinner."

> "Since we have discovered the soul song I am
> sure this must be the heart of it all. I say
> discovered, but perhaps I mean uncovered,
> because it is not a new thing, only a new
> understanding of something that has always
> been waiting for us."
>
> *Sila's Journal : the early years*

Chapter Five

On *Day Bringer* Nemle tried to be sanguine about Marheh's well being. At least she knew now and could try to understand. She had nothing in her own life to draw on for guidance. It had been her duty to care for Hafa who had been her mentor and she had done so. She had loved her first out of duty and love had grown as Hafa had nurtured and respected her. Now she loved Marheh. It had been her duty to love her too, but she had not needed duty to prompt her for long despite a difficult and rebellious beginning to their relationship. If Marheh chose to leave the water road for this Daniel it would break her heart, she thought now, but underneath she was aware that hearts did not break so easily.

She was standing at the sink looking out the galley window when she saw Marheh coming, running, stumbling, her hands outstretched almost as if she needed to feel her way. Then she saw her trip and fall headlong onto the grassy path. For a moment she looked to be struggling to get up then she put her head down and lay still. Nemle caught back an anxious cry and set off to go to her. When she came closer she realised that Marheh was not injured, but crying desolately. Quietly she approached and sat down beside her on the grass. At first all she did was sit and think her concern then she began gently rubbing Marheh's back, making little crooning sounds.

At last Marheh lifted her head.

"Mama Nemle."

It was such a sad, croaky little voice Nemle longed to be able to comfort her but instead she said firmly. "You need to get up now Marheh. Come along inside and wash your face. You'll make yourself sick."

She stood up herself and held out her hand. Like a good child Marheh stood up and went with her.

While Marheh washed her face Nemle cleared away the extra cutlery and crockery that had been set ready and put the kettle on for sperit. She badly wanted to know what had happened but knew she must wait for Marheh to tell her, or not tell her if that was what she chose. Although she ached for Marheh's pain there was a small warmth at the knowledge that Marheh would remain with her.

She was more composed when she came out from the bathroom but she looked very weary. Nemle handed her a mug of sperit and wanted to settle her in the armchair but she shook her head and took her usual place on the footstool. Nemle sat down beside her with her own drink and waited quietly.

"I must be such a fool," Marheh said at last, her voice sounded bitter and exhausted.

Nemle said nothing, but one hand reached forward to touch her shoulder.

Slowly she continued, speaking almost as if the story belonged to someone else. For the most part she controlled herself rigidly, her voice quiet and colourless, but repeating Daniel's ugly phrase "paid to get into my knickers", was more than she could bear. Her voice broke. She put her head down on Nemle's knee her whole body shaking with dry, painful sobs. Nemle rubbed her back between her shoulder blades and said nothing. At last Marheh lifted her head and looked at her.

"So he won't be coming to dinner," she said.

It was a brave attempt at lightness but it did not quite come off and Nemle had time to see her tears overflow before she put her head down again.

Later Nemle insisted she eat something then put her to bed, dosing her with chamomile tea to help her sleep. She went to the galley and began to clear up, her mind full of questions. Was it just random mischief, attempted because Marheh was young, beautiful and different, or was it deliberately aimed at Marheh herself? Who was the wealthy young man? Who was

Daniel? The most urgent question, the one that pushed its way to the surface time and again was how could she help Marheh, how would Marheh be affected? She completed the chores automatically unaware of what she had done minutes after she had done it then she sat down and tried to compose herself enough to enter the discipline of the soul.

She did not sleep much, but the soul song refreshed her and wrapped Marheh and *Day Bringer* in its music. Such an intangible thing, but in her mind's eye Nemle could see the music in beautiful colours infiltrating the darkness that was sadness, pain, even evil and softly but inexorably changing it for the better.

From the moment Hafa, her mentor, had guided her towards the discipline of the soul Nemle had revelled in its enfolding beauty. She had loved the practice. Hafa had watched over her and helped her to explore the soul song so that by the time she had left her Nemle was beginning to feel a degree of mastery. From the day she had finished her apprenticeship until the day Hafa died, eighteen months later they had sung together each evening, a wordless communion that nourished her for those first months alone.

She could not understand how there could be Silberay who found this difficult discipline unsatisfying though she knew there were some who practised it rarely. To Nemle, part of its strength was that so little of herself was involved. Once she had placed herself in that quiet space where she could enter the discipline something outside herself seemed to make the song. Yet it was her song and she knew it would not exist without her. Perhaps it was this relinquishment of self that made it a chore for some who preferred to see a more tangible result for their effort.

"But it isn't an effort," Nemle thought drowsily, finally closing her eyes to sleep for a couple of hours.

It would be the discipline of the soul that would help Marheh most, she decided as she dressed the next morning. That would be the most healing thing she could do, since to practise it she would have to put her feelings aside. When she left her cabin she was not really surprised to find Marheh was still in bed and set about tackling Marheh's morning chores along with her own so they could get away as usual. Everything as normal would be best, she thought, refreshing the fire and putting the kettle on. She went along to the engine room and did the engine checks and as there was still no movement in the back cabin she made sperit and took along her own mug as well as Marheh's.

Marheh's curtains were still drawn and Marheh just an untidy hump in the dim cavern of her bunk. Putting the mugs down on the top step Nemle drew the curtains briskly.

"Time to wake up," she said as the morning light poured in to reveal Marheh's face, wan and red-eyed, blinking at her from the bunk.

"I've brought you some sperit," Nemle said.

Marheh turned her face away.

"You may stay in bed today if that is what you want," Nemle went on. "I'm perfectly capable of taking us on by myself, but I want you to sit up and drink your sperit before you decide."

Marheh burrowed deeper into the bed clothes. Nemle sat down on the bottom step beside the bunk and placed her sperit on the floor at her feet. Marheh's mug she held in both hands. She waited, saying nothing, her eyes concerned, aware that Marheh really was hurting, but aware too that she was inclined to indulge her feelings. If she was determined to be broken hearted life might be a bit difficult for a while.

At last she sat up. Her hair had come out of its plait and tangled itself around her shoulders, her face was white and red in patches and she looked as if she had been crying for hours.

"Here you are," Nemle said, handing over the mug and trying to be matter-of-fact.

Marheh took it without speaking and sipped obediently, carefully not meeting Nemle's eyes. After a few sips and a few minutes she sighed deeply and tried to give the mug back to Nemle.

"You can do better than that," Nemle said firmly and refused to take it. "I know you think I'm being very unsympathetic but you'll be better to get up and go on with your life."

Marheh gave her a look and closed her eyes wearily, but she continued to hold her mug and even to take a few sips. Nemle picked up her own mug and waited.

After four and a half years as Marheh's mentor, living with her, teaching her, making it a priority to know and understand her Nemle was aware of her strengths, her courage and enthusiasm, her ability to feel deeply, but she knew too that she could not always control those same deep feelings when she needed to.

The wait went on and on. Nemle patiently sipped her drink. Marheh remained silent, her eyes closed, her hands clasped limply around her mug. Nemle had almost decided to leave her when she saw the fingers grip the mug more tightly. Marheh's head turned and she opened one eye and then the other and looked at Nemle.

"Am I being melodramatic?" she asked in a little voice that was husky with crying.

Nemle smiled at her though she suddenly felt close to tears. "I think you could say that."

"Sorry."

Marheh took a couple of big gulps from her mug and sat up straighter. Then she paused almost as if she was listening to something in herself.

"I really hurt Nemle," she said, making the discovery.

"I know you do, but I know you have plenty of courage too."

"Don't want courage."

It was a child's response and she knew as soon as she had said it. She finished her drink in one big swallow and swung her legs out from under the covers.

"If I come out to the saloon when I'm dressed please will you brush my hair?"

"Of course I will."

Nemle leaned forward to take her empty mug and give her a kiss.

"I'll make us some toast too," she added as she got up to leave.

Marheh dressed carefully and made her bed. One glance in the mirror had revealed her red eyes and tangled hair and she felt a bit ashamed of how far she had abandoned herself. Then she thought of how he had kissed her and the tears started again. She went to the bathroom and washed her face, rubbing hard with her towel. The smell of toast had begun to filter through from the galley and concentrating on that helped. Grabbing her hair brush and pasting a kind of smile on her face she went through to the saloon.

Nemle had a magic touch with a hair brush and by the time she had sorted out the tangles, brushed Marheh's long dark hair one hundred times, plaited it and finally tied the end with tape Marheh was feeling soothed and loved.

"Time we were going," Nemle said at last, handing back the brush.

Marheh turned around impulsively and gave her a hug.

"Thank you. I'll try not to inflict my feelings on you."

"What else are mentors for," Nemle said lightly. "Come on, hop to it."

Once they were under way Marheh grabbed her brass polish and climbed up onto the roof. The outside brass needed rubbing up every day and it was her job, though not one she particularly enjoyed. There were five new pallets of seedlings on the roof too so when the brass was shining she dipped the watering can and gave them a drink.

These ordinary tasks were not enough to turn her thoughts and she could not help comparing the way she had felt yesterday, eagerly anticipating her afternoon with Daniel and the way she felt today, as if she would never look forward happily again. Tears welled up and she brushed them aside angrily. "But I really loved him," a little voice in her head wailed sadly.

"Too bad," she said aloud and slid down off the roof to the gunnel to be safely out of the way of the bridge ahead.

Nemle at the tiller had been giving Marheh all the attention she could spare from steering. She smiled at her as she edged along the gunnel to the back deck.

"Come and talk to me."

Marheh held up her cloth and can of polish.

"I'll just put these away."

Nemle nodded and watched her down the steps into her cabin, wondering whether she would return. It seemed to her to be quite important to find out who was behind Daniel's actions but she couldn't question Marheh without causing her pain.

She was not long below and Nemle smiled a welcome as she came to join her.

It was a pleasant morning, cool but sunny with a light breeze. It was all new country to Marheh and on any other day she would have watched eagerly and commented on the passing scene. There was an oak wood on their left, the leaves just beginning to colour. On their right quite steep hills rose to a wooded skyline. Their way seemed quiet and remote with few signs of habitation though Nemle knew that beyond the oak wood was a large estate.

Although everything looked peaceful and beautiful Nemle had never much liked the area where they now travelled. It was the sort of place she had not wanted to moor and leave *Day Bringer* to go plant hunting despite the outward attractions of the wood. Ten years ago, the last time she had been this way, she remembered pushing herself to get beyond this rather enclosed valley with a sense of urgency that had kept her boating hours longer than her usual comfortable morning's travel. She wondered now whether Marheh would feel what she felt.

"Have you looked at the map?" she asked her as they stood together. "We are away from everything here."

Marheh looked around without much interest. "It's very quiet. I feel a bit shut in."

Nemle nodded. "I wondered whether you would feel it too. I've never stopped here, always wanted to get past as quickly as I could, but now I'm wondering if perhaps that was cowardly – as if I was not doing my job properly."

A flicker of interest appeared in Marheh's eyes.

"What would you do if we stopped?" she asked.

"Start by practising the discipline of the soul."

Unexpectedly Marheh shivered.

"Something didn't like you saying that," she said, then turned to Nemle as if she had not known what she was saying.

Nemle looked at her sharply for a moment then gave her attention to her steering while she negotiated a narrow channel where bushes had encroached. They wriggled past the obstacle then she turned back to Marheh.

"What did you mean by that?" she asked, but Marheh looked at her helplessly and shook her head.

"I don't know why I said it."

Nemle frowned, wondering whether Marheh's sadness made her particularly vulnerable to atmosphere and if it did, whether it would be better to hurry away or stop and deal with it. Even the idea of stopping was like a sore place she did not want to touch, but sometimes sore places needed touching to heal.

Day Bringer chugged quietly onwards and the knowledge of her sturdy reliability was comforting. The feel of the deck under her feet, the smooth polished wood of the tiller under her hand were like the familiar presence of a trusted friend.

Nemle's silence had given Marheh the opportunity to withdraw into herself. She stared ahead with unseeing eyes, her mind replaying the times she had been with Daniel, not just replaying but questioning, analysing, trying to pinpoint the moment when she should have held back from him.

"Daniel was angry with me. He said I was too trusting," she said at last.

"And were you?"

"I didn't think so." Marheh's voice was small and sad. "I think it is better to trust people."

Nemle reached out and squeezed her hand. "So do I, but sometimes you might be hurt."

"Yes," Marheh said flatly.

Suddenly, unexpectedly, Nemle throttled back until *Day Bringer* was barely moving. Marheh looked up, surprised.

"I can't decide," Nemle explained. "Part of me wants to keep going through here as fast as we can, but part of me thinks that is cowardly and there is work for us here."

Marheh looked down and kicked at something non-existent on the deck.

"Then there's the part of me that thinks it is important to find out who was behind Daniel's actions and why."

Marheh made a little sound of protest.

"I can keep going without your help, but I'd rather stop if I know I can rely on you."

Marheh's right boot was tracing lines on the deck. At last she looked up.

"I haven't been able to do much proper practice, even when I tried."

"But you will try?"

Marheh nodded.

"Good. Then we'll stop as soon as there is a good place. You go to the bow and look for somewhere on the same side as the wood."

Marheh made her way along the gunnel as Nemle opened the throttle a little. She looked ahead at the trees lining the bank and shivered involuntarily. The beautiful autumn colours glowed above the wood where the light caught the foliage but beneath the trunks were dark and tangled with undergrowth.

"It's just a wood," Marheh told herself, but she was aware of feeling afraid and made a conscious effort to acknowledge it and put it aside.

A few minutes later she raised her hand for Nemle, pointed towards a place where the trees receded a little and the bank seemed to fall away sharply. Nemle throttled back again and began to nose *Day Bringer* carefully into the bank while Marheh watched and listened for the sound of the hull scraping the bottom.

The water was deep enough for them to get all the way in and soon they were neatly moored and the engine turned off. It seemed unnaturally quiet without *Day Bringer's* gentle throbbing. There was no birdsong nor any other sound of life.

Nemle and Marheh made their way through to the saloon without speaking and Marheh went to make up the fire.

"It seems cold," she whispered, looking at Nemle with troubled eyes.

"It does doesn't it," Nemle said and her normal voice sounded loud, even harsh in the stillness. "Can you wait for lunch do you think? We will enter the discipline first."

Marheh nodded. She was kneeling by the stove feeding sticks in through the open door. Flames were licking around the opening.

"That's enough now Marheh," Nemle said gently.

Marheh started, glanced up at Nemle then closed the door and stood up.

"Shall I go to my room?" she asked.

Nemle shook her head.

"No, we'll do this together. Can you get comfortable enough on the footstool?"

Soon they were sitting together, Nemle in the armchair, Marheh beside her on the footstool her back against the chair. Breathing slowly and deeply they set themselves to relax and enter the discipline of the soul.

Nemle's portal was the image of a violet that she held in her mind's eye and brought closer and closer until she was lost in its deep purple heart. She found it and held it, waiting, wanting to be sure Marheh could find and use her own portal before she relinquished herself. She could only see the back of Marheh's head, the dark hair in its neat plait lying against the nape of her neck then flicking over her shoulder to be out of the way, but waiting as she was, with every sense heightened, she was aware of Marheh's deep unhappiness. She continued to wait peacefully resting in that in-between place, her attention lightly upon Marheh until she realised she had failed to find her portal. She let go of her own and leaned forward to touch her shoulder. Marheh looked around. Her face was wet with tears.

"I can't do it Nemle," she said, and more tears spilled over.

"Of course you can," Nemle said easily. She fished in her pocket and handed Marheh her own clean handkerchief. "Wipe your eyes," she said. "Now blow your nose, come on big blow."

She might have been talking to a five year old and when she had obeyed Marheh managed a watery smile.

"Come along," Nemle said getting up. "We'll pretend you are back at the beginning."

She took her hand and led her to the table. It only took a moment for her to get a candle and light it then she settled herself opposite Marheh, the candle in between them.

"Remember how you used the real candle to find your soul's light?"

Marheh nodded.

"Look now and let it happen. No need to try, just look."

Nemle's soft voice was almost hypnotic. She saw Marheh begin to quieten, heard her exhale, a long, sighing breath and knew she was on her way. Lovingly she took up her violet again and moved gently towards its heart.

Within this discipline they laid aside what they thought of as self, yet paradoxically they became more essentially themselves. The song Nemle's song encountered faltered at first as if unpractised, the melody halting and uncertain. Nemle wove her own song to support the other in and around, now adding harmony, now ornamenting the melody but always steady and reliable. Gradually the other song, that on some level Nemle knew was Marheh's, gained in confidence until it danced joyfully above Nemle's strong foundation.

Then when the songs were truly intertwined Nemle began to move them outwards. Light and music moved, expanded. It was harder work now to keep the singing alive. There seemed to be only darkness beyond and not a soft accepting dark but a sharp, hard dark that wanted to reject the song, to dim the light. For a time Nemle allowed their song to nibble at the edges of the dark, but Marheh's fragile music must not be tested too far and she was careful to withdraw gently and calmly while there was no need for urgency, no sense of danger.

When they were again aware of their surroundings Marheh looked at Nemle, her expression dreamy and content, then she yawned widely and put her head down on the table, pillowed on her folded arms. Nemle smiled a little, blew out the candle and leaned back. *Day Bringer* seemed held in stillness. Perhaps she would have a little rest too.

Hunger woke them a little later and they decided to combine lunch and dinner and have an early night. Marheh looked out of the window towards the wood, dim and shadowy in the twilight and shivered.

"We could do with a bit more fuel," she said, testing herself. "I might find some out there."

Nemle looked at her from the galley, raised her eyebrows quizzically.

"Perhaps not tonight," Marheh said, turning away from the window.

"I think it is time to draw the curtains," Nemle said. "And you could light the lamp."

It made a difference, Marheh thought as she moved quietly around *Day Bringer* drawing the curtains against the encroaching dark. Usually she loved the night, enjoyed watching the light fade over the fields, the shadows lengthen and merge, the first stars appear, but not tonight. Her cabin, usually so cosy, felt chilly and she was careful to push down the bolts that secured the door to the back deck as well as closing the curtains.

Back in the saloon with Nemle, the lamp lit, the smell of Nemle's vegetable hot pot gently inviting, she began to feel more peaceful, so that when, after they had eaten, Nemle raised the subject of Daniel she was able to respond quietly. She had cleared away their dishes and made them each a mug of sperit when Nemle put a hand over hers as it lay on the table.

"I know it is hard for you," she began. "But I need you to tell me as much as you can. Somehow we must find out who was behind him."

Marheh looked at her mug, turned it where it stood on the table then looked up at Nemle.

"Does it matter?"

"You know it does, not so much if it was just generalized mischief, but very much if you were particularly targeted."

"Why would I be particularly targeted? It doesn't make sense."

"It might to someone who does not want you to reach your full potential," Nemle said quietly.

"Well I think it's more likely that someone just saw the uniform and wanted to have a go. Sometimes I think it's crazy to draw attention to ourselves like that. Look what happened to you."

"We've always worn uniform," Nemle said. "Because we want people to recognise us, but of course sometimes that back fires."

"Daniel called us witches and when I asked why he said it was because we could disappear. People are afraid of witches. Lately it seems as if everywhere I go people are puzzled or afraid of me."

Nemle sighed a little and sipped her sperit.

"It's true that fewer people seem to understand who we are, but if we dressed like everyone else they would overlook our very existence."

"Would that matter?"

"That's an interesting question." Nemle spoke thoughtfully. "Are we more effective or less if people are aware of us, or does it make no difference?"

Marheh thought for a moment then spread out her hands and shook her head. "It depends I suppose."

Nemle smiled at her. "I expect it is a question we could debate for a very long time, but now I want to talk about Daniel."

"Oh yes." Marheh picked up her mug and put it down again. "What about him?"

"I'm wondering whether he gave you any indication of where he came from."

"I told you I met him at Marisford, at the market," Marheh said slowly. "After that he just appeared where ever I was."

"But how did he find you? You said he couldn't see the water road so how did he know where to look?"

Marheh blushed and looked away. "I showed him the map," she confessed. "That day in the pub."

"Oh Marheh!" Nemle said.

Marheh's blush deepened. "He said you ought to give me the whipping of my life for being too trusting. Maybe you should."

"Well it wasn't very sensible was it? Besides being against our usual practice."

Nemle found herself at a loss as to how to proceed. Perhaps Marheh was right and Daniel's actions were inspired by malice against Silberay as a whole. If that was the case then there seemed little point in returning to Marisford and starting a search for him when he could be anywhere. They were both aware of something that needed their attention right here, so shouldn't this be where they stayed. Their song had revealed the darkness surrounding them and it had been difficult to make even the smallest impression on it. Here was where they ought to be, she decided.

She had been silent and thoughtful for quite some time and now she was aware of Marheh looking at her anxiously.

"Are you going to punish me?" she asked.

Nemle smiled. "Send you off to get your slipper?" she teased.

Marheh sighed, her anxious look fading.

"Well I knew I shouldn't have done it," she said. "Showed him the map, I mean."

"Well next time you'll think a bit harder won't you?" Nemle took up her mug and drank the remaining sperit. "I've decided for the moment we are needed here, so can you tell me how you experienced the soul song we just sang?"

Marheh thought for a minute, turning her empty mug in her hands.

"I couldn't find my song at first," she said. "But then your song was there and lifted me up." She paused, remembering. "When we were really together you started to take us into the darkness. It was hard to keep singing then." She paused again and looked at Nemle. "I don't think I could ever be frightened while I was in the discipline of the soul, but that darkness didn't like us."

Nemle nodded slowly. "I felt it too," she said. She stood up suddenly and gathered up the mugs. "Best get to bed I think. We'll need to be fresh in the morning."

"You are the young, our heartbeat, our hope
As you dance let our love partner you
Let it lift and support as you leap into life
To dare, to become and to do."
Songs of the Silberay

Chapter Six

All very well for Nemle to say we need to be fresh in the morning, Marheh thought as she prepared for bed. Her little cabin felt cold and bleak and she seemed to be a long way from Nemle and from the warmth of the saloon. Her candle even seemed dim as if it had taken fright at the darkness. She undressed quickly and pulled on her nightdress. Usually she pottered about the cabin tidying up before blowing out the candle and opening the curtains. Tonight the curtains could stay closed. She just wanted to be into her bunk and hiding under the covers.

Although she had not expected to, Marheh went to sleep quickly, but woke sometime in the night or early morning cold and shivering. She felt as if she had been dreaming, but she could remember only images, oddly disturbing images of stunted plants with grotesque faces, of birds all beak and spiky feathers. She pulled her blankets closer around her and closed her eyes trying to ignore the cold and to replace the uncomfortable flashes from her dream with happier things, but nothing worked. She ought to get up and attend to the fire, she thought, remembering how cross Nemle had been in the first weeks of her apprenticeship when she could not seem to keep the fire in over night. Nemle would not blame her tonight she knew, but it was her job. Reluctantly she pushed aside the covers and swung her feet out onto the floor. It felt like the middle of winter. She fumbled for her slippers and for the candle she left by her bunk.

Her dressing gown hung on the back of her door and she pulled it around her and went through the engine room and the bathroom to the galley. It felt as if the fire must be completely out and she wondered that Nemle was not already attending to it. She knelt to open the door to the fire and gave a little yelp of surprise as she burnt her fingers. She was even more surprised to find the fire still glowing brightly just as it ought to be. Sucking her burned fingers she used her other hand to feed in little sticks, then more and bigger pieces as the fire took hold. She should be feeling warmer in a minute she thought watching the flames. She was so engrossed in the fire she did not hear Nemle's door open nor feel *Day Bringer*'s gentle response to her movement.

"That's enough Marheh," she said. "You'll have us on fire."

"But it's so cold," Marheh said, looking round at her. "Aren't you cold Nemle?"

Nemle shook her head, reached over her with the handle and closed the door. "There is plenty of fire. Something else is making you cold. I think something must be playing games in your head."

"In my head," Marheh echoed.

"You're a bit vulnerable just now," Nemle said, drawing her back from the fire to sit on the footstool.

She sat beside her in the arm chair, turning Marheh so they were facing each other.

"You ought to be able to defend yourself against this one," she said. "Why don't you try? I'll be here to help you if you need me."

"The discipline of the mind?" Marheh asked.

"Yes, you're good at that." Nemle smiled at her encouragingly.

Why had she not known she had been invaded, Marheh thought, trying to find her focus and uncover the intruding idea. She *was* good at it, that was what had got her into trouble at the Gathering, so how was it that she didn't know? She was still shivering and she looked at Nemle helplessly.

"Concentrate," Nemle said. "No point in asking why or how just now."

Marheh nodded and began carefully putting aside her own extraneous thoughts and turning inwards. Once she had found the way of it, it was not so very difficult to sift through and discover the invader. Then she could picture herself gathering it up and disposing of it suitably. Immediately she felt warm, hot even. Loosening her dressing gown she smiled up at Nemle.

"Sorry, I've made the place like a furnace."

Nemle smiled back. "You've done it then."

"Mmm, but I can't understand why I didn't know."

"Your natural defences are down at the moment and we haven't been practising lately," Nemle reminded her. "Perhaps we haven't practised this either. You're so good at keeping me out of your mind that we haven't worked on how to get me out once I'm in."

Marheh grinned. "But I guess we soon will," she said.

Nemle laughed. "I dare say. Now do you think we can go back to bed?"

Snug now and cosy in her bunk Marheh spent a moment or two wondering where the invading idea had come from, who had sent it, but she was too warm and sleepy to stay awake for long. She woke early though as she always did. The fire would not need attention for a while yet so she could sleep in if she wanted, but the curtains were drawn and she never liked staying in bed with the curtains drawn. She'd used up most of their firewood last night too. If she got up now and went out she could probably fill the wood box again before breakfast.

A last little snuggle into the warm bed clothes and then she was up and dressing quickly. One good thing about a uniform was that she never had to worry about what to wear. Ready to go, she pushed open her curtains and looked out to find something had changed during the night. Quickly she unbolted the back doors and hurried out onto the deck. *Day Bringer* was no longer lying neatly against the bank on the edge of the wood, but had drifted out, just a foot or two at the back, more at the front.

"But we moored properly yesterday," she said to herself. "I know we did."

Then she looked down and saw the mooring pin and coiled rope lying neatly on the deck. She and Nemle had known they were not welcome, but undoing the mooring was not very kind and meant that someone could see them, not just any someone either, but someone who did not like them, Yareblis.

She studied the bank carefully, but had no sense that she was being watched nor sight of anyone. Nemle might want to move on in the circumstances, she thought, but there would surely be no harm in collecting a little firewood first. Looking once more at the narrow gap between *Day Bringer* and the bank she decided she could easily jump the distance so she gathered the coiled centre rope loosely in one hand, poised herself on the gunnel and leapt for shore. It was not quite such a narrow gap as she thought and for a split second she was afraid she might not make it, but she did, flinging the coil of rope ahead of her and tumbling onto the grassy bank. The force of her jump had sent *Day Bringer* further away so she scrambled to her feet, took up the rope, braced herself and pulled.

The rope cut through her hands like a knife through butter. For an instant she saw bone and flesh, white and red, then it was all crimson, wet and shining. On the ground at her feet lay the rope and beside it something that had once been part of her hands, her fingers lying lightly curved, looking oddly out of context.

She screamed, and screamed again as the awareness of pain overtook her.

Nemle woke as Marheh was dressing and lay for a moment feeling *Day Bringer* move gently beneath her. An underlying sense of unease encouraged her to get up and dress however and when Marheh's jump set *Day Bringer* rocking violently she was just fastening her belt. When Marheh screamed she was already opening the door to the well deck and she looked out to see her standing on the bank holding her two hands in front of her, her face a mask of terror.

For a few moments she did not understand, then she saw what Marheh was seeing, the mutilated, bloody remnants at the end of her arms.

Now was no time for finesse and she thrust her mind into Marheh's without thinking about laws and permissions. Even the illusion could damage Marheh irrevocably if it took too strong a hold.

Nemle was very familiar with Marheh's mind and it was not difficult to identify where the illusion began, but dispatching it would be a different matter because it had been designed to tap into Marheh's own hidden fears. Somehow Nemle would have to calm her enough for her to be able to act on her own behalf. She would need to uncover the fear and face it in the end or she would always remain vulnerable. Nemle held her mind still amidst the chaos that was Marheh's panic and began by naming her, steadily, lovingly again and again.

She could not go to her physically. *Day Bringer* was too far from the bank and she needed the extra protection built into the boat by years of loving ownership and many hours of practice at the discipline of the soul. She could see her though with the small part of herself that still stood outside. She had stopped screaming and was staring at her hands, mourning with a continuous, keening cry.

Within Marheh's mind, Nemle still spoke her name and now it seemed that she heard. The frantic activity began to ease a little.

"Look again Marheh," Nemle's mind insisted. "Look with your own eyes. Recognise the illusion."

After what seemed a long time the mind she inhabited began tentatively to function again. The anguished keening became a whimper then a hiccup. She saw Marheh's face change, saw her begin to recognise her hands were whole, undamaged, still useful, skilful servants of her mind. She named her again, making herself a bulwark of loving warmth for Marheh to hold onto. Now she could hold on, recognising Nemle, acknowledging her presence. Nemle remained with her, calm and steady, waiting for her to realise the next step, knowing it would be almost impossibly hard.

Gradually she changed the quality of her waiting, became expectant. When Marheh understood what she must do, Nemle almost cried out, her rejection of the knowledge was so fierce, but she stood her ground, still warm and loving but adamant that Marheh herself must finally destroy the illusion by taking up the rope again and pulling *Day Bringer* into the bank.

"I won't leave you," she assured her. "But I won't control your mind either."

Trembling, terrified that this nightmare might repeat itself, Marheh reached down to touch the rope, just touch it then jerk her hand away.

"It's just a rope," she thought and tried again to make herself believe this.

"It's just a rope," she heard Nemle's voice in her mind.

"Just a rope," she echoed.

"Touch it," Nemle said. "Handle it a little. Take your time."

So she did all that and at last, after many false starts, she grasped the rope, braced herself and began to pull.

At first she pulled so tentatively that *Day Bringer* barely moved, but as she began to trust the rope the boat began to come in more quickly until she was lying neatly beside the bank again. Nemle held out her hand to Marheh, but she shook her head and went as usual to the back deck, coiling the line as she went. As soon as she stepped on board Nemle stopped watching her, eased out of her mind and hurried through to join her.

She had placed the rope carefully in its proper place and was sitting on the deck, her hands held in front of her. She was flexing her fingers and turning her palms over then up again. When she saw Nemle she gave her a tremulous smile and began to cry. Nemle lowered herself to the deck and held her until she was calm. *Day Bringer*, neither moored nor attended to, drifted gently away from the bank.

"I'm sorry," Marheh said at last, leaning away from Nemle and reaching for her handkerchief. "I've done nothing but cry over you for days." She blew her nose and rubbed a hand over her eyes.

"I'll be cross and send you to bed later," Nemle said with a smile. "For now you can help me get up, I'm too old for sitting on the floor."

After making her breakfast and insisting she eat it, Nemle did send her firmly to bed. Her white face and bruised looking eyes spoke of the aftermath of fear and shock. She did not put up any serious resistance and once she was asleep Nemle was free to turn her attention to *Day Bringer* who had been neglected for far too long.

Fortunately there was no wind and scarcely any current so she was resting gently against a clump of reeds. Moving quietly around her Nemle did the engine checks then walked along the gunnels looking for anything that might cause a problem. Then she started the engine and eased quietly into the deeper water.

For a time she allowed herself to rest in the task. Steering required little thought on a calm day and *Day Bringer*'s gentle throbbing provided familiarity and comfort. She too was tired, drained by the effort of helping Marheh, but she realised they needed to be away from the wood before they could moor. Whatever or whoever had attacked them was strong and malevolent and they would need to be much better prepared and stronger themselves before they attempted to address the problem.

Gradually the countryside changed. The woods gave way to steeply sloping fields where sheep grazed. The water road seemed enclosed, far from anything that indicated human presence. One or two tumble down structures might once have been shepherds' huts, but not for many years now. Nemle knew another hour or so would take them to the foot of a flight of ten locks. She would moor at the bottom, she decided, knowing Marheh would enjoy helping, but not wanting to wake her especially.

As she travelled onwards Nemle's mind was increasingly occupied with the problems of understanding the nature of the illusion that had fastened itself to Marheh.

She had encountered Yareblis illusions like the chill that Marheh had experienced during the night, though even that was surprising. *Day Bringer* was usually sufficient protection against such attacks. She remembered only once during her years with Hafa when they had needed to work together to dispel the illusion of fire surrounding a bridge they must pass beneath. She had been well into her thirties then. Standing in the well deck she had met the fire first and screamed at the leaping flames and searing heat. At the tiller armed with the knowledge and experience of her more than eighty years Hafa had not been touched, but had entered Nemle's mind to support her as she struggled to see through the illusion.

It seemed as if the Yareblis were gaining strength and skill in using mind control in ways that contravened Silberay law. She would discuss with Marheh a new training regime that would prepare her to defend herself. The difficulty was thinking the way the Yareblis thought so as to pre-empt the next form of attack.

She was still turning over the problem in her mind when they reached the first of the locks. The malign influence surrounding the woods had passed and she moored up without difficulty only about thirty yards from the lock mouth. When all was secure she went quietly into the back cabin. Marheh was just stirring, aroused by the cessation of noise when the engine was turned off.

"Mama Nemle," she said sleepily.

Nemle sat on the bottom step beside her bunk.

"Better?" she asked as Marheh rolled onto her back to stretch and examine her hands.

She looked better. There was colour in her face and her eyes no longer seemed drowned in tears.

"I'm hungry," she said, sitting up and pushing back the covers.

"Good." Nemle stood up. "I'll see you in the galley in ten minutes."

It was not even that long before she appeared, face washed, hair neatly plaited, dressed and ready for anything. Nemle wondered at the resilience of youth and tried to remember how long it had been since she had been able to bounce back so quickly. Of course it was youth that needed the resilience to get itself out of the scrapes it had so unwisely embraced.

"Bread and butter, hard boiled eggs and the last of the tomatoes," Nemle said, waving towards the table. "I'll just make the sperit."

"I'm doing the washing up," Marheh said, slicing her tomato onto a piece of bread. "You're not to spoil me any more."

"I see. So it's back to bread and water and spankings is it?"

"I can take it."

"I'm not sure I can," Nemle said laughing.

"Did you get into trouble when you were an apprentice?"

"Absolutely not… how could you even suggest it!"

"I thought not." Marheh's tone was gloomy.

"Of course I did," Nemle said. "Not quite as much trouble as you and not the same sort of trouble, but I had my share of bread and water."

"Really bread and water?"

"Not really, penitence I mean."

"What was your sort of trouble?" Marheh asked curiously.

Nemle thought for a minute, wondering whether Marheh would understand her younger self.

"I was not very happy at home," she said at last. "I don't think my mother and father really wanted a daughter except to help around the house. I expect they loved me in their own way, but Hafa was kind to me, kinder than anyone had ever been and I worshipped her." She paused, looking back at the plain, needy child she had been. "It isn't a good idea that. If you worship a good person it asks too much of them. Hafa didn't want my worship. I wanted to serve her, slave for her with no reward except her kindness, but she understood herself too well to let me. She could be arrogant. You should have heard her sail into people at the Gathering when they didn't agree with her. She told me later that my uncritical devotion had been bad for her, encouraging the arrogance to become pride. I never saw her as proud or arrogant but I came to understand how difficult I was making life for her." She paused again, remembering how much the realisation had hurt. "I was so ashamed when I saw that idolising her was not love because it was more about what I wanted than what she wanted."

Marheh was looking thoughtful and a bit puzzled and Nemle wondered whether she could understand. Marheh was much more secure in herself than she had been at her age.

"That's enough about me," she said. "It's not very interesting."

"It is," Marheh said slowly. "I don't quite understand, but it is interesting. I can't imagine thinking like that about someone."

No, Nemle thought, but perhaps someone might feel that way about you one day and then you might remember this conversation.

She smiled at Marheh.

"No," she said aloud. "Your troubles are different."

It was mid afternoon by the time they had eaten and cleared up.

"Do you want a walk this afternoon?" Nemle asked as Marheh finished wiping down the sink.

She looked up, opened her mouth to reply then hesitated. Nemle watched sympathetically.

"I'm not sure I do," she said at last. "But I ought to. I'm a bit scared."

"Not surprising. I'll tell you what we'll do. We'll start by practising the discipline of the soul. That will be good for us and help to reassure you that we have left the darkness behind. Then I want you to walk up the flight, it's only about a mile. On the way I want you to look at the locks and see what is different about these and when you get to the top I want you to communicate to me what you see there. How does that sound?"

Marheh smiled. "Very ordinary, and just what I need," she said.

"I'm convinced that if we do nothing but practise the discipline of the soul in the places where we travel this is life enhancing. If we are requested to perform some practical service, or if we see some need we could meet we are merely adding something tangible to our continued offering of ourselves."

Sila's journal: the early years

Chapter Seven

By the time they had sung together and Marheh had studied the map she was quite looking forward to her walk. She set off briskly up the rise to the top of the first lock, turning to wave to Nemle who was sitting in the well deck enjoying the late afternoon light. At first glance the lock seemed similar to those she had previously encountered so she continued on. She would stop and examine the workings more closely when she was out of Nemle's sight.

The first three locks were in a straight line and from each one she could look back and see *Day Bringer* getting smaller and smaller in the distance. Already she was quite high. She knew from her map that each lock raised the water road about ten feet. It was fascinating to see it running away from her into the distance through the landscape she had slept through that morning. On the horizon a smudge of darkness might be the wood. She waved to Nemle once more and turned to continue her walk.

The water road curved around to the left and the next lock was about one hundred yards away. Beside her the land rose sharply almost like a cliff. Not much grew on the steep side except a bit of tufty grass. A scramble of vines seemed to tumble over the edge. On her right, beyond the water road there were steep grassy banks bounded by a hawthorn hedge. The red berries provided a touch of brightness in the rather bleak, unwelcoming landscape.

When she reached the lock she stopped to examine it more carefully and stepped out onto the lock gate to see if there was a view back the way she had come. A narrow gap in the surrounding hills revealed a tiny spire far on the horizon and a distant patchwork of green and gold. The lock itself was half full of water. Moss grew on the stone sides above the water line and dampness glazed the heavy wooden gates.

Marheh liked locks. She enjoyed the challenge of operating the paddles, changing the water level, managing the heavy gates. These ones had a different safety mechanism on the paddles and she saw that instead of the usual single gate at the top of the lock there were two gates, the same as those at the bottom. She smiled, pleased at her discovery, then wondered at the pride that had kept her from checking at the first lock.

On she went, climbing steadily, glad that Nemle had encouraged her to stretch her legs. She had not forgotten Daniel and thinking of him made her sad, but the shock of the illusion had shown her she had things to be grateful for too.

After the seventh lock was a longer space and for a moment she wondered whether she had miscounted, but a couple of minutes more of walking and she came to the last three, very close together, each lock emptying into the one below. She knew it was called a staircase when they operated like that. This was the first she had seen. She walked up beside them trying to understand what she would need to do when *Day Bringer* reached this point. Then she remembered Nemle had asked her to communicate what she saw.

What was special, she wondered, looking around. There was not much view even now. The water road still travelled between high cliffs as far ahead as she could see. Even looking back the view was confined within a narrow gap, the distant patchwork was still there though the spire was hidden. Then she smiled to herself. What if she sent Nemle her memory of a different view? Would she be able to trick her? She thought of an especially favourite place, built the picture in her mind then concentrated on reaching Nemle's mind to show it to her.

A few minutes later she laughed out loud. Nemle had sent her a picture in return. A large and ferocious Nemle held a small and squalling Marheh over her knee. Thinking a quick acknowledgement to Nemle she sat herself on the beam of the lock gate and prepared to be sensible.

What could she really see? Was there anything to be learnt? If she tried to listen with her heart what would she hear? First of all the distant view was filtered through her mind to Nemle's. The sun was low now and she was in shadow but the patchwork field was flooded with gold. Then back to the high hills that framed the view. Nothing moved in the shadows and it was hard to make out the separate components though she was aware of tall trees and dark patches that could have been bushes or perhaps piles of rock. Then suddenly a large bird soared upwards, circling now dark, now golden as it moved in and out of the light. She watched it glide and hover then plunge out of sight and for an instant knew the terror of some small hunted creature.

She drew her attention back then to the locks. The gates leaked a little and the sound of the water seemed to echo in the confined space. It felt as if no one had set foot here for a long time and a kind of brooding sadness hung between the cliffs. It must have cost the Silberay enormous effort to bring the water road to this place, such a difficult landscape and no people. Marheh had forgotten Nemle as she sat and pondered the possible reasons for coming to such a lonely place.

"Come back now Marheh." Nemle's words in her mind almost shouted themselves into her stillness and she blinked as if roused from a dream.

The light was fading quickly now and she realised she would have to hurry if she was to be back before dark. Pushing herself off the lock beam she began to jog down the path. A bit more than half way home, as she was nearing the last group of locks, she saw something moving in the vines. She stopped running but continued to approach quietly and carefully thinking it might be an animal of some kind. Then, as she came closer, she saw it was a small child. She stood still, her heart in her mouth as the child climbed down the cliff face, quite at home amongst the vines, seemingly unafraid. Then she heard the sound of someone calling. The child looked up, responded with an echoing cry not unlike an owl's call and began to go back the way it had come.

Marheh watched until the child was safely over the edge then walked on slowly, wondering.

Nemle had lit the lamp in the saloon and its soft glow beckoned. Marheh quickened her step when she saw it knowing she would be glad of *Day Bringer*'s sheltering warmth and feeling of safety. *Day Bringer* was so small in the surrounding landscape, her light tiny and frail seen from a distance, but once on board she held a world of love and protection. She began to run again pushing herself, all of a sudden wanting to be there with Nemle enclosed, away from the coming night and the strange lonely place outside.

She was still breathing hard when she came into the galley. Nemle had been cooking and the boat was filled with appetising smells. She turned to smile at Marheh as she entered and something about the way she looked, so solid and strong and dependable, prompted Marheh to go closer, then closer to hug and be hugged so the outside was banished.

"Dinner is ready," Nemle said. "Will you set the table?"

"It smells good." Marheh busied herself with cutlery and crockery. "And it's good to be home too. Something feels a bit creepy out there in the dark."

Nemle smiled, but did not reply. She pushed a full plate towards her and moved with her own to sit at the table.

It was not until she had taken the edge off her hunger that Nemle put down her knife and fork and looked across at her.

"What?" she asked quietly.

Marheh began to tell her about the child and the calling voice.

"Just a small child, I thought perhaps five or six, with long straggly hair and ragged clothes," she finished.

"So it's true," Nemle said after a long pause.

Marheh looked at her questioningly.

"There is a story of a group of people, a tribe I suppose you could say, who were displaced from their homes by a rich landowner. They became outlaws, skilled at poaching, thieving, doing what they could to survive outside the law. No one knew whether it was just a legend or whether, if true, there were any of them left. It seems perhaps there are."

"Living out there?"

"That's how the story goes. Hiding in the hills amongst the trees, coming out to rob travellers, living in caves in the hillside."

"I can't imagine there would be many travellers to rob," Marheh said. "Where could they go around here?"

"Now-a-days there would be few travellers," Nemle said. "But one hundred and fifty years ago when Silberay began to make the water road travel was different and beneath the water road is one of the few reasonable paths through these hills."

"Beneath the water road!"

"Yes."

Marheh pulled at the drawn curtain beside her and stared out into the darkness, seeing little beyond her own reflection in the glass.

"But I thought people who can't see the water dimension feel uncomfortable if they are in the same space."

"Yes," Nemle said again.

"Well we shouldn't have done it," Marheh said fiercely. "It isn't fair to make the path uncomfortable when it is the only one."

"Not quite the only one," Nemle said. "But near enough. It would have been a difficult decision."

"Why?" Marheh demanded. "Why are we here? Why did we need to come this way?"

"In the days when we were more visible, when people seemed to value what we offered, we were asked to come." Nemle could see Marheh's crusading instincts were aroused. "Silberay who worked this section would tow another loaded barge filled with goods that needed to be brought through the hills."

"So the outlaws couldn't see them?" Marheh asked.

"I don't think that was the reason," Nemle said. "More that it was a gentler way of carrying things when the roads and paths were so difficult."

Marheh sighed, put her elbows on the table, propped her chin in her hands.

"I just can't help thinking about the child I saw," she said. "I don't care if he or she is an outlaw. We've made it more difficult for them to live. They must hate us."

"I don't expect they know we exist," Nemle said. "Anymore than we knew about them."

But Marheh was not satisfied.

"I think we should help them," she said.

"I'm not sure they will want our help," Nemle said. "I imagine they are fiercely independent. Why else would they still be living the way they do?"

"But…"

"Think a minute." Nemle leaned forward across the table. "Would you like it if someone who didn't know us, didn't know the way we live is our choice, wanted to help us?"

"But we don't need any help"

"Other people might not think that."

Marheh was silent for a while, but Nemle could see she was not happy.

"I don't think that child has enough to eat," she said at last. "That can't be right."

"No," Nemle said. "Of course it isn't, but the solution is not for you to go out there with your fifteen shillings in your pocket and let them take it from you."

Marheh smiled ruefully. "No, I can see that but…"

Nemle reached out and put one hand over hers. "Often you can only help people if you are ready to stand alongside them. It takes time and commitment." She sighed. "It is one of the reasons we keep to the same route for several years, but even then we miss things, and sometimes we hurry past when perhaps we shouldn't."

Marheh looked down at her plate, scraped her fork across the surface and licked it.

"Do we have to hurry past here?" she asked.

Nemle smiled at her.

"We can take two or three days to go up the flight if you like. How would that do?"

"It's a start," Marheh said.

Later, lying snug and cosy in her bunk, Marheh thought about the child and wondered if he was snug and cosy too. She and Nemle had continued to talk as they cleared up after the meal and then sitting by the fire. She felt pleased all over again as she remembered how Nemle had thanked her for challenging the way they were travelling and making her think again about their purpose. She turned on her side and pulled the blankets closer around her. Nemle had threatened all sorts of dire penalties if she stayed awake worrying and wondering, but it was not easy to switch off. They were going to moor at the top of the first three locks and Nemle had promised she could explore if she was sensible.

She turned over again, kneaded her pillow a bit and closed her eyes. What would Nemle consider to be sensible? Could she try to climb the vines, or was there another way to the top of the cliffs. She saw again in her mind's eye the small dark shape of the child, silhouetted against the sky for just a moment as it went up and over the cliff top.

An hour later she was still awake and felt *Day Bringer* move gently. Then Nemle scratched on her door and came in wrapped in her dressing gown, carrying her candle.

"Silly child," she said, setting the candle down carefully before sitting beside Marheh on the bottom step. "Come, practise."

Obediently Marheh turned her mind to search for her candle flame and within minutes she slept.

Working up the locks next morning was rather more of a challenge than Marheh had expected. The paddles were very stiff as if they had not been used for a long time. The gates were old and leaked, making it difficult to fill the lock and reach the balance point where the gates wanted to open. Marheh pulled and pushed, battled with her windlass and struggled mightily at each stage of the process, but at last the first three were conquered and *Day Bringer* moored ready to tackle the next group. Nemle smiled as Marheh, red faced and dishevelled, joined her on the back deck.

"That looked like hard work."

Marheh nodded.

"Fun though."

"I'm not sure I could have managed by myself now."

"Yes you could, but they were pretty tough. Surely the boat who had this route before us should have come through here. It felt like I was the first to raise the paddles in ten years or so."

Nemle shrugged.

"Perhaps other things, other places took priority. I'll have a walk up the next group this afternoon and see if I can do a bit of maintenance, sometimes a bit of grease is enough. Do you still want to go off and explore?"

"May I?"

"As long as you're sensible. I had a thought while I was watching you work. Why not take a basket and do a bit of plant hunting? It might give you a point of connection if you were to meet someone."

Marheh looked down at her boots and blushed.

"I'm not very good at recognising things yet," she said, knowing she could have been if she had taken the trouble to learn.

Nemle laughed.

"Do you think I don't know that!" She had long recognised Marheh would not be earning her living making medicines and tisanes. "I can always use more dandelion though, and even you can recognise that."

"Just as long as you don't make me drink it," Marheh said, remembering how Nemle had dosed her with it when she thought she needed a tonic.

"Get the whole plant," Nemle told her. "It's a good time to gather the root, but don't take too much from any one place, and no cheek or I'll find something much worse than dandelion to dose you with."

Marheh laughed and followed Nemle down to the galley to eat before she set out.

A bit more than an hour later she had found her way to the top of the cliff and was pottering along a narrow path on the edge of a wood. It all looked quite bland up here, she thought, a bit of rough pasture, a few trees, then more trees. She had rather wanted to climb up the vines, but Nemle had been discouraging, and a surreptitious attempt had demonstrated it to be rather more difficult than she expected. Instead she had walked on to discover a steep, rocky track between lock five and lock six. It was quite a scramble, a climb rather than a walk, but it led to the path she was now exploring.

Just ahead she saw a single, bright golden globe. She had an idea that it was not quite the right time for dandelions to flower, but she was grateful for the signal it provided since she was not at all sure she would have noticed the plant without the flower. She put down her basket and knelt, trowel in hand. Soon the plant was in the basket and she was on her way again.

A little further along the path divided. One way continued to skirt the wood, but the other wandered its way between the trees. Marheh hesitated. Probably Nemle would not think it sensible to venture into the wood, but it seemed much more like exploring.

"I'm not old enough yet, for sensible," she told herself, turning in under the trees.

At first it seemed to her that the path was leading her back towards the place where she had seen the child, but soon she had lost all sense of direction as it turned and twisted between the trees, now climbing steeply, now plunging downwards. There was not much undergrowth and the ground was very rocky. Not too many dandelions here, she thought, wishing she could abandon the basket with its solitary offering and use both hands to help negotiate the track.

She climbed down to a little valley and stopped to look around. The path was almost non existent now and she wondered whether she had crossed the line between adventurous and fool hardy. If she got herself into trouble here it was not very likely that Nemle could rescue her.

She rested against a rock and looked back the way she had come. The trees towered above her, thick trunks surrounded her. The ground beneath her feet was damp and covered with leaf litter. Perhaps she should go back now, she thought, not quite liking the prospect of more twists and turns, climbs and scrambles. She reached down for her basket which she had put at the base of the rock. She felt around for the handle then turned to discover the basket had gone.

Surprised, she stared around her then a little giggle alerted her to the presence of a child not far off, half hidden amongst the trees. This child seemed a bit older than the one climbing the vines, but similarly ragged and dishevelled. Realising it had been seen it began to skip away, darting between the trees. Marheh took off after it, determined to retrieve the basket, not thinking about the sense of her actions.

The child seemed very much at home in this difficult landscape, scrambling over rocks, swinging around trees, never quite allowing Marheh to catch up, but not going so fast that she gave up hope. Then, after a particularly awkward scramble down a narrow, rocky track Marheh suddenly found herself alone. She looked around, her breath coming in gasps, the sounds of her exertion still throbbing in her ears. She had a moment to recognise that she did not have a clue where she was and then a figure stepped out from behind a tree and stood before her. He was joined by another and another and in a moment Marheh was surrounded by half a dozen silent figures looking at her gravely. She gulped and tried to smile, but they made no response.

"I think I'm lost," she said at last when the silence extended. "I was looking for dandelions," she added.

"In the wood?" One of the figures mocked her.

Marheh thought perhaps this one was a woman. Her voice was low and oddly accented but understandable.

"No," Marheh said. "I think I was looking for you in the wood."

This statement caused a flicker of expression on those faces Marheh could see.

"And now you have found us?" It was a man who spoke this time.

"I..." Marheh faltered at the look on his face. "I... just wanted to say hello," she finished lamely.

There was a snort behind her, but when she turned the faces were still and unreadable.

"You'd better come with us," the man said.

The surrounding figures moved closer.

"I should be getting home," Marheh ventured. "My mentor will be anxious."

There was no reply, but the figures began to move, herding her forward with them. She had a moment of panic, her mind sending a flash of fear to Nemle. Then she realised she was on her own. Nemle could not come to her here and her mental support would only help if she wanted to use mind control to escape. These people had not actually threatened her and she was curious. She fought down her fear and tried to breathe calmly. She needed to find enough focus to reassure Nemle too.

The figures did not take her far. Behind a pile of big rocks was a narrow cleft almost hidden by vines. There they guided her between the rocks and into a small clearing. The child stood there with her basket and two other children crouched by a small fire with a big kettle at its edge. Marheh looked around. There were a couple of rough shelters built against the rock face and she could hear the sound of water trickling. The man who had taken the lead invited her to sit by the fire. The others gathered around, except for one woman who disappeared into a shelter and returned with a small wooden box. It looked old and worn though it still shone as though it was regularly polished.

"It is our custom to share food and drink with travellers," the man said.

"Oh... thank you."

Marheh looked uncertainly from one face to another. The man was quite old, perhaps fifty. His face was brown and lined and his long matted hair had quite a lot of grey. Another man, younger and two adolescent boys flanked him. The woman with the box also seemed old and beside her was a younger woman. All of them wore ragged clothes, layered for warmth. Marheh wished they would not look at her quite so intently, almost as if they wanted something from her. She tried to smile, but no one smiled back. She could not hope to control them all, even with Nemle's help and anyway she was quite lost. Her smile had somehow fixed itself to her face, but it did not belong to her.

The older woman had been preparing a drink using the kettle and a pinch of something from the box. Now she held out a small wooden cup in both hands and offered it to Marheh.

"Drink," the man commanded.

Reluctantly Marheh took the cup. It felt warm and smelt a little spicy.

"You will drink with me?" she asked, wondering what the drink contained.

The woman handed another small cup to the older man, almost as if she had expected Marheh's question. He raised it and waited. Marheh lifted her cup and together they drank.

Whatever it was didn't taste too bad, Marheh thought, handing back her empty cup. Better than Nemle's dandelion tonic anyway though it left a slightly bitter aftertaste. She smiled at the assembled company.

"Thank you," she said. "It has been nice meeting you, but I think I'd better go now."

"Not yet," said the woman. Her voice was gentle and adamant and for a moment Marheh was reminded of Nemle.

The group still watched her intently, not threatening exactly, but somehow expectant. No one spoke. The silence was uncomfortable and once or twice Marheh opened her mouth then closed it again. She shifted position on the hard ground and then found herself beginning to relax. The arm she was propping herself up with gave way and she subsided slowly onto the dirt. The faces around her seemed to grow larger, the watchful eyes bigger and brighter. A bunch of big brown flowers with shiny black centres, or blue centres, or grey centres or… She sprawled out on the ground and began to giggle helplessly.

The woman laughed softly and held out both hands to her, but her own hands and arms seemed no longer to obey her. She wondered for an instant whether to be afraid but she felt so relaxed, as if she was floating, that she smiled beatifically upon them all and continued to giggle.

"Now you may pay for your visit," the woman told her, still gentle and adamant.

Paying seemed to mean that they took her clothes, her shirt and tunic, her boots and trousers, while she continued to float and smile. When she was stripped to knickers and chemise the younger man hoisted her over his shoulder still gurgling happily. There was a quiet chorus of thankyous and goodbyes as he set off, bearing her away from the clearing and off through the woods unhindered by her weight or the foolish burbling she was making behind his back.

She was flying when he finally lowered her to the ground, soaring above and between the trees, feeling the air rushing beneath her. He laid her on her back amidst a tangle of vines and carefully placed her dandelion in her left hand before jogging away. For a little while she lay there wide-eyed, still flying, no longer in the trees, but in the pale sky that seemed so close above her. Then she stretched out her arms as if to change direction and rolled over. And over. And the earth fell away beneath her.

Sometimes I'm heavy and burdened
Sometimes I'm light as air.
Sometimes I want to go nowhere
Sometimes I'll do and I'll dare.
   Refrain :
         Walk on, walk on through the landscape
         Take another step, step again.
         Feel the earth beneath your feet
         Feel yourself and nature meet
         Walk on, walk on in sun or rain.

Songs of the Silberay

Chapter Eight

Once she had watched Marheh out of sight Nemle gathered together a few tools and a pot of grease, put her windlass in her belt and set off up the flight. She was glad to have something constructive to do to take her mind off Marheh's escapade. Perhaps she had been foolish to allow it, but she knew Marheh would have resented it if she had forbidden her to explore. After all many young women her age had homes and families and expected to take responsibility for their actions. It was a difficult balance. Marheh had placed herself under Nemle's authority but if she exercised that authority too rigorously it would limit her growth and damage their developing relationship.

At the lock gates Nemle put down her tools and went to examine the mechanism of the paddles and test them with her windlass. They were certainly stiff. Just dealing with the four gates of this lock was likely to take all afternoon. She opened her pot of grease and set to work. Tomorrow Marheh could learn how to help her, since it was obvious that all the locks in the flight were in the same state. The gates would need attention too, but that was a job for a specialist. She would need to make a report at the next Gathering.

Steady and determined, she kept her thoughts firmly on the lock and its problems and away from any temptation to seek Marheh's mind. She was just stretching her back and gathering her tools to move to the next lock when Marheh's flash of panic reached her. Already weary she set down her tools again and leaned against the lock beam to gather herself and find her focus. Several minutes later she understood Marheh was sending something that was intended for reassurance and ceased her mental voyaging, but not her worrying. Where was she? What had she got herself caught up in that caused her to panic? She felt so helpless and knew she must contain the anger her helplessness provoked. Best to continue working, though she was tired. She could take out her frustration wrestling with the locks.

The afternoon wore on and still there was no sign of Marheh and no further communication. All her good resolutions about allowing Marheh to take responsibility for herself fell away as her anxiety increased. She finished work on the two lower gates of the second lock and knew she could do no more. As it was she had exhausted her physical strength to the point where it would be difficult to go to Marheh's aid should she need her. Tentatively she sent her mind in search of Marheh's, but found only confusion. After all, Marheh could not really be telling her she could fly.

Wearily she gathered up her tools and was about to head back to *Day Bringer* when a sound above her caused her to look up. The cliff beside her was some eighteen or twenty feet high and vines crawled over the face. She had paid them little attention except to remember Marheh's story of the child climbing. Now however the figure that was descending was not climbing but falling, not fast, held in a tangle of vines that pulled away from the cliff top under the weight.

She hurried forward as the figure landed on the path with a bit of a thump and lay still. Then she heard a giggle from within the mass of leaves and twisted stems.

"Nemmie," Marheh said as she bent over her. "Nemmie, I can fly."

Nemle took a deep breath and sat down rather heavily beside her. What on earth had she got herself into this time? Where were her clothes? She wanted to shake her until her teeth rattled.

Marheh made no attempt to do anything but giggle from within the green tangle. She did not appear to be badly hurt, but there were scratches all over her exposed skin and she must be getting cold.

"I can fly, Nemmie," Marheh sang a little tune. "Fly, fly, fly."

"So I see," Nemle said. "But can you walk?"

There was a convulsive movement then she subsided again.

"Fly, fly, fly," she sang.

Nemle reached out to try to pull away the vines, but they were tough and well twisted around her. She levered herself off the ground and stared down at Marheh.

"I'm going for the secateurs," she said, wondering how much was getting through. "Don't move."

"Fly, fly, fly," was the only reply she received and she was tempted to see if a good smack would have any impact, but she went off as fast as she could to fetch the secateurs.

Getting Marheh back to *Day Bringer* was quite a task and by the time she was tucked safely into her bunk Nemle was exhausted. She moved the kettle onto the hob and sank into the armchair. Probably she ought to bathe a couple of Marheh's deeper scratches, wash her and get her into her nightgown, but without her cooperation it was all too difficult. Perhaps after she'd had a rest and eaten something. But when she went to check on her an hour later Marheh was deeply asleep and Nemle went gratefully to her own bed knowing she would be better able to cope after a night's rest.

She was up early and preparing porridge when Marheh emerged wearing a dressing gown and slippers and a sheepish look. When her eyes met Nemle's they were full of questions.

"Yes, I was worried and angry. No, you can't fly, and no, I don't know what happened to your clothes," she said, answering the ones she recognised.

Marheh sighed and subsided into her seat at the table. She put her head in her hands.

"Oh Nemle!"

Nemle slid a mug of sperit onto the table beside her.

"I hoped perhaps it was a dream," she said. "But I was afraid it wasn't."

"Do you feel bad?"

"Like a horse sat on me."

Nemle gave a little grunt of sympathy.

"And my head doesn't feel like it belongs to me." She looked up then, her face tragic. "And oh Nemle, my boots!" she wailed.

"Yes." Nemle's face was rather grim. "That is the difficulty. You'll have to make do with my spare pair and pad them with extra socks."

Marheh's head went down again for a moment or two.

"I'm sorry Nemle."

"Drink your sperit. You'll feel better when you've eaten. We'll talk after that."

She did feel better after food, and better still after she had washed and Nemle had anointed her scratches with one of her salves. Then, clad in her old, patched trousers, her despised grey tunic and Nemle's well worn boots she worked *Day Bringer* up the locks while Nemle steered. The physical activity helped ease the stiffness she felt from her fall and when they reached those gates Nemle had not had energy to attend to the previous day she was a willing learner. They ascended the group of four locks and moored up again at the foot of the staircase. Nemle heard the story in dribs and drabs as they worked, apart while *Day Bringer* went into a lock then coming together again as she came out. When it was all told she stopped her work for a minute to look at Marheh and be sure of her attention.

"So what have you learned?" she asked.

Marheh looked at her, surprised, expecting to be scolded.

"That I'm not very sensible?"

Nemle gave a short laugh. "Think about it," she said. "I'll want a proper answer after lunch."

Marheh knew she meant what she said and tried to think about what had happened to her and whether she could have acted differently. Nemle surprised her again after lunch by wanting to know first what she had learned about the outlaws.

"You've paid dearly for the knowledge," she said. "What actually did you learn?"

"Now you may pay for your visit," Marheh said unexpectedly, then wondered where the words had come from.

She told Nemle all she could remember but Nemle was still not satisfied.

"You've told me what happened to you," she said. "But what have you learned."

Slowly Marheh began to try to make sense of her experience, to connect the threads between the hidden dwelling, the ragged clothing, the venturing children, even the small wooden box.

"So they've dwindled into just a handful," she concluded. "But they still have the knowledge of their past in some ways, like whatever it was they gave me to drink. And once I had been of use to them they didn't really care whether I lived or died as long as they were rid of me without too much effort."

"So how are we going to use what we know to help them?"

"Help them!"

"You were the one who wanted to help them," Nemle pointed out.

"Well I don't now."

"Don't you?"

Nemle slid out from her seat at the table, signalling the end of the conversation.

"How about we go and look at the staircase and see what is ahead of us?" she suggested.

Marheh was very thoughtful as they worked together through the afternoon. She knew Nemle had challenged her with her final comment and part of her resented it. It wasn't Nemle who was wearing patched trousers and second hand boots. On the other hand it wasn't Nemle who had been so passionate about helping them in the first place and it *was* Nemle who had given over her spare boots without a word of rebuke. She thought she might feel better if Nemle did scold her. She seemed to cause her nothing but worry and expense. Sometimes she wondered why Nemle put up with her, but of course she didn't have a choice really.

Nemle watched her as she worked and worried. She knew her very well. When the silence and the gloomy face continued she called her to her.

"Stop berating yourself," she said, holding both her arms and giving her a little shake. "You are not the worst apprentice in the world and you're worth a little worry and expense."

It was not until they were back on *Day Bringer* sitting by the fire after supper that Marheh voiced the question that had been on her mind all day.

"Can we afford for me to have new boots?"

She felt a little ashamed that this had become so important, but she knew she could not enjoy her usual extended explorations in Nemle's spare pair. Not only were they very worn and not strong enough for rough walking, but they were too big for her and not very comfortable even with extra socks.

Nemle understood the importance of this and looked at her sympathetically.

"Not as things stand, but I've been thinking about what we might do. We can spare five shillings, which might get you a good second hand pair, but there's no town close to the water road until Highington and that is quite a way off yet."

Marheh drooped a little and tried not to look as disappointed as she felt.

"But," Nemle continued. "There is a small market town about five miles away from the water road. If you think you could push the barrow that far you could take the sculptures you have left and some of my tisanes. I'll give you the five shillings and anything you sell can be added to it. Would that do?"

"Can I go tomorrow?"

"Best wait until market day," Nemle said, teasing her. "We'll go up the staircase tomorrow and get you to the nearest point on the water road. Then you may go."

It was still dark when Marheh set off for Market Mondborough. The previous day had been a busy one. First the locks. She had been fascinated by the way each emptied into the other and how she had had to fill the top one first so there would be water to let into the lower ones. Then, while Nemle continued to steer *Day Bringer*, Marheh had set about assembling the barrow and filling it with her remaining sculptures and a big box of tisanes.

Nemle had got up to make her breakfast and wish her well, but she promised Marheh she would go back to bed for an hour or so. She had insisted on Marheh wearing her good boots for the long walk.

There was a hint of frost in the air and Marheh stepped out as briskly as the barrow would allow, looking forward to the sun coming up so she would be able to see the countryside around her. All she could see now was the glimmer of moonlight catching the painted edge of the barrow and the dark shapes of trees and hedges lining her way. It was very still and she was aware of her own warm breath in the chill air.

Slowly the sky lightened and the dark shapes found colour and form. She sang a little Silberay tune under her breath and quickened her step, eager to reach the town. Whatever happened before evening, the morning was a time for looking ahead with anticipation. Then the steep climb flattened out a little. There were cottages clumped together in twos and threes. Then more cottages and some little terraces close to the road. Although it was still early there were people about too, purposeful for the most part, with somewhere to go or something to do. Marheh was aware of a few curious glances and kept her head down and stopped singing.

At last, unexpectedly, the road spilled into the market square, already busy with traders setting up. She knew she needed permission to set up her barrow and probably would need to pay something for the privilege. Hopefully it would not eat too much into the five shillings Nemle had given her. One of the traders pointed her in the right direction and soon she was opening up the barrow and setting out her wares. She would have liked a hot drink after her long walk, but she had paid out two of her five shillings and now felt even a penny more was too much.

When everything was ready she opened the little folding stool Nemle had suggested she take and sat down to wait. Nemle had warned her that she might have a long and sometimes dreary day and she had put a few tools and a ball of damp clay in the bottom of her pack but just now she was too keyed up to think about it. It was a smaller market than the one at Marisford, but the energy was the same, and the noise. She watched, bright-eyed and curious as the market came alive. These early shoppers were very purposeful, consulting lists and going busily from stall to stall. No one much even noticed Marheh, her little barrow dwarfed by the bigger tables and awnings of the regular traders. She had been expecting that. Her customers would be the browsers who came later, their regular shopping done, but it was a bit disheartening.

Sighing a little she dug into her pack for her clay, spread the towel it was wrapped in over her knees and began on a little model of an old woman she could see sitting at the side of one of the vegetable stalls. Soon she was completely absorbed in the work so that her first customer took her by surprise.

"Did you make all them then?" a woman asked, fingering one of Marheh's little models carefully.

"Yes, yes I did." Marheh smiled and stood up, the little figure she was working on held carefully in one hand.

"That's clever, that is," the woman said. "But it's tea that I want. Nice drop of chamomile is good at bed time."

Marheh made a face and put down her work on the top of the barrow so she could extract a packet of Nemle's chamomile tea.

"My mentor makes it," she said, holding it out. "I don't like it, but I know people who do say it is very good."

The woman held the packet to her nose. "Smells alright."

She handed over her sixpence and continued to stand looking at Marheh's work.

"You've got the feel of her, just right. I wouldn't mind buying that one if the price was right."

"I'm sorry. It has to be fired. The clay would just dry out and crumble."

"It's very clever," the woman said again as she departed with her tea.

Marheh picked up the towel from where it had dropped and sat again to her work. By lunch time her net profit was a shilling and though there had been several onlookers and some favourable comments her sales had been confined to Nemle's teas. She had completed a second little market character and was ready for a break. She stood and stretched and reached into her pack for the bread and cheese Nemle had provided her with. Six shillings might buy her a pair of second-hand boots if she could find some her size. Perhaps she should pack up now and go looking. It didn't seem as if she would sell any of her sculptures. She sighed a little. It didn't seem right to take the money from Nemle's work, but she had no choice if her own did not sell. She would finish her lunch and wait another hour, she decided, remembering that the afternoon had been the best time at Marisford.

She was just wrapping up the remains of her clay and her tools and wondering whether she could get the two figures she had made back safely to *Day Bringer* when two women appeared on the other side of the barrow.

"I'll have this one," one of them said, holding out a model of a little dog sitting neatly and expectantly.

"Oh," Marheh's happy smile was like a light coming on.

The other woman chose a robin in a nest. Marheh had hardly finished wrapping them carefully in newspaper when another customer appeared, then another. She could hardly believe it.

In just over an hour she had sold everything she had, even the reclining hound whose front paw had cracked in the firing was purchased at a reduced price, Marheh conscientiously pointing out the flaw. Jubilant, she packed her two new models into the barrow and closed it ready for her journey home. The trader at the next stall promised to keep an eye on it for her while she went looking for boots. He even pointed out the location of the market's clothing stalls when he heard what she was looking for.

She danced off, conscious of the weight of coin in her pocket and there was money carefully concealed in her pack as well. She would be able to give Nemle back the five shillings and more as well as get herself some boots. Perhaps she should get a few provisions too, she thought, looking at the produce, and a treat for their supper. She had room to pack things in the barrow now. Boots first though. She found the little clutch of clothing stalls grouped together at the opposite end of the market and slowed down to look. The first sold new things, mostly big bolts of material. Marheh stopped to finger some of the fabric because she liked the colours, but her sewing skills were very limited and she knew she could keep nothing she did not need in her tiny cabin. There was a shoemaker next and he had a few pairs available, but mostly he took orders and measured and made shoes to fit. Marheh knew she would have to wait until the next Gathering for that luxury. Hesitantly she asked if he had anything that would fit her even something second hand. He didn't, but kindly pointed out another stall that stocked second hand goods.

A little bit deflated Marheh moved across to the stall he had indicated and stood looking at the jumble of goods. For a few seconds she saw only a muddle of colours then she began to distinguish some sort of order. There was a pile of trousers spilling out of a large box and some skirts hanging from the awning. Other boxes seemed to contain jumpers and shirts and on the ground beside the proprietor of this ramshackle affair was a box of footwear.

Marheh looked hesitantly from box to box, wondering whether it was worth her while to rummage. Then, hanging out of a box on the counter, she saw a colour she thought she recognised. Slowly she stepped closer to reach and touch, to draw out from the pile her very own claret coloured tunic. Perhaps if she was really lucky her own, comfortable, made-to-measure boots might be here too. Certainly it was worth going through the box that had, at first, seemed too unsavoury to tackle. She knelt down and began to lift out the oddments of footwear, pairing them when she could, and putting the pairs on the ground beside her. She got to the bottom of the box and sighed with disappointment. Then she began to put everything back, looking a bit more carefully in case there might be something that would do instead.

It was only when she had returned everything to its box and was getting rather despondently to her feet that the proprietor spoke.

"What are you looking for then?" he asked.

"Boots," Marheh said. "Like these I'm wearing. I've just borrowed these."

"And you want that red thing you've got over your arm, do you?"

She nodded. "Yes please."

She wanted to ask where he had got it from and whether he had perhaps had her boots and sold them already, but she was not quite sure how her questions might be received. She held out the tunic.

"How much for this?"

"Two shillings," he said. "And five for your boots."

Marheh's mouth fell open.

"My… my boots?" she stammered.

He reached down to some hidden store and drew out a pair of well worn, but well loved brown boots.

"My boots!" Marheh cried joyfully, hugging them to her.

"Thought as much," the man said. "When you wanted that red thing – boots came in with it. Too good to keep in that box you was looking through."

Marheh transferred the boots to one arm so she could reach into her pocket for her money.

"How did you come to lose them?" the man asked, looking at her curiously.

Marheh blushed.

"They were stolen from me by a kind of trick," she said. "By the forest people."

"Hmm," said the man. "I did wonder, but the youngster who brought them to me looked like he needed a good feed so I didn't ask too many questions."

Marheh smiled radiantly and handed over the money he had asked for.

"It was my own fault," she said. "I'm just so glad to have them back, especially my boots."

Within an hour she was heading back to *Day Bringer*, the barrow packed with produce, her tunic and boots in her pack. She could hardly wait to share her day with Nemle. She whiled away the long walk home by planning how she would surprise her and by singing at the top of her voice once she was away from the town.

It was nearly dark by the time she reached *Day Bringer*. Nemle had lit the lamp in the saloon and left the curtain open so the soft glow shone out to welcome her. She left the barrow on the path close to the back deck and hurried on board. Nemle looked up from the armchair and smiled a welcome as she came into the saloon.

"No need to ask whether you had a good day," she said.

Marheh laughed and held out the five shillings Nemle had given her.

"Returned with thanks," she said swinging her pack off her back.

She pulled out her tunic first then her boots and finally her money pouch. Laughing she emptied it into Nemle's hands.

"I sold absolutely everything," she exulted.

"My goodness," Nemle said. "And you found your own boots. That was lucky."

"And…" Marheh said, holding out her hand to help Nemle up from the armchair. "Come and see."

Nemle put the money Marheh had given her onto the table and followed her out to the back deck. Marheh opened the barrow and took out first her two little models, cradled in the damp towel and scarcely damaged by their journey. She put them carefully on the roof and darted back to the barrow. Then, while Nemle watched in amazement, she took out a bag of potatoes, a string of onions, carrots, apples, flour, nuts, a big piece of cheese and finally a big block of chocolate and a bag of bullseyes.

"My goodness," Nemle said again.

Marheh laughed.

"I could hardly believe it when everything sold, every single thing. So I thought it would be good to get some stores, and a treat."

Nemle hugged her and together they took her purchases down into the galley.

Marheh's pleasure in her success was infectious and the evening was full of laughter and happy chatter as they ate together and found places to store Marheh's purchases. Marheh disassembled the barrow while Nemle washed up and brought in her two new sculptures for Nemle to admire before going to bed tired and happy.

Nemle spent a few moments quietly looking round the saloon and the galley. Everything still seemed to glow with the light of Marheh's happiness. Involuntarily she shivered. Everything sold, it seemed too good to be true. She pushed down the hint of misgiving, closed up the fire, turned down the lamp and went to bed.

"Apprenticeship is like a journey. Do not be impatient if your destination sometimes seems unclear. Trust your mentor to plan the route and set a pace that will suit you best."

The Silberay apprentice: a handbook

Chapter Nine

Next morning they were on their way again, travelling by easy stages to Highington. The weather was not good, wet and colder than usual for the time of year. Nemle thought perhaps there was a cold winter ahead and insisted on husbanding their coal so that she and Marheh both spent time each day in gathering wood to use instead. It took them about three weeks to reach Highington and it seemed to Marheh that there was not a day that passed without wet coats steaming in the engine room and damp trousers draped by the fire to dry.

She missed her long walks and was grateful even for the need to collect fuel. *Day Bringer* never seemed too small when the weather was good, but she and Nemle had to be very conscious of each other when the rain went on and on. Marheh knew she was trying Nemle's patience at times, but she just wanted to push away the walls and get out and go.

It was from Highington that the cargos had come in those long ago days when the water road was made and the small town still kept some of its links with the Silberay. The old wharf was still in place and they could moor there and fill their water tank and buy diesel and coal. Nemle was particularly glad of Marheh's earnings and stocked up with extra coal.

"It can go on the roof," she said. "It's not very good for the paintwork, but I've a feeling we're going to need it."

Marheh hefted the heavy bags that had been delivered to the wharf for them and wondered whether Nemle was right in her prediction.

At first it seemed perhaps not. They left Highington on a beautiful sunny morning loaded to the gunnels with provisions and ready for anything.

Marheh stood in the well deck coiling the front line and stowing it neatly. It was unusual to be travelling so close to the town and she watched curiously as they went slowly past the backs of houses, some with gardens down to the water road, some with high walls around and tall trees reaching above them.

It was a bit like Deerford, where she had grown up, she thought, picturing the family pottery with the water road running past and the old wharf. All her life there had been connections with the Silberay and the times when Jik had visited had been highlights for her. She had been lucky. All her life she had lived by the water road. Her family had supported her decision to become apprenticed to the Silberay and she knew they valued the life she was trying to live. It was not like that for everyone. Nemle's parents had not been able to see the water road and wanted their daughter at home looking after them and there were others whose friends and families considered them misguided fools.

She watched the world go by, listened to the water under the bow, the throb of the engine, not loud here at the front and thought about what she had committed herself to. It was a narrow life for a young woman some would say, no chance of home or family only this continual wandering on the edge. Would she have given it up for Daniel if he had cared for her? She was glad now she had not had to make that decision. Nemle loved her and made her feel valued, but how was she really progressing? She was good at the disciplines, but only because she had a natural talent, not because she worked hard, not because she was disciplined herself. If Nemle was stricter would she learn better? She frowned a little then shrugged off her anxieties to enjoy the welcome sunshine and take pleasure in the journey.

There were two more glorious weeks of sunshine. The water road climbed higher and higher and Marheh forgot all her resolutions in the enjoyment of physical activity, working the locks, walking briskly in the bright chilly air. She wore herself out being and doing and never seemed to have time for those other things that were an integral part of the life she had chosen. Nemle watched her happiness and enjoyed it with her. There was plenty of time.

As they climbed the days became colder though still sunny, but then came a day when Nemle halted their day's travelling earlier than usual. She chose their mooring very carefully and even checked Marheh's knots and the way she hammered in the mooring pins, something she had not done since Marheh began her apprenticeship four and a half years ago. Marheh watched with concern. What did Nemle know that she didn't? She went off to look for wood at Nemle's behest and when she came back, dragging two long branches behind her, Nemle had taken everything except the coal off the roof and had even used the centre line as an extra mooring rope.

"It's coming up to blow," Nemle said, carefully placing fenders between *Day Bringer* and the bank. She had said that before, Marheh thought as she went to get their little hatchet from the engine room, but never before had she made such meticulous preparations.

She went outside again to attack her logs and now she was aware of the sky, heavy and close, pressing down so she had to make herself stand upright and swing at her branch. Little gusts and eddies swirled bits of leaf and twigs around then dropped them. She looked at Nemle wondering whether she should be frightened. Nemle smiled at her and began breaking up the smaller parts of the branches.

"There's time to finish this," she said. "But don't go away again."

Marheh had not thought she could be frightened by a storm, but she had never experienced anything like this. The sky was leaden, the wind howled and *Day Bringer* bucked violently against the restraining ropes. The water road was not wide enough to build up waves, but the water slapped vigorously at the hull adding to the cacophony that built around them. Even though all the windows were fastened, the cold wind seemed to infiltrate making the candles gutter and the chimney smoke. Nemle smiled at her and patted the footstool.

"Now we will practise the discipline of the soul," she said, though Marheh could only guess the words through the noise.

She went and sat at Nemle's knee, turned to look at her. Nemle leaned forward to repeat her instruction.

"Now!" Marheh said, startled.

"Now," Nemle mouthed, and Marheh caught something about a challenge.

It seemed an impossible challenge to find her way to stillness and enter the discipline in the midst of all this sound and fury, but Nemle was looking steadily at her and she could feel her warmth and strength.

"Don't fight the storm. Allow it to flow through you." Nemle's words were placed in her mind. "The noise is bigger than you are. Let it hold you."

She did not want to let herself go. It felt as if it would be a dangerous abandoning, but there was a thread of song beckoning, a golden strand that seemed to need her own song to make the music complete.

She returned in the end to the storm and the darkness, but it seemed as if she and Nemle were still held inviolate. There was no personal attack in the violence of the wind, the swirling sleet. The sound and fury were part of its nature and held nothing malevolent.

They went quietly about the afternoon tasks, Nemle sorting and packaging her remaining stocks of dried plant material, Marheh working with mortar and pestle to reduce dried comfrey to a powder for Nemle to add to her ointment. Then there were preparations for supper and early bed.

The cessation of noise woke Marheh sometime in the early morning and she was aware of a paleness moving against her window, so she was not really surprised to be getting up to a world of white. She dressed quickly and went to attend to the fire. There was more than just a chill in the air today. The sky was grey, almost colourless and the temperature seemed to be dropping. She wondered whether Nemle would want to move on. They were miles from anywhere and the snow was deep enough to disguise any landmarks. It would be good to be nearer a village, or at least some friendly company, but it would be bitter out on the back deck at the tiller.

The kettle was just boiling when Nemle emerged from her cabin, neat and contained as always. Over breakfast she discussed their options with Marheh.

"If this keeps up the water road will freeze," she said. "And we'll be going nowhere. There's a good eight hours of boating before we get as close to the next village as we are now to the last village we passed. We're well stocked. What do you think, stay or go?"

Marheh thought she had probably already made up her mind, but she was also aware that she expected a considered answer.

"How long might we be here if it does freeze?" she asked.

She had not experienced winter at this latitude or this altitude.

Nemle shook her head.

"Only a few days if we're lucky. This is quite early still, but it might be weeks."

"Weeks!" Marheh echoed, wondering if she could bear it.

"We'll be able to do some serious work at the disciplines," Nemle said with a bit of a smile. "I shall be very strict."

"You think we should stay don't you?"

Nemle nodded.

"I doubt we could travel for more than two or three hours today and by tomorrow we'll probably be frozen in. At least here we have a sheltered mooring and we know roughly where the nearest village is if we need it."

Marheh sighed. "I can tell it will be more sensible to stay, but it's going to feel like being in prison if it goes on for long."

Nemle laughed.

"I'll try to be a sympathetic gaoler," she said.

She was to need all her sympathy and her patience for they were frozen in place for six long weeks. At first they kept expecting the thaw to come within a few days, but once Nemle realised respite would not arrive so quickly she knew she must help Marheh to find a way of using the time.

Marheh was pacing the floor of the saloon trying not to grumble while Nemle sat at the table writing. After a while she put down her pen and watched her.

"Can't you sit down?" she asked at last. "You're like a fly in a bottle."

"My legs feel like they have to be moving."

Nemle looked at what she had written then back at Marheh.

"I think we shall be here for some time yet. I've been making a plan."

Marheh stopped her pacing. "What do you mean some time?"

"Weeks."

"Weeks," Marheh wailed. "Oh Nemle."

"It happens. We'll need to set ourselves some challenges and plan how we might achieve them."

Marheh perched on her seat on the other side of the table.

"What sort of challenges?"

"What do you think?"

"Discipline," Marheh said, her face and voice rather gloomy. She felt she had heard enough about discipline.

"The disciplines and the self-discipline to practise them," Nemle said. "Will that be so bad?"

She began to unfold her plan. In spite of herself Marheh became interested.

"It won't be easy," she said as Nemle suggested some possible goals.

"All the more worth while when you succeed then," Nemle said.

"If I succeed."

"You have the ability to succeed," Nemle said bluntly. "But you do lack self-discipline."

Marheh put her head in her hands.

"I know I do," she said. "Sometimes I think I don't even know what it is." She looked up. "When I first became apprenticed I had this idea that I was going to be part of something big and special, but most of it is just ordinary really."

Nemle laughed for a moment.

"And well I remember the consequences of your disappointment." She reached out to cover Marheh's hands with hers. "You are part of something big and special, but it is what you do with the ordinary time that makes it that way."

She patted Marheh's hand and stood up.

"Just a minute," she said, disappearing into her cabin.

Marheh looked curiously after her. A moment later she came back clasping a piece of rope.

"There you are," she said, handing it over. "Go out on the back deck and skip to two hundred, that should take the fidgets out of your legs."

Marheh laughed and slid out of her seat.

"Best put down a mat first. You don't want to slip… and you can be thinking about how to tackle my plan."

"I will," Marheh called back as she made for the door.

Later Marheh was to date her true commitment to the life of the Silberay from these six weeks. Up until then she had been like a child playing at something that intrigued her, but during this long stretch of confinement she learned to work.

The first thing she and Nemle did together was take stock of the store cupboard and ration their food. Nemle suggested they plan for four weeks and take stock again after two. The need for austerity brought home to Marheh the seriousness of their position, but also of Nemle's intent. She suggested a structure to their days, time together and time alone, time for work and reflection as well as time for relaxation.

By the end of a week the days had begun to shape themselves naturally. Marheh woke at first light, not very early these short winter days. She washed, using the cold water sparingly but not giving in to the temptation to omit this part of the program. Then she dressed and went to check the fire. This had been her job since the first week of her apprenticeship and it was second nature now, but it had never been so important. She must conserve their fuel as best she could but the fire must not go out or *Day Bringer*'s water system might freeze and the pipes split.

When the fire was well established she took the kettle and went out onto the back deck. It seemed odd to be moving around *Day Bringer* without her usual gentle shifts in the water. *Day Bringer* was in prison too she thought. The bitter air woke her even more completely than the cold wash and she stood for a moment conscious of each breath before stepping off to fill the kettle with snow.

Nemle was in the galley making porridge when she returned with the kettle. There was no milk but a dribble of honey was still possible. There was no real need for speech. They exchanged a smile and a touch of greeting and saved any words until they were sitting opposite each other with their bowls of porridge and mugs of sperit.

When her bowl was empty Nemle leaned back and looked at Marheh.

"How's my girl this morning?"

It was her usual greeting and there had been times when Marheh resented it.

"I'm not your girl," she wanted to say, but she never had and now she welcomed the love behind the words that acknowledged her as a treasured companion.

"I'm fine. Very glad of my breakfast."

She scraped at her bowl and mimed licking it so that Nemle would laugh.

Breakfast over and cleaning up done they went through the plan for the day together before separating to go to their cabins and find the stillness necessary to enter the discipline of the soul.

Always the beginning was solitary. Each had her own portal and her own song. Marheh felt her song developing, becoming more truly a reflection of the best part of herself. But the soul song was not only self and now she was learning to sing in the dark places. Nemle sang with her at first and when she reflected on where she had been she realised Nemle was always a watchful presence. She was the simple line of music her questing melody rested on.

Occasionally when she sang in the dark she would begin to see an edge of light pushing out from her song like the ripple of a wave and these times helped her to continue in those other times when she struggled to keep singing in the dark corners that seemed to ache with sadness, even pain. The best time came when she and Nemle sang equally together, each tune weaving and dancing around and with the other, sometimes harmony, sometimes counterpoint, first one leading and then the other.

She always relinquished this song reluctantly but when she returned to herself she was exhausted and slept for a short time. Then she took her rope and her mat and went out on the back deck to wake herself up again by skipping until she could skip no more. *Day Bringer* never moved no matter how long and hard she skipped and she understood it to be a measure of the strength of the ice that bound her.

When she went through to the saloon again Nemle was making sperit. She hugged her and handed her her mug. Today there was no need for words though Nemle was ready to listen should she have questions or fears. She did need Nemle's help and advice when she practised her bread making though. She knew it was a necessary skill and she could see the value of it, especially now, but cooking did not come naturally to her and even more than usual it was important not to waste the ingredients.

"Relax," Nemle teased her a little. "Your last loaf was perfect."

"It was just a fluke."

"This one will be just as good, you'll see."

She sighed, closed the oven and pushed back a tendril of hair with the back of a floury hand.

"When you do it it all looks so easy and natural."

"It will be easy and natural for you too if you practise."

"Practise, practise, practise. Everything is practise, practise. I'm tired of it. It doesn't seem as if I'll ever get beyond it."

Nemle laughed at that.

"No I don't expect you will. I haven't."

Marheh stared at her for a moment, almost affronted, then laughed ruefully.

"Of course I know you're right," she said. "When I think about the disciplines, or my clay I hope I'll keep learning all my life and that means practising all my life too."

As they continued to talk the smell of the baking bread began to fill the boat. Marheh sniffed appreciatively.

"The smell is almost enough," she said. "But not quite."

"Why don't you get on with your mending until it's time to eat," Nemle suggested.

Marheh made a face.

"You think of the nicest things to do."

"Bring it out here and we'll work together. I don't believe you have a single pair of socks without holes in them."

"I have so!"

Domesticity ended with the washing up after their meal of bread and jam. Then it was time to practise the discipline of the mind.

"No holds barred," Nemle suggested. There was a lurking twinkle in her eye.

"That just means I agree to let you beat me up," Marheh said grinning.

"You can defend yourself very well when you concentrate."

"You're on!"

She put up both fists and made little punching movements before dancing off to get some clay from her cabin.

Nemle took out a book and sat down in the armchair. Marheh came back and set herself up at the table. The aim of today's practice was to keep a mental shield in place all the time, even when working at something quite different.

Marheh propped up her sketch book and began on a model of a badger using the drawings she had made nearly a year ago. After a few minutes she looked across at Nemle, absorbed in her book. It was a herbal that she had found in a second hand bookshop in Highington and bought for her. She had a pencil and was making little notes in the margin. Marheh thought she might make her turn over two pages at once and prepared herself to ease the suggestion into Nemle's mind. Nemle slapped at the little probe as she might have slapped Marheh's fingers if they were getting into places they shouldn't.

One to you, she sent, and received Nemle's acknowledgement.

A few minutes later she found herself dancing around the saloon, a piece of clay clasped in each hand. Another one to you, she sent, but Nemle kept

114

her dancing and Marheh understood she must release herself. It was difficult to find her focus when her legs were skipping and jumping under Nemle's command but she knew that whatever bizarre movements Nemle might have her perform were nothing to what an enemy might require of her. Breathing hard she tried to disassociate her mind from her dance and find the mental strength necessary to force Nemle out of her mind and close the door.

When she finally succeeded she flopped down on the floor and rolled onto her back only to find Nemle was again in her mind trying to force her onto her hands and knees.

Mean! She sent, fighting against Nemle's command.

Nemle sent her a wicked chuckle. No holds barred, she reminded her.

Sometimes it seemed to Marheh she was wrestling with Nemle, at other times it felt more like fencing. It was not so difficult if she remembered to maintain her shield, but if she didn't Nemle was relentless. The practice ended with Marheh positioned strategically over the footstool. Nemle released her suddenly, gave her a light smack and sank back in her chair.

"Not bad," she said. "You've exhausted me."

Marheh remained sprawled over the stool.

"She is so mean," she told the floor. "First she beats me up mentally and then physically."

Nemle laughed.

"You're getting better, but if I don't bully you you forget to keep shielded."

"I know." Marheh pushed herself back onto her knees. "It is all for my own good." She groaned theatrically and staggered to her feet. "Now I suppose you want me to make sperit."

"I thought you'd never ask."

"I suppose it is naïve of me to assume that the power we continue to develop over the mind's thought will only be used with humility and compassion. Inappropriate use of the discipline of the mind could destroy any credibility we have won through our desire to serve."

Sila's journal: the early years

Chapter Ten

By the time the thaw came they were eating nothing but porridge and beans. Marheh claimed her trousers would fall down if she lost any more weight and Nemle was beginning to think they might have to try to walk back to the last village they passed before they became too weak to make the effort. Then there was a day of sunshine, and another. Neither of them commented, not daring to hope, but that night in bed Marheh was disturbed by odd cracking sounds and next morning when she got up she felt *Day Bringer* move beneath her. Another day of sunshine and they could see and feel the difference. Then at last they were on their way again. Three days of what Marheh called "serious boating" and they were within reach of new supplies, then they could return to their usual pattern.

"Just as well there is no Gathering this year," Marheh said. "Or we would have missed it."

So they travelled on through the seasons and the landscape, unhurried, balancing work and play, practising the disciplines and singing light into dark places. Marheh knew she was growing even as the world around them grew through the first new buds of spring, the spreading green of summer, the autumn harvest. And then it was winter again and another year had gone slipping past and it was time to make their way to the Gathering.

"Will I have to take Silberay law again this year?" Marheh asked one morning as she was standing beside Nemle in the winter sunshine.

"I'm afraid so." Nemle allowed her attention to move from her steering and looked at Marheh. "Are you worried about it?"

"I don't think Hud likes me," she said after a pause. "And I know I won't be able to keep quiet if he goes on like last time."

"Perhaps it won't be him this year. It shouldn't be."

Marheh shrugged. "I guess I'll find out when we get there. I can't do anything about it anyway."

She hoisted herself up to sit on the roof and looked back past Nemle to *Day Bringer*'s wake rippling behind them. She'd almost forgotten her humiliation at the last Gathering, almost but not quite and now she could not keep from thinking of it.

"Let it go," she said at last.

Nemle looked a question.

"Like the wake, let it ripple away and disappear."

Nemle nodded approvingly. She was remembering too, Marheh's eagerness to reach the Harbour, to be first. This time she was not the child anticipating a treat, but an adult with work to do.

"What happens at the Harbour when we go away?" she asked next day.

"The Harbour Master keeps it maintained, makes sure the old ones are cared for, the Apprentice Master travels on the lookout for possible apprentices. Boats come and go if they are near enough. No one has to go out like we do. It is a choice, but one we are encouraged to make."

"Why would anyone stay in Harbour if they didn't have to?"

"Some find a reason I think."

Marheh sighed. "We should be there tomorrow and… and I just can't work up much enthusiasm."

Nemle looked sideways at her.

"Think about new boots," she hinted.

Marheh laughed and gave her attention to the tiller.

They reached Silberay Harbour mid afternoon, not the first to arrive, but not the last either. The Harbour Master indicated a suitable berth and Marheh steered *Day Bringer* neatly into place. They tied up and went below to drink sperit and consider the evening meal. Nemle was rolling out pastry and Marheh chopping vegetables when they saw feet walking past and there was a knock on the roof. Nemle called a welcome and next minute they felt *Day Bringer* dip and rise as someone came on board. It was the Apprentice Master and he wanted Nemle. She looked from the pastry to Marheh and seemed about to make a protest.

"I think I can manage," Marheh said. "You've done the hard bit."

"You're sure. I can't imagine what is too urgent to wait until after we've finished."

"I'm sure."

Marheh waved them off and continued chopping.

The Apprentice Master seemed a bit preoccupied she thought. He barely returned her smile of greeting. No doubt Nemle would tell her when she came back, unless it was a mentor issue. She concentrated on her work and had soon assembled the two Cornish pasties and put them in the oven. Nemle would surely be back before they were ready.

She thought she had earned a holiday then and settled into the armchair with her favourite novel. She had read it many times but still it held her attention and carried her off into another world. The good smell coming from the galley brought her back to the realisation that Nemle had been gone for quite some time. She got up to check the pasties and move them into the cooler, warming oven. Better to wait for them to heat up again then to overcook them.

While she was up she lit the lamp then settled down to her book again.

At last Nemle's feet appeared on the jetty. Marheh was surprised to realise it was quite dark outside and the passing feet were only visible because the lamp light spilled out of the window. What on earth had kept her for so long?

She stood up and went to the galley, put the pan of extra vegetables on to the hob and bent to move the pasties back to heat up. When she straightened again Nemle was standing in the doorway.

"Nemle!" she cried out, startled by her pallor and her grave face. "Nemle what is it?"

Briefly Nemle closed her eyes, turned her head a little as if to avoid some obstacle. Then she opened her eyes and looked at Marheh.

"I tried," she said, a catch in her voice. "I tried every way I could. That's why I was so long. They only got rid of me by threatening to take you away from me."

"Nemle what are you talking about? What's wrong?"

Marheh went towards her. Nemle's arms went around her, but after a moment she pulled back.

"How can they take me away from you? Tell me. You have to tell me."

There was a long, painful pause.

"They are accusing you of using mind control to exploit," she said at last.

It took a moment for the words to register meaning then Marheh spun away from her.

"But that's ridiculous!"

"Of course it's ridiculous, but they wouldn't listen to me." Nemle put out a hand to steady herself. "They claim to have evidence."

"How can they have evidence of something that hasn't happened?"

Nemle shook her head and Marheh suddenly realised how exhausted she was.

"What have they been doing to you?" she asked, leading her to the armchair and settling her into it. "Who are *they* anyway?"

She sank onto the footstool at Nemle's knee and looked up at her.

"The Apprentice Master was talking, but Hud seemed to be feeding him the words."

Marheh was silent for a few minutes. Nemle reached out to clasp her hand.

"What will they do to me?" she asked at last.

She knew it was one of the worst things she could have been accused of.

"They have scheduled a public hearing for the day after tomorrow. The evidence will be presented and you and I will have a chance to speak."

For a moment Marheh put her head down on Nemle's knee then she straightened.

"Well it would be silly to let the dinner burn while we worry about it," she said.

They ate their way doggedly through their pasties, though neither seemed to have much appetite. Marheh insisted on clearing up by herself then she went again to sit beside Nemle on the footstool.

"I'm sure I haven't done it Nemle," she said. "Not even through ignorance like I did in first year."

"I know that. I told them that. They said I would not necessarily know. They said I was blinded by my affection for you."

Marheh smiled a little and rubbed her cheek against Nemle's knee.

"I'll tell them you love me too much to let me get away with anything."

"I don't like what is happening to the Silberay," Nemle said slowly. "There is no trust any more. It should be enough that you and I both deny it. They know us. Instead it is as if we were criminals."

"Not you."

"That's what it felt like when I argued with them."

"I know Hud doesn't like me," Marheh said after a short silence. "But he wouldn't make up evidence against me... would he?"

"If they really have got evidence then someone has provided it." Nemle's voice was grim. "It's the Daniel business again."

Marheh looked startled.

"I thought at the time that was a personal thing – not a general attack on the Silberay."

"But why me?"

"I think someone is jealous of your potential," Nemle said slowly. "Or frightened of it."

"But..." Marheh broke off abruptly.

Nemle reached out to touch her.

"But that must mean I have an enemy within the Silberay."

"Yes," Nemle said at last.

Neither Marheh nor Nemle slept much though they went to bed at a sensible hour and made a point of practising the discipline of the soul. Next morning Nemle could see Marheh was making a valiant effort to behave as if everything was normal but her eyes looked tired and she was very pale.

"We can't pretend it hasn't happened," she said. "And we don't want to, but we will not hide away as if we have done something wrong. I think this morning will be a good time to go and order your new boots."

Marheh looked up from the plate of porridge she couldn't seem to fancy and squared her shoulders.

"Of course," she said. "The boot maker will be here all through the Gathering and I really need them now."

She polished off her porridge with determination.

Half an hour later they were walking together towards the store. Marheh would not be alone amongst the Silberay in needing new, well-fitting boots and as well there would be people ordering provisions or organising specialist maintenance for their boats.

"Will people know?" Marheh asked, hesitating as she saw the activity.

"They may do. They will soon because of the hearing."

"Oh Nemle, I can't..."

"Yes you can." Nemle's voice was stern, but her eyes were kind.

There was a moment of silence as they entered the store then it seemed as if everyone spoke at once. Some greeted Nemle and Marheh but some were very interested in their neighbours' purchases or fancied something that necessitated them moving away to examine it. Marheh felt a hand on her arm and swung around to find Sul and Kel smiling at her.

"Are you still getting yourself into trouble," Sul said.

"Big trouble this time," Marheh replied. "But I didn't do what they say I did."

"I know that."

Sul gave her a bit of a hug and Kel grinned at her. Marheh smiled at them gratefully and found she had to blink back tears.

The exchange had answered people's curiosity and attention seemed to flow back to where it was before Nemle and Marheh arrived. Marheh went to book herself a slot with the boot maker while Nemle picked up a few perishables and chatted to those who had been amongst the greeters. Marheh wondered what she was telling them. She saw her nodding emphatically on several occasions and she was standing straight and determined. She guessed she was defending her and turned back to Kel who had stayed with her, claiming he too needed new boots.

"It seems like something out of a nightmare," she said. "They haven't even spoken to me and they won't tell Nemle any details only that they have evidence."

"I don't care how much evidence they offer, Sul and I know better than to believe it," Kel said.

With the support of Nemle, Sul and Kel and her Uncle Jik, Marheh got through the day better than she expected. There were others too who treated her as they had always done, but there seemed to be currents, disturbances beneath the ordered life of the Silberay that hinted at struggle and darkness.

By the middle of the next morning all the Silberay had gathered in the biggest of the meeting rooms. Marheh sat, stiff and silent in the front row with Nemle on one side and Jik on the other. She thought if anyone was to touch her, the control she was struggling to maintain would shiver into a thousand pieces.

Last Gathering this same room and these same people witnessed the humiliation of her probationary promotion. Now she was to be questioned and examined and there would be those who would wish her guilty. Her hands clenched momentarily and she made herself relax them. She had done nothing wrong. She would not let them make her feel ashamed.

The Apprentice Master came in with the Harbour Master followed by Hud and with him a tall young man in the uniform of a first year apprentice. Marheh looked at him curiously. He was very fair with a bell of smooth fine hair, a small pointed beard and light blue eyes. He seemed to be deferring to Hud and the two sat together at a table on the side. Hud had the large volume Marheh recognised as the Book of Rules he had read from in the Silberay law classes.

The Apprentice Master beckoned to her. For a moment she wondered whether her body would obey her, but she managed to stand and walk across to where he stood with the Harbour Master. She was very conscious of the weight of the collective gaze and lifted her chin with what Nemle and Jik both recognised as her Marheh the Great look. She was directed to a solitary chair facing the assembled company then the Apprentice Master and the Harbour Master took seats at a central table and began the proceedings.

"Marheh, you are accused of using the discipline of the mind illegally, in order to exploit people with no defence against you," the Harbour Master said. "This is a very serious charge, but because you are still in the early years of your apprenticeship this will be a hearing conducted by the Apprentice Master rather than a formal trial."

These remarks were addressed to the whole group but now the Harbour Master turned to Marheh.

"Do you understand what it is you are accused of?"

"Yes," Marheh said quietly.

"And are you guilty?"

"No I am not."

With a nod to the Apprentice Master, the Harbour Master sat down.

"Marheh," the Apprentice Master said, crossing to stand beside her. "Can you remember visiting Market Mondborough, eighteen months or so ago?"

For a moment she could not remember then she felt Nemle's sympathetic gaze and steadied herself.

"I think it was more like fourteen months," she said. "But yes, I went there."

"Could you tell us what happened that day?"

"I took some of our goods to sell at the market."

She answered carefully wondering why they were asking, not wanting to volunteer more than necessary in case they could use it against her.

"Market Mondborough is quite some distance from the water road. Why go there to market instead of waiting till Highington?"

"My clo… my boots were stolen," she said, blushing at the memory. "I don't have a spare pair so Nemle lent me hers and let me go and see if I could earn enough to buy some for myself."

"And did you?"

"Yes, I did." The thought of that success gave her confidence. "Why are you asking me? What has this got to do with… with anything?"

"In fact you did quite well that day, didn't you?"

"Yes I did." Marheh lifted her chin. "I sold everything I had."

There was pride in her voice. The Apprentice Master looked at Hud, who nodded. Marheh glanced at Nemle whose grey eyes were steady and reassuring.

"I suggest to you Marheh that you sold everything because you used mind control to force people to buy from you."

"I didn't!"

Marheh stood up angrily.

"I did not."

There was a moment of silence.

"Sit down please Marheh."

When she had obeyed the Apprentice Master continued.

"We could perhaps be sympathetic if you were prepared to admit what you have done. We do understand how important it was for you to replace your boots."

124

"I did not use mind control to make people buy," Marheh said. "I did not. They bought because they wanted to."

The Apprentice Master looked again at Hud. He nodded to the apprentice beside him and he left the room by a side door. Hud approached Marheh, the book of rules clasped to his chest. The mellifluous voice began to describe Marheh's iniquity in such colourful and emotive terms that Nemle could not restrain herself.

"You don't know what you are talking about," she said loudly, standing up, strong and determined. "Marheh glowed with happiness when she returned that day. She could not have been that way if she had done something wrong."

She turned to address the Silberay gathered behind her. "You know me, you know Marheh, why are you allowing this nonsense to undermine our community and waste our time?"

There was a restless murmur but Hud raised his voice and spoke over it.

"You are deluded Nemle. She did it and we have evidence to prove it."

He turned and there in the doorway as if on cue, stood the apprentice and behind him a small group of people. Hud beckoned and the apprentice urged two of the group forward. The two looked at Marheh. One seemed merely curious, the other resentful.

"Do you remember this young woman?" Hud asked them.

"She was selling at the market," the curious one said. "I watched her making a figure out of clay and selling them too. They were clever and I liked them."

"But I wouldn't have bought one," the resentful woman broke in. "I don't have three shillings to waste. I'd never have bought one."

The first woman shook her head.

"It hasn't been a good year."

Marheh's face paled and she looked at Nemle. Could she have influenced them without knowing what she was doing as she had done before being apprenticed?

Almost imperceptibly Nemle shook her head.

"Well Marheh?" Hud said and the satisfaction in his voice was very thinly disguised.

She was silent for a moment then she looked steadily at him.

"If they were influenced it was not by me."

"Who else would have a reason?"

It was not a question she could answer and he knew it.

Hud and the Apprentice Master questioned the women a little longer then went on to question three other citizens of Market Mondborough who had been brought to the Gathering for the purpose. All of them said that although they liked Marheh's work they would not have spent money on it that could have been better spent on food or necessary items of clothing. They had no money to spare for luxuries.

Nemle, watching Marheh saw her close in on herself, the memory of her happy day tarnished and the weight of evidence against her frightening. When the witnesses were finally dismissed the Apprentice Master turned to Marheh.

"We can understand your need," he said. "But you can see now the hardship you caused."

"If they were influenced it was not by me," Marheh said again.

Nemle was aware of how hard she was fighting to control herself but sensed that her cold, clipped tone was losing her the sympathy of the Silberay.

"You still deny it?" the Apprentice Master said.

Nemle too was fighting for control. She wanted to spring up and shout against these careful, logical men who seemed to have condemned Marheh.

"I deny it."

Again the hard bitten off tone that was Marheh's way of hiding her feelings. The Harbour Master beckoned Nemle, spoke to her then turned to the Gathering.

"Nemle and Marheh will leave us while we decide what is truth," he said.

"When to be silent, when to speak out?"

Sila's journal: the early years

Chapter Eleven

They walked out together, Marheh's natural grace a little marred by the effort of control, Nemle angry and determined beside her.

"Decide what is truth," Nemle muttered as the door closed behind them. "What nonsense."

It was nearly two hours before they were called back into the meeting room.

"Guilty," the Harbour Master said and pronounced her sentence.

Jik told them later how the verdict had been reached. How he and Sul had fought for Marheh. How they had voted three times before a sufficient majority had been reached. How persuasive Hud had been.

"And they claimed to be deciding what is truth," Nemle said again. "What nonsense."

"We know it is nonsense," Jik said. "But the result is not nonsense."

Marheh had pulled herself together after the initial shock of the sentence and the realisation of what it meant. She had removed herself from Nemle's lap and was busy making sperit for the three of them.

"I didn't mean to go to pieces," she said, giving careful attention to the spiced berries she was spooning into their mugs. "I had not quite understood what I have chosen. I do now and I still choose it."

"But Marheh," Nemle protested. "A beating can't be undone when we find out the truth."

"But Nemle," Marheh said in the same tone. "We would have no chance of finding out grounded here at the Harbour."

She looked from one to the other.

"I know there is not much chance that there will be new evidence in time."

"Sul was going to try to speak with the witnesses, but I think they've already been dispatched back to Market Mondborough," Jik said.

"Of course they have," Nemle said. "That Hud would be afraid to let anyone else question them."

Marheh poured boiling water into mugs and handed them round.

"Can we not talk about it," she said a little catch in her voice. "It is going to happen and I'm... I'm very afraid, but I will just have to bear it."

The day of her sentence seemed both too far away and too soon and bearing it was difficult. There was little to distract her mind from the approaching ordeal. Since her apprenticeship was to be extended by two years she would not be promoted this Gathering and she was not permitted to attend classes.

"Just as well I got my tunic back then," she said to Nemle when they told her. "Can you put up with me for two more years?"

"It will be my joy and delight."

Her loving words tested Marheh's fragile control, but she blinked back her tears and lifted her chin.

She busied herself fetching and carrying, stocking *Day Bringer* with non-perishable provisions, giving the engine and the engine room a thorough clean, washing down the hull and polishing the paintwork, but though these activities kept her occupied they did not engage her mind. She was aware of Nemle's watchful presence and her loving concern and drew on these when she needed.

All her physical activity meant she was tired enough to fall asleep when she went to bed, but she could not stay asleep. She dreaded the four o'clock wakening when all her fears came to a head and she made wild plans for running away and hit at her pillow as if it were Hud and ended up stifling her sobs under the blankets so as not to disturb Nemle. She was ashamed of her fear and fought it, but she grew pale and her eyes looked bruised.

Friends tried to support her and she was grateful, but kindness undermined her self control so that she appeared cold. Nemle and Jik alone were permitted to provide comfort. Even Kel and Sul were shut out though Kel came and worked beside her when she was polishing the hull and Sul went daily to battle with the Harbour Master on her behalf.

The three days passed somehow and the appointed hour arrived.

Marheh struggled to put on the penitential garments and tried not to think of them being unfastened so her unprotected skin would receive the blows of the cane. Her fingers would not obey her and Nemle had to do them up at neck and waist and pin up her long dark plait.

Now that the moment had come she was strangely calm, almost detached and it was Nemle who wept as they walked together to the meeting room.

They waited outside the door. At the stroke of ten it opened on a sea of faces. Marheh gripped Nemle's hand very tightly for just a moment then lifted her head and stepped into the room. Steadily she walked the dozen or so steps that brought her to the scaffolding. Obediently she faced the frame and stood on tiptoe, stretching out her arms so Nemle could fasten her wrists. She moved her feet so Nemle could fasten her ankles. She even managed a tremulous smile as Nemle came to slip the half moon of blue rubber between her teeth.

She felt curiously detached, outside herself. Nemle's tears were nothing to do with her although somewhere she was aware of being grateful that it was Nemle lovingly preparing her and not some stranger or adversary. The rustle of sound as her clothes were folded back was nothing to do with her either or the voice proclaiming the crime and its consequences.

Then came the first blow and she was jerked back to herself and to the awareness of pain. Ten stripes were placed deliberately between her shoulders and the top of her thighs. Ten blows that spread into each other, that stung and burned.

There was a few minutes respite then and the realisation that the blows would come again and again. She whimpered a little at the thought, then as the next stroke landed gripped the rubber between her teeth and set herself to endure.

Nemle, watching from the front row, saw her skin darken to an angry red, saw her body twitch and jerk involuntarily, and as the punishment continued, heard the sounds that were forced from her. She was scarcely conscious of the tears that ran down her cheeks though she heard the sound of sobbing from several places behind her.

She was angry. Cruelty went against everything the Silberay believed in and this was cruel. And it was her beloved Marheh who was suffering.

Why was she sitting here allowing it to happen?

She turned to Jik and felt the strong warm pressure of his hand clasping hers. It is too late to stop it now, he seemed to be saying. Keep your anger and your strength for Marheh. She will need it.

It was a very long hour.

By the end Marheh's legs would not support her and she hung by her wrists. The cane had broken the skin in two or three places and a little blood, scarcely darker than the angry red flesh, scribbled a small scarlet trail over her back and down one leg.

At last Nemle was allowed to go to her, to cover her, to unfasten her ankles and her wrists. She managed two steps before she staggered and would have fallen if Jik had not sprung forward to catch her and lower her gently to the floor.

Nemle crouched beside her scarcely aware that behind her a riot had erupted as the Silberay faced the reality of what they had been a party to. Later it might be important but now all that mattered was Marheh. From somewhere a blanket appeared. Jik laid her on it, willing helpers lifted it by the four corners and carried her away to *Day Bringer.*

They put her on Nemle's bed. It was softer and easier of access than her own. Then Jik shooed the helpers away and stood guard while Nemle tended to her, washing her with cool water and smoothing ointment over the inflamed skin.

When she had made her as comfortable as possible Nemle carried the footstool into her cabin so she could sit beside Marheh and watch over her. She sent Jik away.

"Go and find out what is happening," she said. "I can't believe I allowed that to take place. I'm ashamed I did not fight harder. I hope I'm not the only one who is ashamed."

Jik nodded, bent to caress Marheh's cheek and left them.

He returned several hours later. Marheh seemed to be sleeping and Nemle still sat beside her. She had given her a few mouthfuls of porridge and helped her to take a few sips of sperit but she had not left her for more than the few minutes it took to prepare these. She looked questioningly at Jik as he stepped into the cabin.

"We've looked beneath the surface and found something very nasty underneath," he said. "We none of us like ourselves very much."

Nemle nodded. "Good, neither we should."

They were speaking quietly so as not to disturb Marheh, so they both heard the little sound from the bed.

"The stick," Marheh said. "Now the water has flooded the banks, but who put the first stick in place?"

"Today has been a difficult day. I didn't understand that there would be those who could not accept that trust and kindness should be our only guiding principles. It seems even a small community of like-minded individuals are still as different as they are alike."

Sila's journal: the early years

Chapter Twelve

The controversy raged.

"She chose her punishment." That was Hud and the Apprentice Master.

"She could have chosen to be grounded."

"Doesn't that show that grounding is not appropriate either?"

"She broke our most important law."

"Did she?"

"That's irrelevant."

"Are you saying she shouldn't be punished at all?"

"It should be up to the mentor."

"The mentor should have prevented the crime."

"The mentor would know best if there *was* a crime."

"If there is need for punishment then the mentor should be responsible."

The mentors would have been unanimous about this only it was discovered that Hud was now a mentor, his apprentice the young man beside him during Marheh's hearing.

Nemle stayed apart. Her priority at the moment was Marheh. She realised the mentors were now determined on change and trusted Sul to push things on and to let her know if her voice was needed. It was important, but more important for her was the need to discover who put the stick in the water. Somehow Marheh was the key. There had been too many attempts to inhibit her potential. Her courage and determination had been enough to enable her to overcome these so far, but she should not have to suffer any more.

She spoke of this only to Marheh and to Sul and Jik.

"We are being undermined from within," she said. "No amount of anger and argument will make real change. We have to discover who is responsible."

They were all gathered in Nemle's cabin. Marheh lay face down on Nemle's bed, her head resting on her folded arms. She was healing, but still uncomfortable sitting. Nemle sat beside her on the end of the bed, Sul had the footstool and Jik the floor. The cabin was crowded and they felt like conspirators.

At first Sul was inclined to disagree, but when Nemle had summarised for him the events since the last Gathering he was persuaded.

"Market Mondborough," Marheh said, lifting her head a little. "Nothing happened after Market Mondborough."

She paused, took a breath. Nemle's hand rested lightly on the small, bare foot beside her.

"Perhaps someone thought they had succeeded in getting you off the water," she said, smiling fondly at Marheh.

"No chance."

"Don't be too cocky young woman," Jik said.

"Whoever it is must not be given the chance to try again," Nemle said.

"And you think Market Mondborough might be the place to start investigating?"

Sul stretched out his legs, kicked Jik and apologised.

"And Daniel," Marheh said suddenly then blushed. "Daniel might help if we can find him."

Nemle nodded agreement with this comment and they went on debating and planning for sometime before Nemle shooed the men away.

"We need some time to find out," she said. "See if you can help the others to come to the conclusion that an extra-ordinary Gathering in three months time would be a good idea."

"Well it would give everyone time to think," Sul said, struggling to his feet.

"We'll see what we can do." Jik joined him.

"And tell Kel what we've been discussing," Nemle added as they moved out of the cabin.

"And don't break any laws."

Marheh's voice sounded light and teasing, but when the men had gone her head went down on the pillow with a little sigh.

"Tired daughter?"

The dark head moved in agreement and Nemle thought she heard the word sore. She stood up.

"Bed for you then," she said, shaking out a blanket and laying it over her.

Then she closed all the curtains, kissed her lightly and disappeared into the saloon.

It was a week before Marheh could move with reasonable ease and even then she was reluctant to leave *Day Bringer*. Nemle watched her with loving concern, understanding how she felt, but knowing she must face the Silberay some time. Sul and Kel and Jik all came to visit but otherwise they were left alone. Once she no longer needed Nemle's ministrations she moved back into her own cabin. When she was strong enough Nemle encouraged her to practise the discipline of the soul. There would be encounters there, other souls for Marheh to sing with, without the awkwardness of ordinary meetings.

"Do we have to stay until the end of the Gathering?" Marheh asked at breakfast one morning when she was at last able to wear her uniform and sit for short periods without too much discomfort.

Nemle had been expecting the question and had her answer ready.

"No, I don't think so," she said. "Just long enough for you to collect your new boots."

"Oh."

Marheh was tempted to ask Nemle to fetch them for her, but she knew she would refuse.

"You have done nothing to be ashamed of," Nemle said, understanding her response. "You don't have to go alone, but you can't hide away for ever. Better to have the first encounter over with before we go."

Marheh thought about what she had said. It was true she had no reason to feel ashamed but somehow she did. If she went with Nemle she would be like a child shielded by her mother.

"I'll go for my boots tomorrow," she said with her characteristic lift of the chin. "Do you think Kel would come with me?"

She went for her boots, conducted the several encounters with quiet dignity and found mostly friendly sympathy. Then, very early the following morning *Day Bringer* slipped quietly out of her mooring and away. Sul and Kel and Jik would stay until the end so as to have a voice in the discussions and keep watch. Nemle and Marheh would set out for Marisford to begin their investigation.

After the last Gathering they had spent most of spring and summer making their way to Marisford, now they had three months to get there and back and make their inquiries as well. Perhaps she should have pushed for six months, Nemle thought, but the matter was urgent and even three months would be long enough for the issues to fade in importance.

"We'll take things reasonably easily until *Storm Cloud* and *Autumn Wind* catch up with us," she said to Marheh when she came up to take the tiller. "That will give you a chance to rest a bit if you need to."

The tension was already leaving Marheh's face and now she raised both arms and stretched luxuriously.

"Almost back to normal," she said.

Nemle thought she would never be back to normal in the sense of being the person she was. Daniel would not be telling her she was too trusting if he met her now.

"Good," she said, smiling.

Impulsively Marheh came closer and put her arms around her.

"Thank you Mama Nemle."

For a moment Nemle enjoyed her embrace then she took Marheh's face in both hands and looked intently into her eyes.

"My dear good daughter."

Perhaps they might have stayed longer looking affectionately at each other, but *Day Bringer* had a mind of her own and decided attention had been turned away too long. They both laughed as Nemle wrenched the tiller round and managed to avoid the bank.

"An hour will be enough for you this morning," Nemle said when *Day Bringer* was back on a straight course. "Call me if you need me," she added as she went below.

Marheh grasped the tiller eagerly. The smooth wood of the handle felt comfortable in her hand. It was still warm from Nemle's grasp and Marheh thought she could feel not just Nemle's firm, capable grip but that of all the women who had owned and loved *Day Bringer*. This part of her life had never let her down. *Day Bringer* was outside all the troubles and difficulties she had been experiencing. She stood firmly in her new boots, feet a little apart, spine straight, head up.

"It was worth it," she thought suddenly, and now all this meant more than ever because she had paid so much for it.

The spring morning was cold and overcast, not springlike at all, but there was a softness in the air and already the trees and hedges were veiled in gauzy colour, delicate greens and a pale hint of pink. Ploughed fields too seemed to hold out the promise of growth. She breathed deeply, feeling herself washed through with newness. After a while she found she was singing under her breath and opened her mouth to make the sounds, consciously claiming her happiness in being. Nemle, walking through from the galley with a mug of sperit, heard the song and felt her eyes fill with tears.

It was three weeks before *Storm Cloud* and *Autumn Wind* caught up with them. Nemle was grateful for the respite and although she insisted Marheh make time to practise the disciplines and kept them boating a good five hours each day she otherwise encouraged something of a holiday mood.

They were comfortably settled in their overnight mooring. They had eaten a late lunch and were lying on the roof, warmed by the first spring sunshine. Nemle was almost asleep and Marheh was hovering on the edge of the portal through which she entered the discipline of the soul. She seemed to rest there often of late. The candle flame was bright and warm and beckoned. She was on the point of entering when she heard the sound of an engine and drew back. The sound grew louder and she sat up. Nemle opened her eyes. They looked at each other then Marheh scrambled to her feet hoping the height of the roof would be enough to provide her with a view over the hedges that lined this section of the water road.

"It's them," she said, grinning at Nemle. "I'll put the kettle on."

By the time *Autumn Wind*, who was leading, had rounded the nearest bend, the kettle was on, the mugs prepared and Marheh back on the bank ready to welcome Jik. Nemle climbed carefully off the roof and went to greet *Storm Cloud* who was coming up behind.

Soon all five were squeezed into *Day Bringer*'s saloon sipping sperit and talking. News from the Gathering was disappointing at first.

"Somehow they changed their minds about the need for an emergency meeting," Sul said. "People are still shocked at the violence done to Marheh, but have decided to believe she should not have been given that choice. No one else will be."

"It's too confronting," Nemle said, nodding. "Grounding is easier, out of sight, out of mind."

"I tried to hint at the possibility of problems within the Silberay," Jik said. "Just to one or two who I thought might be sympathetic, but no one seemed prepared to consider that and I thought it better not to persist."

"Much better," Sul agreed. "We don't want anyone getting the idea that we are planning to investigate."

Kel grinned at Marheh.

"You should have seen us getting away from the Harbour - saying goodbye to each other, pretending to be heading off on our assigned routes. It wasn't too bad for us, but Jik had to sneak back in the dark."

"Maybe it's for the best," Nemle said thoughtfully. "We can be a bit more careful, take our time planning."

"But not too long," Sul said. "Marheh still has an enemy."

Marheh shivered involuntarily.

"Do you think it might be Hud?" she asked. "I know he doesn't like me."

"He has certainly managed to acquire a great deal of influence lately," Sul said.

"And an apprentice," Jik added. "I didn't think he was old enough."

"Old enough but..." Nemle paused. "Does he ever take his boat out of the Harbour?"

"That apprentice reminds me of someone," Kel said. "But I can't think who. I keep trying to get a good look at him, but he stays in the background."

"Even at the closing ceremony?" Marheh asked. "What about when he got his tunic?"

"Only his back view and then only briefly."

"I feel sorry for him if he wants to go boating," Marheh said. "But perhaps Hud will change."

"He'll have to." Nemle was adamant. "The mentors have standards."

"But do you think it could be him?" Marheh said again.

"He's the obvious person, but I don't think we are looking for the obvious," Nemle said.

Sul nodded. "He has perhaps allowed himself to be influenced. He might not even know. I doubt he practises the disciplines over much."

There was a brief pause than Marheh summed up the feelings of them all.

"Then why be Silberay," she said.

Next day they set off again towards Marisford. Now that the pressure of time was relaxed Nemle was anxious to continue with the work that earned them their keep as well as making progress with the investigation. The men were understanding though it was not as important for them. Nemle's work was seasonal and if she did not use the spring and summer well there would be nothing to work with in autumn and winter.

Sul and Kel worked with wood, making small, beautifully crafted pieces. Jik added to the small inheritance he had from his parents by labouring at markets or on farms. Sul too had a small inheritance but Nemle's parents had not approved of her life choice and had left what little they had to a nephew.

They developed a pattern of travel that meant they kept in touch with each other without being tied together. A three day target was set and they planned their own journey to accommodate that.

Usually Sul and Kel reached the target first and spent a day moored up, working, acquiring provisions and exploring the landscape listening and observing. Jik waited, perhaps as much as an extra day before setting out, spending his time with the disciplines, making himself an extra shield for Marheh. *Day Bringer* travelled between them, her journey varying according to Nemle's needs.

They took an extra couple of days in one place so that Marheh could make contact with the pottery she had used before and again offer her labour in exchange for firing. She had quite a collection of fragile little pieces and also needed some more clay. She wanted to contribute, but also felt she needed a good excuse to spend time at the market.

Three days away from Marisford they paused again to take stock. Their investigation was about to begin and it seemed important to take time to practise the disciplines together and discuss what they were planning. Nemle felt that Marheh needed more challenge in the discipline of the mind than she alone could give so she arranged for Jik and Sul to practise with her. Kel had one practice with her too, but although he was much further on in his apprenticeship his skills could not approach hers.

They were all aware that the Yareblis had no qualms about using mind control in anyway that would benefit them. Silberay restrictions on its use meant they were disadvantaged often because they lacked experience. Marheh understood why they were making her work so hard and she was grateful but the first couple of days they spent together left her so exhausted that Nemle decreed a day of rest before they proceeded to Marisford.

They were in two minds about travelling as a group. They knew their enemy could see the water road and the sight of three Silberay boats together was as good as a red flag but in the end they reasoned that if their enemy was near enough to see them it was already too late and the added protection would be critical.

So they set off, *Storm Cloud* leading, then *Day Bringer* with *Autumn Wind* bringing up the rear. Three long days of boating and they were at the mooring for Marisford. Next morning Kel, Marheh and Jik would make the long climb up to the market with the barrow filled with their various wares, lots of Marheh's sculptures, some of Nemle's herb teas and even a few of Kel's little carved and inlaid wooden boxes.

Marheh couldn't help feeling excited. The morning sky was filling with soft light as they set out, Kel pushing the barrow, all carrying loaded packs. The men walked on either side of her and she felt very safe though it crossed her mind that these two protectors would also keep Daniel away should he see them with her. Of course Daniel might not be anywhere near but this was the place to start looking.

It was not long before they were setting up the barrow in the place assigned. Jik went off to see if he could earn a few shillings lifting and carrying, not because he really needed the money but because it gave him a degree of anonymity if he could become part of the background to the market. His Silberay uniform did not mark him as different in the way it did for the women and when he had a crate of vegetables on his shoulder or a piglet under each arm he disappeared. The work left his mind free too and he was accustomed to listening to his environment as he worked. Nothing yet gave him cause for concern.

Marheh insisted on taking the first shift at the barrow because she thought if Daniel were to come it would be later in the day. Only minutes after Kel had left to wander round the market a woman came to look at her sculptures. She owned a little local shop and was interested in negotiating a price for a dozen pieces that she would buy to sell on.

Marheh was happily discussing which pieces would be included when suddenly she drew back. What if this was another attempt to incriminate her? She looked at the woman who seemed so eager. How could she tell if she was being controlled without entering her mind, the very thing she must not do?

"What's the matter?" the woman asked. "I've offered a fair price. I can't offer anymore."

"The price is fine," Marheh said, continuing to study the woman's face. "I just want to be sure you really want them."

"Of course I want them. I wouldn't be here if I didn't."

She seemed genuine. There was no hint in her eyes that she was being controlled. Marheh swallowed hard. This was her livelihood. She had to proceed.

"I… I'm glad," she said, then added hastily. "I'll be here till the end of the day though, so if you should want to change your mind…"

The woman raised her eyebrows.

"I like the pieces, I want the pieces and I think they will sell." She handed over the thirty shillings they had agreed on. "And if you are here again in a couple of months or so come and see me. I may want more."

Marheh began carefully wrapping the pieces in newspaper and putting them in the bag the woman held out to her.

"If you were to think of providing little boxes for them that would make them even more marketable," the woman continued.

The transaction concluded the woman smiled, put a little card with the address of her shop on the barrow and departed.

Marheh pocketed the card and began to think about little boxes. She could make boxes out of strong white cardboard and draw a little pen sketch of the contents on the side of the box. It would be fun to do, but probably not feasible while she was an apprentice. There was so little storage space available and Nemle's work had to come first.

She was still designing little boxes in her head when Kel returned carrying a mug of tea and a bacon sandwich.

"What does he look like, this Daniel of yours?" he asked passing over the mug and half the sandwich.

Marheh bit into the sandwich and considered her answer. It was more than a year since she had seen him and the image she had of him had faded. The feel of his mouth on hers, his touch on her skin, these were what lingered, but she could hardly explain that to Kel.

"He's not as tall as you," she said when her mouth was empty. "But older, with dark curly hair." She looked apologetically at him. "I'm sure I will recognise him, but it's difficult to describe him so you would pick him out."

"You'd better go and have a scout around then. I'll mind the shop. But finish your breakfast first."

Ten minutes later she was away. Would he be here or was the first encounter something so structured that he had come with one purpose only. She took the mug back to the trader who had sold Kel the tea and set off to scour the market without success. Disappointed she returned to Kel and the barrow. He was deep in conversation with an old man who was holding one of his boxes and rubbing the smooth polished surface gently with his thumb.

"Lovely work." Marheh heard him say.

He turned as she approached and she saw his face change as he recognised her.

"It's the apprentice who delivers free," he said.

Marheh grinned. "Strong and willing," she said, remembering how he had described her.

"Where is the boss then? And where are the seedlings?"

"It's too early, they are barely shooting."

The man shook his head.

"And is this your young man?" he asked, winking at Kel.

Marheh blushed. "He's an apprentice too," she said. Then, because that did not seem quite enough, she added. "We're friends."

The man laughed and winked at Kel again.

"Just friends, "she said firmly.

"Just friends," the man repeated. "Well your friend is a very good workman

142

and I wish to purchase this lovely little box."

Marheh beamed at Kel.

"And I think my badgers would appreciate some company," he went on, picking up a model of a hare and holding it out for Marheh to wrap. "Tell the boss I did well with her seedlings."

The transaction complete the man put his purchases into the pockets of his coat then bent to pick up the bags and bundles at his feet.

"May I help you with your parcels?" Marheh asked.

"You, not him?"

"It's my turn to be out and about," Marheh said, glancing at Kel.

"Free delivery," she added.

The man nodded and Marheh took a bag in each hand and followed him through the market to the back of the pub where his horse and cart waited patiently.

His was not the only conveyance waiting there and people seemed to be coming and going all the time. Marheh remembered how Daniel had invited her to have a drink with him. It would be a logical place to look she thought, putting the old man's parcels in his cart and saying goodbye.

She began to walk away then made up her mind to go in. Turning sharply she made for the front entrance. She saw through the window that it was crowded and heard the noise of many voices and hesitated for a moment before pushing the door open.

There were two steps up into the dim, smoky interior and she paused in the doorway reluctant to tackle the unfamiliar crowded space. Then a couple of men pushed in from the street and she had no choice. There was so little space that she scarcely knew how to proceed. The mass of people felt intimidating, alien even, and she could see that any attempt at moving through them would involve contact she did not want to initiate. Then she felt a hand rest on each shoulder. She started, turned her head then allowed herself to ease back against her Uncle Jik.

"I thought he might be in here," she said, tilting her head back. "But it is so crowded I don't know where to start."

"We could ask if anyone has seen him," Jik suggested. "If this is his local he would be known."

"I never thought of that. I was just going to look around."

Jik began to guide her towards the bar. Somehow a path seemed to open before him and soon they were leaning against the polished wooden surface and Jik was asking Marheh what she would like to drink.

"I thought we were going to ask about Daniel," she said.

"We won't get much attention if we don't buy something," Jik said.

When the barmaid turned to them he ordered a beer for himself and a shandy for Marheh and only when she returned with the drinks did he ask after the friend he made last time he visited, a dark man with a good line of talk, called Daniel.

She took his money and nodded her thanks for his tip.

"Don't know," she said. "Could perhaps be him in the snug. His name is Daniel, but he hasn't said much this twelve month or more."

Marheh looked back at Jik, her face worried. He squeezed her arm.

"We'll go and have a look," he said, giving the barmaid another coin.

He picked up their drinks and led the way through the crowd, Marheh close behind him, glad to be able to bob in his wake.

There were two steps down into the small, rather dark and smoky space that was the snug. It was not as crowded as the front bar and much quieter. Marheh, peering around Jik, saw small tables with men, mostly elderly, nursing their tankards or glasses, some talking to each other, one or two smoking pipes. A rather sulky coal fire struggled in the small fireplace.

Jik stepped down into the room and moved aside so Marheh could see.

"What do you think?" he asked after a minute. "Can you see him?"

Marheh shook her head slowly.

"I don't think so," she said, continuing to scan the faces. "I would have thought he would be in with the crowd, not out here."

She was about to turn away when a solitary figure in the darkest corner of the room caught her eye. He was tucked against the wall behind a tiny table.

A pewter tankard stood in front of him and he stared blankly into it.

"That might be him," Marheh whispered, nudging Jik. "Only…"

Jik looked at her.

"He was happy and funny," she said.

"Come on."

Jik began to move across the room then Marheh, growing more sure, darted out from behind him and almost ran to the still, silent figure.

"Daniel?" she said, kneeling to look up into the unresponsive face. "Daniel?"

Jik came up beside her and put their drinks down on the little table.

"May we join you Daniel?" he asked in his pleasant, low voice.

There was no response.

"You'll not get an answer from that one."

A man seated nearby indicated an empty chair at his table. Jik reached over to pick it up and put it opposite Daniel. Marheh shook her head when he offered it to her and he saw she had tears in her eyes. He sat down.

"He didn't do what they wanted and they've hurt him," Marheh whispered. "Oh Jik, we have to help him."

Jik nodded. "Of course, if we can."

"Friend of yours is he?" the man asked curiously.

Marheh turned to respond.

"But he wasn't like this when I knew him before."

"Come on slowly it has. Used to be he were full of talk. Popular with the lasses too. Now he just sits staring at nothing no matter what."

The man edged his seat closer to them and looked critically at Marheh.

"You one of those water gypsies?" he asked.

"I'm an apprentice Silberay," Marheh said, not quite liking the look in his eye.

"Maybe it was you lot put a spell on him."

"Of course we didn't. There's no such thing."

"Not what I heard."

Jik glanced at Marheh and spoke quietly. "We don't do spells, there's no such thing, but we might be able to help him."

The man continued to look sceptical and turned to draw other drinkers into the conversation. Discussion became general and increased in volume. There seemed to be a degree of antagonism in the air and Marheh was becoming defiant. Jik stood up slowly and looked around. His manner was not threatening, but his size and quiet confidence had an effect and the voices died away.

"Daniel was my niece's friend," he said to the room at large. "And we would like to help him if we can. Is there someone responsible for bringing him here?"

At last after more discussion a small man with a brown, weathered face took his pipe from his mouth, looked disapprovingly at Marheh and spoke to Jik.

"Woman brings him, parks him here, pays for his pint. His sister I think. She'll be back to pick him up when the market closes."

"Then we'll come back to speak with her then," Jik said. He picked up his beer and drained it. "Come along niece, drink up."

Marheh frowned, got up from her knees and took a couple of big gulps from her glass. Bother Jik, she wanted to stay with Daniel and see if she could encourage a response. She looked up to protest and changed her mind.

"Goodbye Daniel," she said, putting down her glass. "I'll be back soon."

"Surely compassion is first for us, a deep love for humanity that is nourished by the soul song. Without it we can do nothing."

Sila's journal: the early years

Chapter Thirteen

Marheh scurried out of the pub in Jik's wake and ran after him, grabbing at his sleeve to get his attention.

"You might have asked me if I wanted to leave instead of ordering me about like an infant."

"You are an infant," Jik teased, then sobered at the sight of her furious face.

"You have to remember how you look to them," he said. "They don't know it will probably be you who heals him. Most of them disapprove of your trousers and expect me to keep you in order. Sometimes you have to play it the way they expect."

She considered this and nodded a bit reluctantly.

"I suppose so."

He was leading the way back to Kel and their market stall and she had to walk fast to keep up with his long stride.

Kel seemed pleased to see them and Marheh saw that there had been a couple more sales. She listened while Jik explained what happened and offered to mind the stall again.

"Maybe Kel could go and get himself a drink and keep an eye on Daniel," she suggested. "They won't know in the pub that he's with us."

She settled herself behind the barrow as the other two went off in different directions. Jik's comment that she might be the one to heal Daniel needed thinking about. She had once been able to free two servants who had been controlled by the Yareblis and Nemle had encouraged her to develop this

147

ability by going with her each year to Haven Cottage where damaged Silberay were cared for. There they offered their labour so Deyah and Gyp who ran the hospice could have a break. There she became accustomed to entering damaged minds to direct and guide them in the necessities of living. Those Silberay were damaged past healing though and her activities were more about making them comfortable – and sharing the soul song, she thought, they could still sing with her, but Daniel did not even know his soul name.

She thought about Daniel all afternoon as she sat behind the barrow. Customers came and went and she made some sales but these hardly registered. What seemed of first importance was to keep Daniel in her mind, rebuild her image of him and prepare herself to enter his mind and offer herself, her love and sorrow for his healing.

Towards the end of the afternoon Jik came back to help her close up the barrow. The food stalls were mostly packed up and the numbers of potential customers had dwindled. Together they pushed the barrow around to the pub and Jik went in to find Kel. He was to take it back to the boats and reassure Nemle and Sul while Jik and Marheh remained to meet Daniel's sister and persuade her to permit them to try to help him.

Daniel still sat in the same dark corner with the same tankard in front of him. Kel told Marheh he had barely moved all the time he had been watching. She joined Jik in the snug, which was now nearly empty, though the small man with the pipe remained. They sat together talking quietly and watching. Jik had provided himself with another beer but he arranged a cup of tea for Marheh and she was glad of its warmth.

"Never thought you'd come back," the small man commented, having studied them for a few minutes.

"Why not?" Marheh asked.

The man shrugged.

"Don't trust you lot. Here one minute, gone the next and what's gone with you is the question."

Marheh opened her mouth to argue, but a glance from Jik was enough to make her pause.

"I'm sorry you feel that way," Jik said. "We came back because we hope to be able to help Daniel and to discover who was responsible for making him like this."

"And we are not thieves either," Marheh added, unwilling to let this accusation pass unchallenged.

The small man shrugged again and sucked on his pipe, clearly sceptical. Marheh might have continued to argue, but just then a woman came into the room and walked across to where Daniel sat. She wore a dark blue scarf over greying hair and her heavy coat was also blue but not quite long enough so that her brown woollen skirt showed beneath it. She put a hand on Daniel's arm and began to encourage him to rise.

Marheh glanced at Jik then stood up and went towards them. The woman looked up, her face expressionless, as if she had put up a barrier against curiosity. For a moment Marheh did not know how to proceed she felt so sorry for them both.

"I... I... Daniel..."

The woman continued to stand looking at her. Marheh tried again.

"Daniel was my friend. I'm so sorry."

Again she paused and still the woman waited.

"I might be able to help him. I was hoping you would let me try."

"No one can help him," the woman said, turning back to Daniel.

"Please let me try."

"Why should I? What's in it for you?"

"He was my friend," Marheh repeated. "I care about him."

She didn't know how to begin explaining that Daniel's condition might have been brought about by her own enemies, but she looked into the woman's eyes and put all she could not express into her gaze.

"Please," she said.'

The woman made an impatient movement, turned to Daniel then back to Marheh.

"I don't know," she said slowly.

There was a long silence.

"You got nothing to lose," advised the small man, removing his pipe for the purpose.

Suddenly it was agreed. Marheh looked back at Jik with a moment of panic then took a deep breath. She could see there was no chance the woman would allow her to go with them to a more private place. She would have to do it here. Jik stood up and moved towards the entrance to the snug. Quietly he stood, filling the doorway and watching Marheh. She drew up a chair opposite Daniel and motioned to his sister to do the same.

"I need to be quiet," she told the woman and sat for a few minutes breathing deeply and looking at Daniel. Then she began to feel her way into his mind.

Dark, oily sludge met her. She could scarcely find a place that was not contaminated by it. She had never met anything like it she knew, yet there was an odd feeling of familiarity. Then she remembered cleaning up after an oil leak in *Day Bringer*'s engine. There could hardly be an oil leak in Daniel's mind, she thought, trying to understand what she was seeing, but something was leaking poison.

Focusing with mind and soul she studied the sad, polluted space where she found herself. Healing meant cleaning, she understood, cleaning gently and thoroughly and she had never been much of a housekeeper but somehow she must not only clean, but remove the waste. The task seemed almost overwhelming and she ached with pity for Daniel's poisoned mind. Then, without really understanding how it had come about, she found she was filling a bowl with her tears. Kneeling, she allowed a tear to fall at the edge of the sludge and was not really surprised to find it a solvent.

On hands and knees she distributed her tears and watched as the sludge dissolved. Then she crouched even lower to use the end of her long plait to mop the resultant liquid and wring it into the bowl. Gradually the space around her began to be clean and she could move further into his mind and trace the source of the poison. It might well have been an oil can leaking she thought, discovering the small, strangely shaped container that had no place in Daniel's mind. As she watched a tiny bubble of darkness dribbled out. It couldn't stay there she knew or all she had done would be for nothing. Cautiously she reached out to touch it and drew back at the pain.

Then she gathered herself, gripped the container and plunged it into the bowl. Her hand stung and burned but the liquid in the bowl was enveloping the poisoned container and changing it until it became translucent then transparent then disappeared.

For a few moments she rested, there in the refreshed space of Daniel's mind then she reached for the candle flame that would admit her to the discipline of the soul. Once there she began her soul song, spinning the music that she hoped would call Daniel's soul to hers and allow her to discover his soul name. It was a lonely task. At first she seemed to be singing in dark emptiness, the golden thread of her music struggling to hold its own. Then, faint and unpractised, she heard Daniel's song, a rhythm more than a tune, but one that built in strength as she wove her song around it.

She resolved the music at length and eased back the first step. In Daniel's mind she still held the bowl of treated waste. She gathered herself to draw it back with her into her own mind then she pictured herself placing it on the coal fire that still sulked in the fireplace.

Only Jik noticed how for a moment the flames leapt blue and green. Daniel's sister, the small man with the pipe and the two or three other patrons in the snug were watching Daniel waking. His eyes, that had been so blank and dim, lit with new awareness. He stretched and breathed deeply as if enjoying even the rather stale and smoky air around him.

"Edith," he said turning to his sister. "This is a strange place for you to be."

His speech was slow as if each word needed concentration.

Edith stared at him. There were tears in her eyes and her mouth opened and shut without forming words of her own.

"Call him Dal," a weary voice beside her spoke. "His soul name is Dal."

Jik crossed the room in two strides and stood protectively behind Marheh. She looked up at him with a small smile.

"It's my little witch," Daniel said then, discovering her.

Marheh shook her head.

"Hello Dal."

She was suddenly so tired she barely knew how to form the words. Jik put a hand on her shoulder and spoke, looking first at Daniel then at Edith.

"May we meet tomorrow? She needs to rest now."

It was quickly arranged then Jik helped Marheh to her feet and supported her out into the street. He was anxious to get her away before the silent wonder of the few witnesses turned into noisy celebration and demands for attention.

Twilight was nearly gone now and the high street was empty of market stalls and busy shoppers. They moved away from the pub and off towards the boats as fast as they could. Marheh was exhausted and the walk was almost more than she could manage, but Jik was at hand to support her, glad that Kel had taken their packs with the barrow. He would have carried her if she had permitted, but she was too tired to be quite rational and wasted her energy in protesting when he suggested it.

The lane down to the water road was dark and shadowy but at the bottom was a tiny pinpoint of light coming from one of the boats. It was a welcome sight.

As they came closer they saw it came from *Storm Cloud* and framed in the lighted window they could see Nemle, Sul and Kel waiting for them. Marheh stumbled and would have fallen without Jik's support. Nemle looked up as if listening and Jik saw her stand and take her leave of the others. By the time they had reached the boats she was waiting for them on *Day Bringer*'s back deck. Jik gave Marheh a hug and handed her over to Nemle. She didn't need questions and company this evening.

Nemle shepherded her down the back stairs and through to the saloon where a lamp glowed softly. A pot of soup was keeping warm on the edge of the stove and the good smell filled the boat. She placed Marheh in the armchair and stood back to look at her. Then, still without speaking, she filled a bowl with soup, took a spoon and went to sit on the footstool beside her. Marheh's eyes opened for a moment and she made a small movement of rejection.

"You can go to bed in a minute, but you must eat something first," Nemle said.

With coaxing noises and teasing words she fed her from the bowl until the colour began to come back into her face and she was ready to take the bowl herself.

"More?" Nemle asked when the bowl was empty and happily refilled it.

When she had finished eating Marheh gave a little sigh and leaned back.

"I didn't know how hard it would be," she said.

Nemle patted her hand. "Kel told us what had happened. I knew you would manage. I want to hear about it, but not tonight."

"Not tonight," Marheh agreed, closing her eyes.

Nemle stood up, took her hand.

"You'll be more comfortable in bed," she said, tugging gently.

As tenderly as if she were recovering from an illness Nemle guided her to her cabin, helped her out of her uniform and into her night dress and tucked her into the hard, narrow little bunk.

"Sleep as long as you want in the morning," she said, bending to kiss her goodnight.

Then she blew out the candle and left her to sleep.

While Nemle was tending to Marheh, Jik went along to *Storm Cloud* knowing they would be anxious. They had waited to share their meal with him and while they ate he told them what had happened.

"We've arranged to meet him tomorrow," he concluded. "Marheh was too tired tonight."

Sul nodded thoughtfully.

"I'm not sure that's wise," he said.

"But our whole purpose was to question Daniel."

"I don't mean we shouldn't meet with him, but Marheh might be better to stay away from the town. If people think she is some kind of miracle worker she is likely to be mobbed."

Jik's eyes widened.

"I hadn't thought of that, but you're right. They won't understand that what damaged Daniel was not an illness."

"She must not go," Sul said. "The more I think about it the more strongly I feel."

"You'll have a job persuading her of that," Jik said.

"Perhaps I could go and bring him back here," Kel said. "I'm not likely to be linked with her the way you are."

"That would be best," Sul agreed. "But we had better not make firm arrangements before we talk with Nemle."

"And Marheh," added Kel.

"And Marheh," Sul repeated. "She will be sure to have an opinion on the subject."

Marheh's opinion was loudly expressed, but in the end Nemle's quiet "I think you would be very foolish" was enough to win her reluctant agreement to the arrangements. She walked a little way up the hill towards the town with Kel and was tempted to protest when he suggested she had come far enough.

"You all treat me as if I was a child," she said.

Kel raised his eyebrows and shook his head.

"You know that is not true, or you would if…"

"I would if I were not behaving like one," Marheh said with a flash of self knowledge. "Sorry."

Kel laughed and continued on up the hill. Marheh watched him for a few minutes then returned to the boats. She knew Nemle wanted to hear how she had released Daniel and to check that she had not drawn any of the poison into herself as she did so.

Daniel and his sister came hurrying down the hill with Kel an hour or so later. Marheh stepped onto the bank as they approached so they would be able to see her. Kel picked up Edith and stepped on board with her.

Marheh heard Daniel's gasp of surprise as she disappeared. She held out her hand to him.

"Look only at me," she said. "Let me lead you, or close your eyes if it's easier."

"I'd rather look at you," Daniel said taking her hand.

A moment later she had guided him onto the back deck and down into the back cabin.

It was not long before they were all squeezed into *Day Bringer*'s saloon, Daniel and Edith at the table as befitted visitors, Nemle in the armchair, Sul on the footstool and Marheh and Kel on the floor. Jik had provided himself with a small folding stool.

"I feel as if we'll leave to find a hundred years have passed," Daniel said looking around with interest.

"Don't be silly," Marheh said crossly, wondering how she was going to talk to him with all these people about.

"This could not possibly be fairyland with me in it," Jik said, grinning. "No pots of gold, no magic."

"Just a beautiful maiden," Daniel said looking pointedly at Marheh.

"Don't be silly," Marheh said again blushing.

"We're all perfectly ordinary," Nemle said. "We just happen to see a different dimension."

"And heal people," Edith said, the words bursting out. "And disappear."

"You might find that we don't disappear if you look," Sul said kindly.

"Particularly if you think about using your soul name sometimes," Nemle added.

"I don't know what you're talking about. I don't know why you brought us here and I want to go now."

Edith slid off the seat and stood up.

"Please don't. We really need Daniel's help."

A surprised stillness.

"My help?"

"Marheh has an enemy," Jik said. "We think the person who offered to pay you has been responsible for other attacks on her and caused your mind to shut down in retribution. We hoped you might be able to tell us who it is."

"The person who paid me?" Daniel said.

"Yes," Marheh said. "You told me someone had paid you to… to… and would pay you more if you did. Don't you remember?"

There was a moment of silence.

"But that was months ago, more than a year," Daniel said.

"But do you remember?" Marheh asked again.

"Yes, I remember," he said. "I felt ashamed."

Again a silence as the listeners felt with him.

"Who was it Dal?" Marheh asked at last.

"A young chap," Daniel said slowly, obviously thinking back. "Pale hair, little fine short beard, told me I could collect my money from Belaven Manor, but he never said who he was. Not one of the family at the manor, I knew that."

"Did you never wonder why he wanted you to seduce Marheh?" Nemle asked when it was clear he had finished speaking.

"Not then," Daniel said. "Then it was just a bit of a laugh. Only when I got to know her it stopped being funny."

"You never said." Edith eased back onto the seat.

"Well I wouldn't would I?"

"Is there anything more you can tell us?" Nemle asked.

"He looked like he had money. Well cared for, smooth, good clothes."

"And young?" Nemle asked.

"Very," Daniel said. "No older than Mary I would have thought."

"Not Hud then," Marheh said, voicing what was in all their minds.

Nemle levered herself out of the armchair and looked around at the crowd in the saloon.

"Would you like to eat with us?" she offered. "I think we can manage soup and bread and cheese."

"For seven!" Jik raised his eyebrows.

"I persuaded Marheh to do some work while Kel went up to meet Daniel."

"Persuaded! Got out the whip more like."

"Poor little kitchen maid."

"Don't mind them," Nemle said, looking at Daniel and Edith. "There is plenty of soup and I made a loaf while Marheh was still asleep. You would be very welcome to share it with us."

Edith was a bit reluctant at first, but Daniel was keen and soon they were enjoying the food and becoming more at ease with the five Silberay. When the last mouthfuls had been scraped from the bowls and Nemle's good loaf was gone Marheh and Kel gathered up the crockery and cutlery, some of which had come from *Storm Cloud*, and put the kettle on for sperit.

Edith leaned across the table and spoke softly to Daniel.

"Go on then," he said. "You ask."

The others looked at her and her face seemed to close.

"Ask me," Jik said, leaning towards her from his stool. "Never mind them."

She looked to Daniel then back to Jik.

"Please," said Jik.

"It was something she said yesterday when Daniel was coming back. She called him Dal and said it was his soul name, and Nem ... Nemle said it too. What do you mean, soul name?"

Jik looked across to Nemle and Sul to see if they wanted to answer then spoke, choosing his words carefully.

"It is the name that belonged to you before you were born, the name that speaks to the essence of you, the name of your soul."

Edith and Daniel looked at each other.

"What good is it?" Edith asked. "Why have two names?"

Again Jik deferred to Sul and Nemle.

"The good is just that," Sul said. "The soul name is part of what is good in you." He smiled. "The kind of goodness like Nemle's loaf, simple and wholesome."

"It doesn't mean we always live up to our ideal self," Nemle said.

"You only have to look at me to know that," Marheh put in.

"But using it calls to the best in us and perhaps safeguards us a little too," Nemle went on. "Certainly we know that our enemies, the people who damaged you Daniel, deny the soul and it seems perhaps that is because the soul keeps trying to call you back to what is good in you."

"And you say my soul name is Dal?" Daniel asked.

"Marheh say so, she went looking. Does it feel right to you?"

"Do I have a soul name," Edith asked, not waiting for Daniel's response.

"Everyone does unless they choose to deny it."

"Well why don't I know what it is?"

Nemle looked sad.

"Over the time I've been Silberay people seem less and less interested in the soul. If parents don't seek to learn the soul name from the baby who still remembers it then as the child grows it is forgotten. Then, when that child becomes a parent he or she will never know there is something to be learnt."

There was a short silence when Nemle finished her explanation. Marheh looked at Edith who was looking inward, obviously considering. Jik and Nemle looked at Marheh guessing what Edith's next question might be. Sul and Kel looked at Daniel and smiled a greeting.

"Can Mary find Edith's soul name too?" Daniel asked.

"If Edith wants me to," Marheh said. "Or one of the others could. It doesn't have to be me."

Edith looked around at the five Silberay. She looked a little trapped Jik thought. He smiled at her.

"You mustn't feel pressured. You don't need to know your soul name to be a good person. You've cared for Daniel all these months, he knows your goodness."

Edith's rather stern face relaxed a little, a faint flush coloured her cheeks.

"Will it be difficult to find it?"

"Not if you want it found."

"Will you find it?" she asked Jik.

"Of course."

He looked around at the others who smiled their support.

He was the best uncle, Marheh thought, remembering the times he had patiently answered her questions when she was a child. How he had allowed her to explore *Autumn Wind* and even taken her boating. She was so lucky to have grown up with family who valued the water dimension even if they couldn't see it and who respected and acknowledged the life of the soul.

Jik spoke softly to Edith for a minute or two then fell silent, looking at her intently. Edith looked suddenly young and a little awed, then she smiled, a small inward smile of recognition. The other Silberay waited, actively supporting Jik so that to Daniel it seemed as if the sun had come out filling *Day Bringer* with light and warmth. He found he could rest there with them and time rested too.

"I'm Dytha," she said into the quiet, timeless light, her voice solemn, but glad and accepting.

There was an easing, like a gentle sigh, then smiles and words of welcome.

"Dytha," she said again, savouring it. "And Dal. We'll remember."

There was more quiet talk then it was time for Daniel and Edith to go. Marheh and Jik went with them a little way.

"Are you sure a hundred years have not gone by," Daniel joked as they said goodbye.

"You'll soon find out, won't you?" Jik teased.

"It seems like something out of a dream," Edith said. "And the boats and the water have vanished."

"We'll be back," Marheh said.

She and Jik stood and watched while Daniel and Edith continued the climb up to Marisford.

"If it isn't Hud, who could it possibly be?" Marheh said when the brother and sister were out of sight. "That's the worst part, not knowing."

"It must be," Jik said.

"Maybe not quite the worst part," Marheh said as they turned to walk back to the boats. "The really worst part is that whoever it is must be hiding within the Silberay."

Her footsteps slowed as she thought about what she had said. It was as if something foul was polluting the water road.

Jik gave her a friendly pat and waited for her to continue.

"It's like a betrayal," she said. "Being Silberay was my ideal, something bright and shining to look up to. The Silberay were my family and now I can't trust anyone except you and Nemle and Sul and Kel."

"The description Daniel gave us reminds me of someone, but I can't think who for the moment."

Marheh stopped and looked at him.

"You know who it reminds me of," she said slowly. "That apprentice of Hud's. But that doesn't make sense... unless..." The idea spilled out. "Unless Hud is controlling him. Could it be that?"

"It's a possibility I suppose." Jik seemed to be considering her suggestion. "But how could he have been fifty years a Silberay and not discovered if he really is aligned with the Yareblis? He's a mentor now. It couldn't happen."

"Couldn't it?" Marheh asked. "What's to stop him?"

"We would know," Jik said. "Surely we would know. He couldn't practise the discipline of the soul. We would know that."

"He doesn't behave as if he practises the disciplines," Marheh said. "How would we know?"

"There are times when the soul song is required, at graduation, on becoming a mentor. I'm sure we'd know."

Marheh sighed.

"I suppose so. I just wish I knew who it is. I suppose I hoped Daniel could tell us and we could go and confront him or her and it would all be over."

Jik put an arm around her and gave her a little hug. He did not say what he was thinking, that this had been an insidious and subtle long term campaign and getting behind it was never going to be easy.

"Come on," he said. "We'll get to the bottom of it before long."

Marheh smiled at him and leaned in to him for a moment then they set off down the hill to the boats.

When they arrived back on *Day Bringer* they found Nemle, Sul and Kel poring over a chart spread out on the table.

"I'm sure there is a big estate behind the wood here," Nemle was saying. "I wonder whether that might be Belaven Manor."

Marheh and Jik crowded in behind. Jik could see over Sul's shoulder but Marheh was not tall enough. She squeezed in beside Nemle and tried to orient herself on the map.

"But that's where…"

Nemle nodded.

"Where you lost your hands? I know that's one reason why I'm wondering."

Marheh shivered as the memory came flooding back and then had to explain to the others what had happened. Sul sent Kel off to *Storm Cloud* to get a road atlas of the countryside that he thought he had.

"It doesn't show the water road," he explained. "But with the chart and the map we should be able to identify the place."

It was soon accomplished. The road map showed the estate, quite clearly named and it was not difficult to see where the water road would lie.

"It's quite close to Market Mondborough really," Jik pointed out. "See how the water road curves around so it seems further."

"There's probably a bus," Nemle said. "And nowhere is very far if they have a motor, or even just a horse and buggy."

"We'll need to go there then," Marheh said in a rather flat voice.

Nemle glanced at her and spoke firmly.

"We don't need to decide what to do now. Why don't we move on? There's a nice mooring an hour away and it will give us some quiet space. We can talk again after supper."

"Which will be on *Storm Cloud*," Sul said. "*Day Bringer* has provided enough hospitality today.

Supper that evening was something of a celebration.

Kel had purchased a leg of lamb at the market the previous day so he and Sul prepared a roast dinner with all the trimmings and apple pie and cream to follow. Jik contributed a couple of bottles of red wine. Marheh and Nemle were not permitted to bring anything, although Nemle had been asked earlier to supply some of her mint.

Marheh was very cheerful, clowning a little, flirting with all three men. Nemle watching her saw that Daniel had taught her how beautiful she was and that she was enjoying being the centre of attention. Kel and Sul were laughing as she described an interaction at the market, taking all the parts. Jik laughed too, but he turned to wink at Nemle.

There was not room for them all to sit at the small fixed table but Kel had set up the bench he and Sul used for their work and their guests had provided folding stools so they were all accommodated after a fashion, very cosy, even squashed, though no one thought of complaining.

As the meal progressed and the wine bottles emptied Marheh became more and more outrageous. She was not very used to wine nor to an audience. The first course was cleared away and Kel was serving the pie. Marheh wriggled round to watch him holding up her glass and looking at him over the rim.

"I think I should always be waited on," she said. "You do it so nicely. Perhaps I could visit Belaven Manor and you could be my servant. Do you think I could be a fine lady?"

Kel did not answer, but passed a serving of pie to Nemle across the table.

162

"Watch me," she said, holding her glass with her little finger cocked at an exaggerated angle and taking a tiny sip.

"Very nice," Kel said passing her some pie.

She gave him a beaming smile then wiped it from her face to replace it with an exaggerated simper. Kel chuckled and she batted her eyelashes at him. Nemle thought it best to ignore her and for a time she was quiet, occupied with eating. Once her plate was empty though, she swept a limpid glance around the company, gathered them all into her orbit and proceeded to entertain them.

She really was very funny, Nemle thought, but there was something unsettling about her as well, a kind of wildness that made Nemle anxious for her. There was lots of laughter, some talk, but no chance for planning how to work with Daniel's information. Then, almost in mid-sentence, it seemed as if the source of Marheh's heightened energy had run dry. She stopped talking, started again then stopped.

Nemle stretched and stood up.

"I'm sorry to break up the party," she said. "I'm feeling rather tired now."

She smiled at Kel and Sul.

"It's been a lovely meal, a real treat."

Then she looked at Marheh.

"Will you come home with me daughter?"

It was said very lightly as if she did not care one way or the other, but she awaited Marheh's answer with some anxiety. In this mood Marheh could well be unreasonable, even a bit irrational and it would be so much easier for everyone if she did not have to assert her authority.

Marheh pouted and looked around at the others as if for encouragement.

"Good night niece," Jik said, giving her plait a gentle tug. "Sweet dreams."

For a moment Nemle thought she was going to rebel but then she smiled at Jik and rubbed her cheek against his sleeve with a small, tired sigh.

Nemle held out her hand.

"Come and give your old tired mentor a hand back home."

Marheh made a face, aware from this that she was being managed and wanting with part of herself to resent it. She looked at the others, kind, understanding friends, and capitulated.

The cool darkness outside was peaceful after the heat and noise. Marheh sighed but did not speak and Nemle walked quietly behind her on the narrow path. When they reached *Day Bringer* she stopped. Nemle waited then heard a tiny sound like a whimper choked off and saw Marheh put her hands to her face and sink to her knees. Without haste Nemle went to her, put her hands gently on the bent head and crouched down to hold her as she sobbed.

After a minute Marheh sniffed, rubbed her eyes and looked up, her face a pale oval in the darkness.

"Oh Nemle," she said. "Why me? I'm so afraid. Why me?"

"Good motives are important, but not enough. A Silberay apprentice is expected to be humble and self-effacing so that the needs of others are understood and not assumed to be the same as those of the apprentice."

The Silberay apprentice: a handbook

Chapter Fourteen

How to proceed?

Nemle was still awake hours after she had seen Marheh into bed and off to sleep.

Marheh's fear was real and justified. Did she need time to find her courage again or would it be better to act quickly so she had no time to think about what it meant to have an implacable enemy? Could they in fact act quickly? Did they have enough information to take the next step? Had they really decided what the next step was? She knew she had no answers and that she would be better occupying herself with the discipline of the soul, but Marheh's behaviour that night had shown her just how much the half-understood threat was undermining her confidence.

She slept at last and woke to *Day Bringer*'s gentle rocking as Marheh moved around the boat doing her customary morning chores. She ought to be getting up she thought, but closed her eyes again and knew nothing more until Marheh scratched on her door and came in with a steaming mug and a look of concern.

Nemle smiled at her and pushed herself to a sitting position.

"Too much excitement for an old woman," she said, mocking herself. "I couldn't seem to get to sleep last night."

"You are not an old woman," Marheh said, emphasising each word.

Nemle took her mug and patted the bed.

"Come and sit with me," she said. "Then I can be lazy with a clear

165

conscience."

It only took a few seconds for Marheh to fetch her own mug of sperit and perch on the end of Nemle's bed.

"I'm sorry about yesterday," she said after a short silence. "I behaved badly."

Her head was down and she seemed to be watching her hands turn her mug around and around.

"I didn't think so," Nemle said.

Marheh looked at her and back at her hands. Nemle watched her sympathetically.

"Anyone would be afraid," she said.

Marheh glanced at her then away. Nemle sipped slowly at her sperit.

"I was pretty silly though, clowning, showing off."

Nemle continued to sip and watch.

"I didn't want you to know I was afraid." Marheh spoke as though she was making discoveries. "I think I didn't want to let myself know."

She stopped speaking and looked helplessly at Nemle who stretched out a hand and patted the bit of her that was nearest.

"You were doing your best not to burden us with your fear. You entertained us delightfully and if you got a bit carried away we all understood. Silly child, we're all your friends and we love you."

She watched a moment then pushed back the covers.

"Now hop off and get us some porridge while I get up. I've been lazy long enough."

They met with the others after breakfast, had their discussion and decided to go straight on to the mooring for Market Mondborough. From there they would have reasonable access to Belaven Manor and hopefully more information. It would be a journey of several days, even if they travelled all the daylight hours. Luckily the days were lengthening although still sometimes wet and chilly. The three boats travelled together this time which meant that Marheh or Kel could give Jik a break when he needed it.

Early on the afternoon of the fourth day they reached the foot of the locks. Nemle called a halt then suggesting they wait until the next day when they could be sure of completing the ascent in daylight. When all three boats were moored Marheh, Kel and Jik set off to walk up the flight.

"This is where I first saw the forest people," Marheh said as they passed the place where she had glimpsed the climbing child.

She told them the story of her adventure as they continued on. Jik frowned as she completed the tale.

"And then you found your boots at Market Mondborough," he said. "Someone must be keeping a very close watch to have used that incident to hurt you."

Marheh looked at him, a bit startled.

"Watching me!"

"Or else it was just chance that…" He stopped. "Either way is difficult to come to terms with."

"Perhaps it isn't me particularly, perhaps it is Silberay in general who are the target and I've just been unlucky."

Marheh did not know how much she had wanted him to agree with her until he shook his head slowly.

"Silberay in general perhaps, but through you in particular."

She stopped in her tracks, gave him a little push and began to run ahead up the path. Kel was about to run after her, but Jik stopped him.

"Let her go. She won't go far. She needs to come to terms with it."

The two men walked on slowly, following her.

"She is … special, don't you think?" Kel commented after a few moments.

Jik did not answer immediately.

"I've know her since she was a child," he said at last. "She's my only niece. She has always been special to me. Such a funny little thing she was, big brown eyes, two little plaits sticking out, that enchanting smile and always with a little brother or two tagging behind. Her brothers called her Marheh the Great. She bossed them all and led them into all sorts of mischief."

He smiled reminiscently.

"She was two before I met her. I was still an apprentice then and I couldn't get home any sooner, but her first word was boat they say. The pottery has always had strong links with the Silberay, most of the family can see something of the water road, even if it is only a shimmer of light. They knew how best to nourish her ability."

The two men rounded a bend and found they had reached the staircase locks. Marheh sat perched cross-legged on the lock beam of the top lock, staring out over the landscape. She waved and jumped down when she saw them, then leaned against the lock beam waiting for them to reach her.

Jik looked at her intently for a moment and saw a suggestion of acceptance in her smile of greeting.

"Alright?" he asked quietly.

"Alright," she agreed. "For the moment anyway."

She waved towards the view, the narrow glimpse of distant fields, the high dark surrounding hills.

"I saw a beautiful eagle when I was here last, circling, riding the air. I seemed to be nearly on a level with it then it swooped and was gone."

The others turned to gaze back the way they had come.

"We're going to have our work cut out getting all three boats up the flight tomorrow," Jik said. "These lock gates are in very poor condition."

Marheh nodded.

"Nemle and I greased the paddles when we came eighteen months ago, but she said the gates needed a specialist."

They wandered around the top locks of the staircase and Kel climbed out onto the gate.

"Really they ought to be replaced," he said, leaning over to watch the water escaping from one lock to the next, but I think we can do a bit of repair work if necessary."

They began to head back down the flight, Marheh leading, tossing the occasional comment over her shoulder, not really caring whether she was heard or answered. She kept up a good pace and it was not long before they were back at the boats. Just as they were about to separate she stopped and turned to them.

"I think we should look for the forest people. I expect they know lots about Belaven Manor. Part of the forest is on the estate."

She said the same to Nemle when she went on board.

Nemle nodded.

"But not by yourself this time," she teased. "No more flying for you."

Marheh blushed and gave a little giggle at the memory.

"It would be nice to fly though, wouldn't it?"

The others came to *Day Bringer* for a convivial hour before supper but ate on their own boats and had a quiet evening and early bed before the energetic day ahead.

They woke to a perfect spring day, cool and sunny, the blue sky clear and high above them with just one or two small white clouds marking time on centre stage. Marheh and Kel set off with their windlasses as soon as breakfast was over. They had plenty to do; empty the lock, wait for the boat to go in, close the gates, open the paddles, run to prepare the next lock, run back and empty the lock again for the next boat. Nemle, watching Marheh with loving concern, thought this purposeful activity was just what she needed.

Day Bringer was leading the way this morning with Jik following in *Autumn Wind* and *Storm Cloud* last. Marheh and Kel seemed to have worked out a way of complementing each other's strengths and they jogged back and forth and swung windlasses with energy and enthusiasm.

Marheh was the forerunner, working one or two locks ahead. Nemle found every lock empty and waiting. Then, by the time *Day Bringer* had slid past the gates and into the lock Marheh was back ready to close the gates behind her.

Somewhere round about the fourth lock Nemle looked up from her position at the tiller. It was a deep lock and taking its time to fill. Marheh was leaning against the lock beam, breathing hard and grinning. Nemle saw her looking back to see where *Autumn Wind* was and give a quick thumbs up to Jik or perhaps Kel. As *Day Bringer* rose in the lock she set her back against the gate ready to push it open. Nemle climbed onto the lockside and went to take up a similar position on the opposite side.

"I hope there is enough water for all this activity," she said.

Marheh looked at her, a bit surprised, then thought about what she had said.

"I suppose we are doing rather a lot of emptying."

She grinned.

"No point in worrying about it though and we are being as frugal as possible."

Nemle laughed at her and they began to push together, walking backwards as the gates eased open. Moments later Nemle was steering *Day Bringer* out of the lock. Marheh closed the gates and ran back to open the bottom paddles for Jik then she darted past *Day Bringer* on her way to the next lock.

With all this energy and efficiency all three boats had completed the ascent by early afternoon. They picnicked briefly, moored together at the top of the staircase then continued on for a few hours to reach the best mooring for Market Mondborough. Another shared meal and a brief planning session and all of them were ready for an early night.

Next morning Jik and Marheh set off at dawn to make the long walk back to the forest. Jik carried a small pack with some lunch for them both and a few extras Marheh and Nemle had decided might be acceptable to the forest people. Nemle had reminded Marheh that she wanted to help them and encouraged her to make the decision herself. She had chosen mostly Nemle's medicines. Comfrey ointment especially would be useful she thought, but at the last moment she also included one of her little sculptures.

"They can always sell it if they don't want it," she told Nemle, hoping really that it would appeal, wanting to give something of herself.

They walked with long steady strides, pacing themselves for what would be a return journey of perhaps fifteen miles.

The first part of the walk was along small, little used lanes. Jik had scribbled a sketchy map from Sul's roadmap and they felt confident of reaching the edge of the forest within a couple of hours. As they swung along side by side Marheh thought how much she was enjoying spending this time with Jik. He was her special uncle who had loved her and spoiled her at all stages of her growing up, but his life as Silberay had meant all the early encounters were brief and irregular, and it was no different now.

She said as much when they paused for a breather after an hour of solid walking.

"I was thinking much the same," he said, handing her the water bottle.

She took a long drink and gave it back to him.

"One good thing out of all this," she said.

"I remember how you always used to let me hide from the boys on *Autumn Wind*," she went on as they continued on their way. "You let me get away with a lot too." She grinned. "Except once."

Jik laughed remembering the small girl who had crept away from a convivial gathering in the family kitchen planning to take her own, unauthorised jaunt on *Autumn Wind*.

She had succeeded in untying the mooring lines which she had coiled very neatly. Then she had taken up the steerer's position on the back deck and begun to use the tiller to waggle the rudder. Fortunately she had not known how to start the engine and Jik had noticed her absence and gone pounding down the path to the wharf before the stern had drifted out too far.

"Such a spanking father gave me," Marheh said reminiscently. "And then I was not allowed to go near *Autumn Wind* for the rest of your visit."

"You deserved every whack," Jik said. "Such a fright you gave us."

"I only wanted to do it myself," she said plaintively.

Jik laughed.

"You're always wanting to do it yourself," he said. "Still."

They reached the edge of the forest soon after this. Here the way was narrow and they went in single file, Marheh leading. They were approaching from a different direction and she did not expect to be able to find the place where she had met the forest people, but she hoped they might come across some sign of their presence.

It was comforting knowing Jik was close behind her. He was right, she did always want to do things for herself, but she was aware that she had been rather foolish a year ago when she explored the forest for the first time. She had been lucky not to lose more than her clothes. She paused to look back over her shoulder and smile at Jik.

"We are not likely to even see them if they choose not to let us," she said.

"Then perhaps we should get a bit further in and just sit and wait," Jik said. "Unless you think you can lead us to their hiding place."

Marheh shook her head.

"Not a chance. I was completely lost before I reached it and away with the fairies when I left."

Jik laughed and followed as she continued deeper into the trees.

The track had almost disappeared and Jik was just about to call a halt when they saw a flicker of movement ahead of them. They stopped. Still and silent, they waited, not sure what they had seen. Then they heard a faint whimper, quickly stifled. They looked at each other then Marheh went towards the sound. Jik waited watchfully, aware that his size could make him frightening. Moments later he saw her crouch down beside the broad trunk of a large oak. He went closer and there, huddled against the tree trunk was a small, thin child, scruffy, tear-stained and obviously fearful.

"I think she is hurt," Marheh said, looking briefly at Jik then turning back to the child.

"We won't hurt you," she said. "Please don't be frightened."

Jik crouched down too, keeping back and trying to project friendliness as Marheh continued to speak soothingly. He could see blood on the child's knee and one ankle was badly swollen.

Marheh was beginning to ease the child's fear and he saw a grubby brown hand wipe itself across the damp eyes and then grip the hand Marheh was offering.

"You know he could carry you," Jik heard her say. "If you could tell us the way."

Jik crept closer and held out his own hand, palm up as he would to reassure a frightened animal. It was a big hand, strong and comfortable looking. The child looked at it, waiting, calm and friendly, then back at Marheh. She nodded. Tentatively the child put one finger out to touch Jik's palm, then trace a line.

"Will you let me carry you?" Jik asked quietly.

They waited for the answer which came not in words but in a hesitant smile and a tight clasp around Jik's forefinger.

Moving slowly and calmly Jik reached out to the child.

"Up you come then," he said, taking her in his arms. "Now you will have to show me where to go."

Marheh scrambled to her feet and smiled at the child.

"I will be just behind."

As if she had at last understood they meant her no harm she smiled back and made herself comfortable against Jik's broad chest. Then she took a deep breath and called, the owl call Marheh remembered from her previous experience. There was no answering cry and Jik set off carefully along what remained of the path, Marheh following.

Twice more the child called as they made their way deeper into the forest and then, the third time, there seemed to be an answering cry. Marheh, a little behind, saw Jik bend his head as if to listen to the child. Then he nodded. The path had all but disappeared now and the ground was increasingly steep and rocky. Marheh looked around curiously wondering whether she would recognise any landmarks but nothing seemed familiar as yet. She watched Jik negotiate a particularly steep and rocky descent and was about to start after him when she heard a slight sound behind her.

It was all the warning she had before she felt herself gripped from behind. A hand covered her mouth, pulling her head back and a guttural voice muttered something incomprehensible. She froze then gathered herself to use her mind to control her assailant, but she heard the child's voice.

"Papa, no papa!"

There was a slight easing of the hand across her mouth, something that had pricked at her throat was removed. She opened her eyes and saw Jik and the child facing her, looking up.

173

"They help me papa," the child said.

The hand fell away from her mouth and she was pushed aside as a thin, ragged figure took the descent in two, seemingly impossible leaps and stood before Jik, grabbing at the child.

"Gently," Jik said offering the child in his arms.

The man drew back a little then and seemed to take in Jik's size and the fact of the child's ease with this large stranger. He took one of the child's hands and held it in both of his, studied the child's face, then looked up at Jik.

There was no question, Marheh thought, holding onto a nearby tree, glad of the opportunity to collect herself, it would be far more sensible for Jik to carry her. She was breathing rather hard and not quite confident of her ability to tackle the descent.

The child's father turned then to look at her and she saw the dawning recognition in his face. She held out her hands placatingly.

"Please, we need your help," she said.

The man looked round at Jik then back to her. He seemed very young to be a father she thought but perhaps it was his thin frame and short stature that made him seem little more than a boy. She did not remember him specifically from her previous encounter with the forest people, but she was uncomfortably aware that there was much she did not remember about that occasion.

"You want my help?" the man asked at last.

"You and your people," Marheh said. "Please."

She began to make her way down to where the others stood.

"Don't you think you owe me your help?"

The man stared at her speculatively for a moment then gave a short laugh.

"Owe you?"

Marheh continued to meet his eyes.

"I don't want much, just information."

She completed the descent and stood beside the two men and the child.

"Please," she said again.

The man looked at Jik who nodded.

"It would help us if you could answer some questions."

The child shifted a little in his arms and he smiled at her.

"And perhaps I could help you get your daughter home where her ankle can be bandaged."

Another short hesitation and the forest man made up his mind.

"If you will follow and bring Thanata that will be best."

It was perhaps another twenty minutes of walking before they reached the cleft in the rock that formed the entrance to the forest people's camp. Jik and Marheh waited with the child Thanata, while her father slipped through the narrow space to warn his people. Perhaps five minutes later a woman came through to them. This person Marheh did recognise. It was the older woman who had prepared the drink for her.

For a moment they studied each other in silence then the woman smiled slightly.

"You wish to leave us more of your garments?" she asked. "Or are you still seeking dandelions?"

Jik laughed and the old woman turned to him.

"Thanata is fortunate to have so strong a bearer."

She cupped the child's bare foot and injured ankle gently in both hands and smiled at her then stood aside.

"You may enter," she said.

The clearing was much as Marheh had remembered, the small fire, the rough dwellings, but there were fewer people, only the old woman and two very young children.

"All seek for Thanata," the woman said.

She turned to the child's father and gestured towards one of the shelters. Marheh wondered whether they were to be offered a drink as before, but the man took a horn from under the low eaves and raised it to his lips. Twice it sounded in a long, mournful call.

175

Jik put Thanata down beside the fire and they all gathered around her. Marheh went to stand behind Jik as he crouched down and fossicked in the pack he carried on his back. She found the jar of comfrey ointment and offered it to the old woman.

"Perhaps you have your own remedies," she said, trying to frame her words so there could be no suggestion of patronage. "But my mentor makes this and it is very good for bruises and sprains. It's made with comfrey."

The woman took the jar, unscrewed the lid, sniffed at it then looked back at Marheh.

"Why should I trust you? We did not treat you well."

Marheh looked a bit uncomfortable.

"I was foolish then," she said.

"And not now?" the woman teased.

Marheh grinned. "Now my uncle looks after me."

While they were speaking some of the forest people began to return to the clearing in answer to the call of the horn. In ones and twos they drifted across to the fire to speak to Thanata and her father and look curiously at Jik and Marheh. Marheh took the ointment and rubbed some into the back of her hand.

"I promise it will not hurt her," she said.

The woman smiled and held out her hand for the jar.

"I believe you."

She was just preparing to smooth some over Thanata's ankle when a scuffle by the cleft in the rock distracted them. An adolescent boy, thin and scruffy as they all were, was struggling in the grip of an older man.

"I must go!" he shouted. "They are here. I must go."

He seemed almost beside himself, shouting and trying to wrench himself free.

"Go where?" the man holding him was asking. "Why go?"

But the boy paid no attention to his questions.

Jik and Marheh looked at each other then at a nod from Jik Marheh eased herself into the frenzied mind. She was not experienced enough to understand immediately what was happening but after a few moments of observation she identified the stranger planted to command the boy. It was a simple affair and not difficult to dismantle and carry away to put on the little fire.

As she slipped out of his mind their eyes met. The boy was quiet and seemed a little puzzled but Marheh saw that for a moment at least he recognised something within her.

"What was that all about?"

The older man still gripped the boy and now gave him a little shake. The boy shook his head, obviously uncomprehending. Marheh stood up and walked across to them.

"What happened when you took my clothes to the market?" she asked, going straight to the point.

The boy looked at her uncertainly but she had not spoken in anger. The man however seemed to see some kind of accusation in her words and pushed the boy away.

"Go to the fire," he said. "Thanata is found. You do not leave now."

Marheh stood without speaking her brown eyes studying the man, calm and speculative. Her steady gaze seemed to make him uneasy and he pushed past her without speaking, following the boy.

Marheh thought she would burst with the effort of being a calm, quietly spoken, well mannered guest. She bit her lip, clenched and unclenched her hands and turned towards the group by the fire. The boy had encountered Yareblis somewhere. Someone had planted a control in the boy's mind. She thought perhaps the sight of her and Jik had triggered it. Probably he had been instructed to inform the controller of the presence of Silberay in the forest. He would not respond now she had removed the command but he might remember the encounter.

As she reached the fire she saw that Thanata's ankle had been treated. Jik was standing holding the pack and talking to Thanata's father. The old woman looked across and their eyes met.

177

"You wish for our help," she said, speaking only to Marheh.

"Please," Marheh said.

"You shall have it if it is possible."

The woman patted the ground. Marheh went to sit beside her and explain a little of her need.

"It seems as if someone must have known that my clothes would be at the market. Someone who knew the Silberay would recognise the uniform. I was hoping perhaps the person who took them could tell me," she finished.

The old woman nodded.

"It is always the older children who go to the market. The stall holders deal more kindly with them. Tomila looks young but he is nearly eighteen now and well able to negotiate a sale, even when you left us your garments."

Marheh rather wished that the woman did not feel the need to keep reminding her of her past folly, but was not in a position to say so.

"Do you think I might speak with Tomila?" She asked instead.

"First you must drink with us," the woman said and gave a short laugh at Marheh's involuntary gesture of repudiation.

"Not as before," she said. "We will not catch you again I think."

Marheh smiled and did not say what she was thinking, that she probably could be caught again because she would continue to trust people. She did however watch the preparations carefully and this time there was no small polished box and this time all drank.

The old woman again caught her eye and smiled a rather teasing, almost mocking smile.

"You are safe from us now," she said.

The ceremony over the group gathered around the fire to listen to Marheh question Tomila. He understood he had approval to speak and seemed unconcerned by the audience though Marheh found herself suddenly shy in the presence of so many earnest listeners.

"I have an unknown enemy," she began. "But I think you met him on the way to the market with my clothes. Can you remember?"

The boy studied her for a moment as if trying to place her and Marheh wondered how many other travellers had been caught the way she was.

"You laughed," he said. "All the time you laughed."

Marheh blushed.

"Did I?" she said. "But what happened after?"

"Grandmother took the clothes and gave me the shirt for my own. She gave the trousers to Yanisy I think, but we had no use for the other things so she sent me to a trader we know who buys from us."

He paused and it was clear the next memory was an uncomfortable one.

"I was careful, but there was a hunting party from the Manor. I was not afraid because I know the forest well and can run, but then I could not run."

He paused again.

"My feet would not move. They came around me and made jokes that I was caught by the hunt and would make good eating."

He faltered.

"I was afraid that perhaps they did not joke."

There was a murmur from the listeners and Marheh wondered how much of the story he had told before.

"Then they took my bundle and opened it. At first they laughed then one took the lovely red tunic. He looked at it and looked and he was not laughing. 'Where did you get this boy?' he asked me. I told him a young lady gave it to me to sell, payment for hospitality, I told him. Then he looked at the boots and gave me back my bundle. He said they would not eat me today, but I must take the things and go."

Marheh and Jik looked at each other at the end of this recital.

"What did he look like?" Marheh asked.

"The one who frightened me was young, perhaps not much older than I am, but he was smooth and clean and finely dressed."

The memory seemed to be disturbing and Tomila stopped speaking. Marheh waited for him to continue unaware that she was holding her breath.

"He had pale hair and blue eyes and the others seemed to … to want to please him."

Tomila shook his head and paused again.

"I do not like to think of him," he concluded at last.

Marheh breathed out in a long sigh.

"Thank you for helping us," she said.

There was quiet talk from the forest people. Tomila's story was new to them.

"You did not speak of this," the old woman said. "Why not?"

Tomila shrugged, clearly he did not know.

"I think perhaps he was encouraged to forget. These enemies of ours are clever at making suggestions. He will not know why, just as he will not know why he wanted to leave just now."

The woman studied Jik as if to ascertain the truth of his words. At last she nodded.

"I do not understand, but I see it is the truth as you know it."

Behind Jik's back Marheh was fumbling in the pack. She brought out another jar of comfrey ointment and some packets of borage tea as well as the package containing the model she had made. She held Nemle's offerings out to the old woman.

"My mentor made these things. She is known for her skill. Please may we give them to you?"

The woman studied Marheh for a moment then beckoned to the oldest of the men.

"Shall we accept these gifts?"

"We will not be in debt to these strangers?"

"No debt," Jik said. "But an offering of friendship."

Now the other forest people were watching and listening.

"Friendship," the man said, chewing on the word as if to extract all of its meaning.

"These are the gifts of your mentor," he said then and it seemed as if he would reject them.

"But this is from me," Marheh said holding out the package. "I made it."

The man took it and unwrapped it carefully, handing the paper to the woman as if it too had value. When the model was revealed the man held it for a moment then displayed it to the forest people. It was an owl, not the sleepy daytime owl, but the alert and skilful hunter, still, but poised for action.

Marheh saw it afresh and felt content with her work.

The man looked at Marheh then at Jik.

"You have given us your strength," he said to Jik, then turned to Marheh. "And you your skill. And you have considered well, for we know ourselves as the People of the Owl."

After some more rather ceremonious exchanges Marheh and Jik understood themselves to be accepted as People of the Owl. Then Tomila led them out through the cleft in the rock and guided them to where the path became well defined and they could find their own way. Not until the edge of the forest however did they stop to share the food they had brought and discuss what they had learned.

As they set off again on the long walk back to the boats Marheh looked back as if saying goodbye to the forest then turned to Jik.

"A fair young man," she said, then added almost to herself. "Whoever he is, the same mind is behind it all, isn't it?"

> "Why would we have enemies when all we want is to serve?
> I asked Lor that question and he said I'm naïve. He pointed
> out that we can't even agree amongst ourselves. That's why,
> it seems, there must be rules. But if there are rules there
> must be sanctions and that worries me."
>
> *Sila's journal: the early years*

Chapter Fifteen

Nemle and Kel set out a little later than Marheh and Jik leaving Sul to guard the boats and keep them all in his mind and heart. The long walk to the small town was a challenge for Nemle but they took it steadily and rested when necessary.

"It must be twenty years since I came as far as this," she told Kel as she stood leaning on his arm.

"It's all new to me." Kel was looking down the lane at the distant view. "Sul and I have not been this route before."

"Sul must have surely!"

Kel shrugged.

"He hasn't said."

"It seems as if we have neglected this part of the world."

As they turned to continue the climb to Market Mondborough Nemle's thought remained with this neglect. Was it a contributing factor? Had the Yareblis been able to establish themselves here because of some oversight of the Silberay? Was the persecution of Marheh only possible because of where they were travelling?

Her deliberations lasted the rest of the way but she came to no real conclusion. They were here now with a job to do and she could hope that if they found Marheh's enemy there might be a positive benefit that would be more far reaching than just safety for Marheh.

It was not market day and the town, when they reached it, was quiet. Nemle was glad to find an empty bench and sit watching the few shoppers passing along the high street. The grocer seemed to be doing a steady trade and the bell on the door to the butcher's shop jingled at frequent intervals. Kel went off to investigate the possibility of a bus to Belaven Manor or, more probably, to the nearby village of Belaven Rise.

He was not long away, returning with the news that a bus ran every two hours and would leave in twenty minutes from in front of the post office.

"It runs between here and Marisford," he said. "And stops at the Manor if required and in Belaven Rise."

He gave Nemle his arm and they walked together towards the post office.

"We might perhaps pick up some groceries on the way home," Nemle suggested. "If you don't mind carrying them."

There was another bench outside the post office and they sat quietly together to wait.

"Perhaps it would be best if we went to the village first," Nemle said. "We might find somewhere to have a cup of tea and a bit of a gossip about the people at the Manor."

Kel nodded. "That seems like a good idea."

"I'm beginning to feel as if we might be reaching some understanding," Nemle continued. "Even a solution if all goes well here. I'm so grateful to you and Sul and Jik. Marheh and I could not have accomplished anything on our own. I would have had to spend all my energies protecting her and helping her defend herself."

"I can't help feeling a bit anxious about Sul," Kel said.

Nemle looked at him in surprise.

"His hearing is going."

"He hides it well."

"I think he uses his mind and his eyes to help interpret speech, but I've noticed that other sounds are missed."

"But he has you," Nemle said. "And his wisdom and skill are formidable."

Kel smiled at that. "He says the same of you."

Nemle gave a little shrug and shook her head.

"He is too generous."

"Marheh and I both know how lucky we are," Kel said, standing up as the bus appeared and helping Nemle to her feet.

They had a little while to wait before the bus actually left and Kel had a chat with the driver, asking about the route and the locality. He and Nemle were able to sit right in the front of the bus and on the side which would give the best view of the Manor and its grounds. Two or three more passengers got on, locals who knew each other and looked curiously at Nemle and Kel. Then they were away.

There were two stops in the town and then they were in open country, farmland, green with new spring growth. They passed fields where young lambs staggered about on unsteady legs or butted energetically at their mothers' sides. The day's promise had continued blue and bright. Then, on their left, the fields and farmhouses gave way to trees, scattered at first but becoming denser. This perhaps was the same forest Jik and Marheh were exploring, Nemle thought, wondering how they were faring.

Before long an old wall appeared, enclosing the trees. A pedestrian would have seen only the tree tops with their delicate veil of new green, but from the bus it was possible to see over the warm brick and glimpse the dark trunks and shadowy undergrowth. The bus trundled along beside the wall. Nemle and Kel were watching carefully guessing that the manor would appear behind the wall before long. They had just caught sight of its high chimneys and the pediment that half concealed the sloping slates of the roof when the bus began to slow down. Kel looked a question at Nemle, but she shook her head.

"Best approach less visibly."

In front of a pair of ornate wrought iron gates a woman was hailing the bus. She was drably dressed and carried a big shopping basket. Kel and Nemle did not spare her more than a glance however. Their attention was focused on what they could see beyond the gates.

The house was not very far from the road. It was square and imposing with a wide flight of steps up to the front entrance. A circular drive led from the gates around a formal garden, very symmetrical with a bed of daffodils in a green lawn and a central fountain. A motor was moving slowly from somewhere behind the house and, standing on the steps awaiting its arrival, was a fair young man. As they watched he made an impatient gesture towards the car then turned to call back through the open door. The bus was just beginning to move away again when two other men appeared behind the first. Nemle gasped and looked at Kel, but he was still staring out of the window.

It was not until the house and its inhabitants were out of sight that he turned to Nemle.

"Hud's apprentice," he said his voice rough with tension. "I've just realised who it is."

Nemle's eyes widened and she waited for him to continue.

"That's the first time I've got a good look at him. I said he reminded me of someone."

"Yes but who?" Nemle demanded when he seemed to be lost in some far away place.

"It's Samuel."

"Samuel," Nemle breathed. "Are you sure?"

Kel nodded. "He's changed of course, he was only fifteen all those years ago, but he lived with us on *Storm Cloud* for three months don't forget."

Nemle nodded slowly.

"He hated Marheh then, saw her as responsible for destroying his way of life."

"Sul and I tried our best to give him a different focus and show him the value of a different life. We thought we were beginning to succeed, but perhaps not."

"What happened to him after he left you? Do you know?"

"We left him at the Harbour. It was just too crowded on *Storm Cloud* and we were neglecting our other responsibilities. The Harbour Master promised to look after him until he could be placed with a family. We called back to see how he was about six weeks later and he was gone. A pleasant couple, comfortably off, with no children of their own the Harbour Master said."

"He would know quite a lot about the Silberay then, how we work, what we believe."

"Yes, yes he would."

The bus drew up at the edge of the road beside a neat, green painted bus shelter. The driver turned to Kel and Nemle.

"You wanted Belhaven Rise?"

Kel stood up and helped Nemle to alight. She smiled and thanked the driver as she passed him but her mind was engaged with what they had discovered and with what she had seen.

"I'm not sure whether you noticed," she said as they walked slowly away from the bus stop. "You were looking at Samuel, but I'm sure one of the men who came out just as we were leaving was Hud."

Back at the mooring, Sul was moving quietly around *Storm Cloud* clearing up the breakfast things and centring his mind so he would be ready to respond to any hint of threat to the others. He had already visited *Day Bringer* and *Autumn Wind* and as he had checked the fires and tidied the evidence of early departures he had gently drawn a degree of protection over them. Once he would have been away with the others but his job was here now and he knew they would be better able to carry out their own tasks because he was caring for the boats.

And for them, he thought, wondering how Nemle was managing the long walk. He held her in his mind for a few moments, feeling her weariness and something of her anxiety but getting no sense that she was in danger. It had been a good friendship, over many years. It still was, the kind of deep, calm strength that could be relied upon. She had her hands full with Marheh, but he could think of no one better to manage her passion and idealism and teach her to understand and use her natural ability. His focus flowed on then to hold Marheh for a moment of warmth and support.

He finished his tidying and took up a comfortable position in the big arm chair that was part of the furnishings on every Silberay boat, just one, there was no room for more. Possession of the armchair was one of the benefits an apprentice could aspire to. The thought made him smile and for a moment he enjoyed it then he set himself to enter the discipline of the soul.

This would not be a time of joyful communion with other souls, but a solitary, demanding distribution of light in dark places and the dark places seemed very concentrated hereabouts.

Sul's portal was the imagined heart of a tree and he seemed to see it with his fingertips as much as in his mind's eye. For a few minutes he held the portal, building concentration, honing the focus that he needed, then he entered and began to sing.

No one of evil intent could enter *Storm Cloud* against the power of his song and its light. No casual passer-by would even see the boats. He settled into the place where he was held and allowed the song to build within him until it had shape and strength enough to push outwards into the dark.

He had no sense of time passing. The work of the song was everything, beyond time, outside place. The loud knocking on *Storm Cloud*'s roof seemed to come from somewhere else, somewhere distant and irrelevant, but it persisted and Sul gradually absorbed its insistent demand and pulled himself back until he again felt the armchair beneath him and around.

He got up slowly and made his way towards the back cabin where the knocking was loudest wondering who or what was living in the water dimension. When he finally pushed open the door and climbed out onto the back deck he found Hud hovering beside *Storm Cloud* his hand raised to knock again.

The soul song was still close and pervasive so that he did not feel surprise but a sense of inevitability.

"What can I do for you?" he asked mildly, his shaggy grey eyebrows lifting a little to emphasise the question.

"I was just passing," Hud said. "It seemed only right to offer a greeting."

"Passing?"

The single word expressed polite disbelief.

Hud stepped onto the back deck. He was not dressed for boating. Sul looked him up and down then stepped back inside to allow him to enter.

"Not boating though," he commented when Hud was standing beside him in the back cabin.

"My apprentice has family nearby," the reply came smoothly. "They have allowed me the use of their motor."

He ran a hand over his tunic and allowed it to rest with the thumb tucked into his belt. Sul began to move through to the saloon Hud following.

"I see you are travelling in company," Hud said.

Sul inclined his head.

"Nemle has been too lenient with her apprentice in the past. No doubt she looks to you to help discipline her."

Polite still Sul offered Hud the armchair and stood leaning against the sink in the galley.

Hud sat and continued to talk. Sul watched and wondered at the mellifluous, meaningless flow.

"Why have you come here," he asked at last.

The flow of words stopped. Hud looked inward for a moment then began again.

"I was just passing," he said. "I see you are travelling in company."

Sul studied him thoughtfully as the words continued. Something was wrong here, off-key. If Hud had not been Silberay and a mentor Sul might have suspected he was being controlled, but practice of the disciplines should have prevented that. Silberay of Hud's age and standing might be broken in the struggle against control by the Yareblis, but there would be a struggle.

Sul watched and listened for a few more minutes, then, although he was very conscious he was breaking Silberay law, he began to edge his mind towards Hud's. He was surprised at how easy it was, how unprepared Hud was. He entered Hud's mind and Hud was completely unaware, but something else acknowledged his presence. Quickly he withdrew, but he knew he had been discovered and was not surprised when Hud broke off his speech in mid sentence and stood up.

"Time for me to go," he said, unconscious of anything unusual about his behaviour. Sul once more inclined his head and followed him through *Storm*

Cloud and out onto the back deck.

Hud made suitable statements of farewell and stepped onto the bank. Sul stood and watched as he walked rather stiffly along the path and started up the lane. Then he realised that there was a large motor parked in the lane, not quite hidden by the hedge. Hud walked towards it. There was the sound of a door and then the engine started and it moved slowly away. For a few minutes Sul still stood gazing after it and wondering. Then he made his way slowly back inside.

Once off the bus Nemle and Kel strolled along from the stop looking about them and trying to absorb the knowledge they had gained. Samuel was Hud's apprentice and he and Hud were here at Belaven Manor.

"Have we already learned all we came for?" Nemle said, thinking aloud. "Perhaps it would be better not to go back to the Manor, but try to talk to people here."

Kel nodded.

"We've over an hour before the return bus. You said something about a cup of tea earlier."

"It would be nice," Nemle said. "I'm getting a bit old for all this adventuring."

Kel shook his head.

"If there isn't a bakery or a tea shop we'll try the pub, but why don't I find someone to ask?"

As they continued slowly along the road a woman with a shopping basket overtook them, looking back curiously at the two Silberay. Nemle smiled and greeted her.

"Can you help us?" she asked. "We've just come off the bus. Is there somewhere I can get a cup of tea?"

The woman hesitated, looking from one to the other. Then she shrugged.

"The bus doesn't go into the high street. You'd better come with me."

She led them a short distance along the road they were following then turned into a narrow lane between two cottages. At the end of the lane they could see a lynch gate and the square tower of an old church.

"Not many strangers come here," the woman said, falling back to join them.

It was a clear invitation to state their business. Nemle wondered just how much to say. Kel, she knew, would be content to leave the talking to her.

"We had thought to visit the Manor," she said. "To enquire after a young man we used to know, but it looked a bit off-putting from the bus, a bit too grand for us."

The woman pushed open the gate into the churchyard and held it for them to follow.

"The church faces onto the green," she said. "The bakery is on the other side by the post office. You can get a cup of tea there."

"You've been very kind," Nemle said. "Perhaps you would join us."

They continued between the headstones and around the little stone church.

"Please" Nemle said as the woman made no response.

"You seem like a decent woman," their guide said at last. "Even if you do wear trousers. What would a decent woman want with the Manor?"

Nemle and Kel looked at each other then Nemle turned back to the woman.

"We are concerned about the young man," she said. "We don't know anything about the manor. It would be a great kindness if you had time for a cup of tea and could tell us a little."

As they reached the front of the church they could see why the bus avoided the high street. The village green ahead of them was yellow with daffodils and there was a narrow lane that split to either side then joined again as it left the village. The bus would have found passage difficult if not impossible though it suited the cyclist who progressed steadily along the track and nodded amiably to their guide. Two or three other shoppers dotted the landscape. They walked with their guide around the green.

"It would spoil this to have the bus coming through," Nemle said. "It is so pretty and peaceful like this."

"We like it," the woman said.

There was a small pub, the Belaven Arms, set in a little garden, then a general store, post office and finally the bakery. All were small and neat and freshly painted.

"I'll just pop in here and get my bits of shopping," the woman said. "Then come on and join you, if you really mean it."

Nemle confirmed her invitation and she and Kel walked on to the bakery. They paused in the doorway and Nemle looked around with delight. Inside were three small tables each with four chairs. The tables were covered with red and white checked cloths and had a small vase with a few bluebells as well as a sugar bowl and salt and pepper shakers. The room was warm and filled with the smell of baking. Behind the tables was a long counter and behind that, shelves with loaves and buns displayed. They sat down at a table in the window, the only customers.

"This is nice," Nemle said. "I've almost forgotten why we're here. It's so seldom we have a treat like this."

Kel smiled and tried to find space for his long legs.

"I expect you would have been happier in the pub though," she went on. "Thank you for indulging me like this."

A small, plump woman in a big white apron came out from behind to greet them and ask how she could serve them. Nemle explained that they would like tea when their friend joined them and perhaps something light to eat. The woman chatted for a few minutes welcoming them and suggesting the scones that would be out of the oven in ten minutes.

When she had gone Nemle turned again to Kel.

"It would be interesting to know whether Samuel has been here since you said goodbye to him at the Harbour."

Kel nodded.

"Do we tell the truth or some of it or have we a story made up?"

"Some of it, I think," Nemle said. "Just that we knew him when he was younger and are concerned for his welfare. I don't think the woman recognised our uniform so she perhaps has not met Silberay before."

"We are quite far from the water road," Kel agreed.

They spoke quietly together, preparing their story and deciding what they hoped to learn.

They did not have long to wait though before the door opened and their guide entered with another older woman behind her. They both came over to the table.

"I met Mrs Bennett in the shop," the woman explained. "She used to work at the Manor."

Kel stood up, not without difficulty in the small space, and helped to seat them both.

"It is good of you to join us," Nemle said.

She smiled a welcome at Mrs Bennett who was looking closely at her, studying her attire.

"You're dressed like one of those Silberay," she said at last. "It must be twenty years since one like you came here."

"We are Silberay," Nemle admitted. "This is Kel and I am Nemle."

The woman came from behind the counter then, to confirm the order for tea and scones. Nemle could see that the woman who had been their guide was full of questions, but found that Hilda Bennett was ready with explanations of a kind.

"You've never heard of Silberay I suppose Mrs Price. Don't seem to be many about now. They sometimes come when there is trouble."

"No wonder they're wanting to know about the Manor then."

Gradually, over the cups of tea and freshly baked scones, the two women discussed the Manor and its inhabitants. At one point Mrs Price even appealed to Mrs Nugent, behind the counter, for confirmation.

There had been incidents in the village, vandalism, petty theft and hints that the Manor had been the source of the trouble. Certainly there was an attitude of arrogance and aggression from the young people there that kept the villagers out of their way wherever possible.

Kel said little but looked and listened and admired Nemle's skill in encouraging the conversation and directing it so they would learn what they needed.

It was Hilda Bennett who remembered the bus in time for Nemle and Kel to pay the bill and get to the stop and she insisted on accompanying them back through the churchyard and along to the stop on the other side of the road.

"I never told anyone," she said. "But I left because of that boy, Samuel. Came with the new gardener and his wife, poor things, but within a month he was at home in the house and expecting to be treated like a prince."

The bus appeared in the distance and she began to make her farewells.

"I never thought to see Silberay here again," she said as the bus pulled up. "But you're certainly needed."

Nemle and Kel arrived back at the boats before Jik and Marheh although they had spent an hour in Market Mondborough stocking up on provisions. Kel was heavily laden as they walked home and even Nemle had a couple of small bundles. They came to *Storm Cloud* first and joined Sul for sperit, but agreed to keep their news until Jik and Marheh were with them.

After half an hour or so Nemle got up to continue to *Day Bringer*. She thought a little rest might be nice and was looking forward to her comfortable chair or even perhaps, her bed. The others felt *Storm Cloud* move as she stepped off the back deck then a few seconds later they heard her cry out. Kel was up and out in a moment and Sul not far behind.

The three boats were moored one behind the other with *Day Bringer* between *Storm Cloud* and *Autumn Wind*. When Kel and Sul reached her Nemle was standing on the bank staring at a big black cross that had been roughly painted over the side of *Day Bringer*'s back cabin. It obscured Marheh's window and part of the decorative paintwork.

"Poor *Day Bringer*," she said and Kel and Sul knew the words were not for them.

Sul went to stand beside her in silent support, but Kel reached out to touch the ugly disfigurement.

"It's quite soft," he said, showing them black fingertips.

"The protection would prevent it from hardening," Sul said. "I suppose someone got past *Storm Cloud* while Hud was visiting. I wondered at the purpose of his visit."

Nemle had been standing stunned, but now she came to life.

"Marheh mustn't see it," she said. "Can we get it off?"

"Try filling a bucket from the water road," Sul said to Kel.

He ran back to *Storm Cloud* to get their bucket and knelt to dip it into the water. Nemle had gone into *Day Bringer* for rags.

"It's on the other side as well," she said as she came out. "I could see it on the window."

She rubbed her eyes and sniffed.

"How dare he go on board."

Fierce and determined she plunged the rags into the bucket and began to attack the side of the boat. Kel tried to take them from her, but she resisted.

"You do the other side Kel," Sul suggested.

Nemle glared at him for a moment then realized what she was doing and sighed.

"Yes please. That will be harder for me."

They began the work, confident now that it would come off, but the task was scarcely begun when Marheh and Jik appeared from the lane. Sul saw them first, moving steadily but clearly feeling the effects of the long walk. He started towards them as Marheh came running up.

"What's wrong? What are you doing?"

Nemle turned wearily to answer her and found herself unable to speak. Marheh stood studying the remains of the graffiti then bent to take Nemle's cloth.

"You've done enough, Mama Nemle," she said. "It's my turn now."

Nemle and Sul sat on the bank while Jik, Marheh and Kel worked until there was no black paint left. Then Sul decreed they all rest for a while before meeting again to share their news.

We were all so tired, Marheh thought much later as she lay waiting for sleep.

The news that Samuel was at Belaven Manor with Hud was deeply disturbing as was the challenge that had been so arrogantly displayed on *Day Bringer*. Sul was distressed that he had allowed it to happen though no one thought of blaming him. Kel and Jik had what would have been an argument over nothing if their innate commonsense had not rescued them in time. Nemle was grey with fatigue and her careful patience had snapped when she, Marheh, had pushed too hard.

She moved restlessly under the covers, pressing her hot face into the pillow. She had been shrill and obnoxious and it was her fault that they could not agree on a course of action. She had pushed and pushed and seen the surprise in Kel's eyes and the disappointment in Nemle's and it had only made her worse. It was no excuse that the sight of that black cross over her window had jolted her like nothing else had. It was so malevolent and so personal.

Her sigh almost became a whimper and she turned over again, unable to settle. Jik had been disappointed in her too but there had been understanding in his quiet reprimand and his hug was warm and strengthening. Resolutely she closed her eyes, knowing she needed to sleep. Samuel had been at Belhaven Manor for five years Nemle had told them. He must have been working with mind control all that time to have become so skilled. He must have been the one who put the control in the boy from the forest. He must have manipulated the family at the Manor so he became accepted as one of them, but where did Hud fit in all this. She thought Samuel might be controlling him, though Sul and Nemle were doubtful. Her eyes opened and she stared into the darkness.

Sul and Nemle had broken up their disastrous evening with the quiet, firm instruction that they should all sleep and be rested before coming to any decision, but she could not sleep. She closed her eyes then opened them again. No, she could not sleep. She stretched out onto her back and willed herself to be still. It was all her fault anyway. Samuel hated her, just her, because she had challenged him in the past.

Challenged him and won, she thought suddenly, thinking back to the first year of her apprenticeship. He'd been about fifteen then and his Yareblis teachers had been instructing him not only in the skills of mind control but more particularly in the philosophy of power that determined their use of it. She still remembered how he had explained it to her when she had been pretending to be a student no older than he was. "We have been given the power to command. It is our right and responsibility to use it," he had said.

She and Nemle had discovered the school and rescued the children but Samuel had not wanted to be rescued. She had already begun to practise the discipline of the mind within the limits set by the Silberay and she had been stronger than he then. Nemle had kept her practising since so why should she be so afraid now, she thought. It was only Samuel.

"It is only Samuel," she said aloud into the darkness. "It is only Samuel."

She sat up. She was not afraid of Samuel. It must be the anxiety of the others that was making her afraid. Nemle was always inclined to treat her like a child. Her own mother had been married with two children by the time she was her age. At home she had been the oldest but now she was the youngest and they all treated her like a child. She pushed back the covers and swung her legs out of bed. She would take responsibility for her own life. She would stop all the arguments. She would go now, while they were all asleep. She would go and confront Samuel and make him stop.

Very carefully, knowing that any movement that set *Day Bringer* rocking would wake Nemle, she eased herself to a standing position in the middle of her cabin. From there she could reach all the clothes she had put ready for the morning. There was enough moonlight coming in her window so she did not need her candle and slowly and painstakingly she dressed, stopping occasionally to listen, keeping to the centre of the boat to lessen the possibility of movement. When she was dressed she took her boots in one hand and edged towards the steps leading from her cabin to the back deck.

Getting off the back deck would be the hardest part, she thought, trying to work out how best to stop the dip and rise as her weight left the side of the boat. Nothing sudden, she decided, and forced herself to make every move in slow motion.

At last she was standing on the bank. She could feel the dew dampness, cold despite her thick socks and hurried to put on her boots.

There was no sound or movement from any of the boats and she gave a satisfied smile as she walked, still moving quietly and carefully, past Nemle's cabin at *Day Bringer*'s prow, past Kel's cabin at the back of *Storm Cloud* and finally past Sul's cabin at *Storm Cloud*'s prow. When she reached the lane she turned to look back at the three boats still sleeping peacefully on the dark water. Moonlight glinted on the polished brass and shone on each painted roof but the bright colours were hidden. Then a cloud moved slowly across the moon and all was dark.

Marheh sighed, shivered a little and turned to begin the long walk to Market Mondborough.

At first she spent time rehearsing her grievances and justifying her secretive departure. Once or twice she considered the nobility of her self-sacrifice but the modicum of commonsense she still retained discouraged this indulgence. Then she pictured herself confronting Samuel and persuading him to stop persecuting her. This too was an image she could not sensibly sustain. In the end she settled into a kind of walking trance, one foot after the other without thought.

It was still dark when she reached the small town, dark and still. Only once was there a light escaping from an upper window and she saw a woman, sharp and clear, with a child held lovingly in her arms. For a moment she felt very small and lonely, jolted out of her trance to an uncomfortable reality. She found the bus stop where Nemle and Kel had described it and sat down. All her stubborn determination seemed to be draining out of her, leaking through the soles of her new boots and disappearing. She was so tired and the bus would not come for hours yet and she should not have left the others and she would not give up and go back. She lifted her feet onto the seat and put her head down, curling up as small as she could for warmth. She would not give up and go back, not give up, not go back, not.

She woke to find a man prodding her.

"What do you think you're doing?" he was asking, but not unkindly. It seemed more as if he was anxious for her.

She tried to collect herself, to sit up and look like a respectable bus passenger. She had no way of knowing how white she was and how her eyes were set in dark smudges. She guessed her plait was coming undone and knew she felt stiff and sore from sleeping on the hard bench.

"I'm waiting for the bus," she said, when she could frame the words.

The man snorted. "You'd better get on then. We'll be off in ten minutes."

She blinked and took in the fact of the dark blocky shape and the low engine rumble waiting in the road nearby.

"Are you the driver?" she asked, feeling in her pocket for the few coins she had put there and holding them out to him.

"Where are you off to then?" he asked, looking at her curiously.

"Belaven Manor," she said. "Can you put me off there?"

He took one of the proffered coins.

"Hop on. You'll be more comfortable finishing your sleep out of the cold."

Marheh thought he was looking sorry for her and she lifted her chin to be Marheh the Great, but he was unimpressed, just waving her on board and taking his pipe and tobacco pouch out of his pocket.

Marheh climbed onto the bus and took a seat in the front. It was just beginning to be light and she watched the driver filling his pipe and holding a match to it. The flame lit his face momentarily and carved deep shadows that made him look fierce and concentrated. He drew on it and puffed out a little cloud of smoke then he settled himself against the bonnet of the bus. Marheh felt cold and stiff and shut her eyes, but there was no more sleep in her. Not long now and she would be confronting Samuel, making him stop tormenting her.

The bus was rumbling away, its gentle vibrations interrupted occasionally by a change of tone. It felt almost alive. She felt it dip, just like *Day Bringer*, as another passenger got on. It was a man wearing a heavy coat and a cloth cap. He looked at her curiously as he made his way past to a seat behind. Then two women came hurrying up and a young man sprinted behind them. As soon as he was on board the driver climbed up and into his seat. Marheh heard the other passengers greeting each other and felt more than ever alone. The bus lurched, the engine note changed purposefully and at last they were away.

Nemle woke as the early morning light eased into her cabin. She lay for a few minutes feeling a little stiff from her exertions of the previous day and uneasily conscious that she had run out of patience with Marheh the previous evening and spoken unsympathetically when she ought to have shown understanding. Fortunately Jik had been there to repair her failure. She stretched carefully and got up to begin dressing. There was no sound or movement from the back cabin and she decided to let Marheh sleep as long as she needed. It was not surprising that she was worn out.

She moved quietly around the boat doing some of Marheh's morning jobs, making up the fire, boiling the kettle. When an hour had passed and still no Marheh had appeared yawning and apologetic she made a mug of sperit and carried it through to the back cabin. The door was closed and she knocked lightly before pushing it open.

An unmade bed, a discarded nightdress and no Marheh. She frowned. No doubt she had gone for an early walk, but it was not like her to leave her cabin untidy. For a few moments she stood looking around the small space as if it could tell her what had been going through Marheh's mind then she moved back through to the saloon and sat down to drink the sperit herself. She would be foolish to worry.

Half an hour later she was still telling herself she was foolish to worry as she went along to *Autumn Wind* to see if she was visiting Jik. He shook his head at her questions and came with her to *Storm Cloud*.

"I don't like it," Nemle said, trying to be calm. "She's been gone too long. She's been in a difficult mood lately. We've all seen it." Her voice was rising with anxiety and she heard it and tried again. "I'm afraid for her."

Sul put an arm around her shoulders.

"What are you thinking?" Jik was saying when Nemle paled and swayed as if she might faint.

"I heard her scream," she whispered.

> "As an apprentice you are expected to consult with your
> mentor before taking any action alone. Your mentor will
> be able to advise you on your readiness and support you if
> support is needed."
>
> *The Silberay Apprentice: a handbook*

Chapter Sixteen

As the bus approached Belhaven Manor Marheh huddled further into her
seat, wrapping her arms around herself as if for warmth. Although the sky
was lightening now she had no eyes for the landscape. She seemed to be
carrying a big ball of clay in the pit of her stomach and she wondered
whether she might be sick. All too soon the roof and chimneys of the
manor appeared, dark against the pale sky. Then the bus slowed and
stopped outside the elaborate gates.

"Manor," the driver grunted, then again, looking over his shoulder at
Marheh. "You wanted the Manor?"

Marheh stood up, straightened her spine and lifted her chin.

"Thank you," she said as she passed the driver and climbed down. Then
she stood and watched as the bus pulled away and bustled off along the
road. She watched until it rounded a corner and was out of sight then she
turned her attention to the gates, examining the decorative ironwork as if
that was all that interested her, pushing aside the knowledge that she
planned to enter and walk up the curved driveway, to climb the steps to the
front door and knock for admittance.

It was too early to go in yet she thought, retreating to the bushes on the
other side of the road. She was not quite sure what the time was, but she
would wait at least until it was fully light. Settling herself against a tree trunk
she tried, not very successfully, to prepare her mind for the confrontation
with Samuel. She had time now to acknowledge her fear and to wonder
about the action she planned to take. Nemle would probably have
discovered her absence and be worried, but it was too late to turn back.

At last the sun was up and she could put off the confrontation no longer. She tried to remember she was Marheh the Great as she made her way around the bed of daffodils just turning to face the sun. She hoped she looked confident at least and boosted her courage by walking in time to the words repeating themselves in her head.

"It's only Samuel, it's only Samuel."

She climbed the wide low steps and stood looking at the heavy wooden door, carved and polished and the shining brass knocker in the centre. Then she took a deep breath, grasped the knocker and banged it loudly.

The door was opened surprisingly quickly. A uniformed man stood looking at her, his face was bland, unsmiling, revealing nothing.

"I need to see Samuel," Marheh said, trying to sound polite but firm.

The man inclined his head and opened the door wider to admit her.

She hesitated for a moment then stepped inside. The man closed the door. It made a quiet click that seemed to underline the folly of her behaviour. She swallowed. The man stepped around her, confident, at ease and she followed him across the black and white tiled floor to a small sitting room.

She had more time than she wanted to look around. The room was quite ordinary really. A dark red patterned rug covered the tiles. Two big leather armchairs faced the hearth where a small fire burned. The mantelpiece was black, some kind of stone with veins of white, and above it a large mirror in a gilt frame. There were no ornaments, but on the hearth were fire irons and a coal scuttle. A tall window in the wall opposite the door looked out onto the side garden. A small table and three small armchairs with polished wooden arms and red brocade upholstery stood there catching the morning sun. Dark red curtains framed the window. Several paintings hung on the wall opposite the fireplace, still lifes with food; fruit, cheeses and dead animals all painted with passionate attention to detail.

She moved restlessly around the room wishing Samuel would appear. It was hard to believe anything bad would happen to her here, but still she held herself in readiness for a confrontation. The mirror showed her, white, a little dishevelled, incongruous in her plain Silberay uniform. She was still looking in the mirror when she saw reflected a door opening in the wall behind. She spun around as Samuel entered.

He's grown, she thought involuntarily.

"Good morning Kathleen," he said, watching her.

"You know quite well I am not Kathleen," Marheh said.

She would have known him before if she had seen his eyes, pale blue, cold, revealing nothing. He was taller than she was now though and the small beard disguised his mouth and chin. As she watched, his mouth opened slightly and his tongue flicked in and out. It was hard to stand quietly waiting, expecting to have to defend herself, yet uncertain of how or when she would be attacked.

"I hoped you might visit after my greeting," Samuel said. "I thought the cross a distinct improvement to the décor."

Marheh said nothing.

"So why don't you sit down and tell me why you have come," Samuel continued, circling around her.

She knew he was mocking her, wanting to provoke her into breaking Silberay law and attacking him. She moved slowly towards one of the leather chairs until she was standing behind it, her hands resting on its curved back.

"Come to your senses have you?" he asked. "Thinking of joining us? You and I together would be quite a force."

His words took Marheh by surprise, distracted her so that his sudden powerful thrust towards her mind was almost successful and they spent minutes locked in mental combat before he drew back. Both were breathing heavily. She watched him warily. His skills had obviously been developed since she last met him six years ago.

"It was worth a try," he said, controlling his breathing with an effort. "I did not really expect to succeed this time, but I will succeed." He studied her in silence for a minute. "You and I together," he repeated and smiled slowly.

Marheh continued to watch him. Her hand pressed down on the back of the chair gave her the illusion of support.

Rapid footsteps sounded outside in the hall and a moment later the door swung open.

"There you are Ess. You wanted us?"

A man and a woman of about Marheh's own age stood staring at her.

"Is she the enemy?" the woman asked, staring at Marheh and giggling.

Samuel did not look at them but answered smoothly.

"It's time to try that little experiment we talked about. Can you remember?"

The woman giggled again. Marheh glanced at her uneasily, newly conscious of her vulnerability, more than ever aware of the need to defend her mind. Then Samuel attacked her again, his mind laying siege to hers with all the power and skill at his command.

She needed everything she had, all the focus and concentration, all the skill and determination Nemle had honed in her to keep him at bay, so she was only aware on the edges that she had left her body vulnerable and she had nothing left to stop Samuel's two friends as they laid hands on her and pulled her to the floor. Fighting Samuel was the most important thing now. Not just defending herself, but fighting to defeat him, but he fought with a brutality she could not match. No practice with Nemle could have prepared her for this and in the end she could only focus on shielding herself from the onslaught.

It was surprising when his attack eased a little. She had not expected any respite. Then she had room to understand what had been done to her and knew that this respite had only been offered for this purpose.

She was lying face down on the red rug in front of the fire. Her wrists were bound to the front legs of one of the heavy leather arm chairs, her feet to the other. She moved her head a little and heard the woman giggle again.

"Can we do the other thing now?" she asked.

"In a minute," Samuel said aloud. "Get everything ready and find a nice bit of skin."

"You see Kathleen," he said then, into Marheh's mind. "One way or another it will be you and I together. In the end I will take what I want from your mind and add it to mine."

Marheh was still primarily focused on keeping Samuel out of her mind, but somewhere on the edge of consciousness she understood the man and woman to be fumbling with her clothes. Then, almost simultaneously she felt Samuel renew his attack on her mind and felt a searing pain across her lower back. She screamed. It was a scream from mind and voice, but the convulsive response of her body to the pain was involuntary whereas her mind's response was active and drew on her skill and ability. The struggle was powerful and intense and she was losing when she felt Nemle's response to her cry. Nemle's mind eased into hers to become a fortress within which she could shelter, from which she could attack.

Still Samuel seemed to be defeating her. She knew her strength was waning and more and more she needed to take refuge. There was physical pain too that increasingly undermined her focus. She knew she had screamed a second time and felt her mind's focus slipping out of her control when suddenly Samuel's mind seemed to turn to a different target. With all she had left she struck at him, fear and pain making her desperate. She struck again as his mind returned to hers and she saw him acknowledge her with a small grimace as he crumpled and seemed to fade.

When Nemle heard Marheh's scream her response had been almost immediate. The three men understood she had left them and Jik guided her carefully onto *Day Bringer* and eased her into the armchair where she would have no physical distractions. After a brief consultation Jik and Kel left Sul to enter the soul song and build protection in that way while they set out to search for Marheh. It seemed impossible that she could have gone as far as the Manor, but they both felt sure she must have gone looking for Samuel. Together they set off for Market Mondborough, striding out with long, easy steps, pacing themselves, knowing they must still keep strength for what they might find. There was no need for speech and talking would take energy, but as they climbed Kel could not help voicing his anxiety.

"Why? Why go off on her own? What could she have been thinking?"

Jik did not reply, knowing Kel did not really expect it, but he remembered the conversation of the previous day.

"You're always wanting to do it yourself... still," he had said to her. You fool, you little fool, he castigated her mentally, anxious and angry because of it.

Kel had been trying to remember the bus times from his experience the previous day.

"If we can make it to Market Mondborough in half an hour we might just catch the next bus. Otherwise it's a two hour wait."

They both pushed themselves into a jog. A two hour wait would be impossible when every minute might count.

As they neared Market Mondborough Kel drew ahead, his youth giving him the edge.

"Go," Jik panted. "Hold the bus for me if you can."

He knew he could go no faster, but still his pace did not slacken as Kel moved steadily onward until he was out of sight amongst the houses on the outskirts of the town.

It was a near thing. Kel was standing in the road, his hand on the bus, ready to jump on if the driver insisted on leaving. Jik saw him gesture to the driver as he came into sight and pushed for his last ounce of energy. Kel had to help him up the steps of the bus but he had made it. The jerk of departure almost threw him into the seat Kel had chosen and he collapsed into it gratefully and concentrated on getting his breath back.

"She came this way," Kel said when Jik's agonised gasping had eased a little. "I spoke to the driver. She was on the first bus four hours ago."

Jik nodded, still unable to speak.

"Four hours," Kel repeated almost to himself.

"The little fool," Jik said, his voice strained and anxious. "The little fool."

The sight that met them when they finally reached Belhaven Manor shocked them into stillness for a moment.

The bus ride had been long enough for Jik to recover from the run and once off the bus they wasted no time getting into the Manor.

The front door had been unlocked when Jik tried the handle and they had no compunction about entering quickly and quietly. The door to the sitting room was open and attracted their immediate attention. Moving carefully, conscious of an intense silence, they approached the door, one on either side. From the doorway they saw, almost at their feet, the sprawling figure of a man in Silberay uniform. Samuel stood in front of the wall of still lifes, frozen, a look of mild surprise on his face. A man and a woman knelt at the hearth. The woman held a poker raised in one hand. They too seemed frozen in place. Between them was a figure spread eagled, face down on the floor.

Marheh's eyes were closed, her face white and still. Her tunic was rucked up above her waist, her trousers pulled down around her hips. Across her lower back was an angry, blistered red slash. Jik was beside her in a moment while Kel closed and locked the door against interruption. Whatever had gone on here, it seemed the enemy was, for the moment, controlled. Jik placed a finger against Marheh's neck feeling for a pulse. He looked up briefly to meet Kel's anxious eyes and nod reassurance then he applied himself to the twine that bound her.

Kel began by removing the poker from the woman's hand then he placed the man and woman in the chairs by the window where they were out of the way. They showed no sign that they were emerging from the control placed on them but he reinforced it with his own command nevertheless and wondered at Marheh's strength. She must have dealt with them, he thought, looking again at the slim figure on the floor. Jik had untied her and placed a cushion under her head, but it seemed best to leave her where she was for the moment.

The silence around them was unnerving and they came together to speak in an undertone.

"What can have happened?" Kel asked.

Jik shook his head. "We may never know."

He walked across to the man on the floor near the door. There was something familiar about the dark blue tunic and silver belt. Crouching down he touched the man's shoulder, then gently eased him onto his back.

"It's Hud," Kel said.

Jik felt for a pulse, listened for breath or heartbeat, then tried to connect with his mind.

Nothing.

"He's gone," Jik said, standing up.

"Dead!" Kel's exclamation was loud in the quiet room.

"Who's dead?"

The voice from the floor drew them both back to her side. She struggled to lift her head.

"Be still," Jik said. "Little fool."

His voice was rough but he touched her cheek very gently. She sighed briefly and closed her eyes.

Jik spent a moment more crouched beside her then he stood and stretched, looked around the room from one still figure to the next, then spoke in his normal voice.

"First priority, Marheh. We need to get her home to *Day Bringer*. Then we have to find out what went on in here."

"Do you think she killed Hud?"

"I don't know, but if she did there'll be hell to pay."

Kel took a moment to assimilate this then looked across to the window where he had placed the man and woman.

"Who are they do you suppose?"

"It might be useful to find out," Jik said. "Sul said they have a motor. It might do to get Marheh home but we would need one of them to operate it."

"The woman held the poker. She must have burned Marheh's back."

"We'll try the man then."

They went across to the window. Jik sat in the remaining chair facing the young man while Kel stood watchfully behind him. Cautiously Jik eased himself into the man's mind and set about removing the control Marheh and then Kel had put in place. He understood very quickly that this was not a Yareblis mind and his exploration revealed another, more subtle control beneath the other two. He removed this also and gradually relinquished the mind to be itself.

Kel, keeping watch, saw the man's face change as first movement then emotion manifest itself. He saw him register their presence in the room and

207

the still figure of the woman in the chair beside him.

"Who the devil are you? What have you done to Poppy?"

He tried to get up but subsided as Jik applied a gentle command. He continued to look around the room.

"And Ess..." His voice sounded bewildered. "What's going on?"

"We hoped you might tell us that," Jik said. "There's a woman hurt and a man dead."

"Dead! Who's dead?"

Jik indicated Hud's body where it lay.

"Oh him. I saw him come bursting in yelling at Ess to stop. Old fool! He thought he was Ess's teacher but Ess just played with him. He won't be dead, that's just Ess showing off."

"I assure you," Jik said. "The man is dead."

"Gosh!"

It was a narrow, pale, rather vacuous face, Kel thought wondering at the inadequacy of this exclamation and the kind of mind that would consider it an appropriate response to news of a man's death.

"That's too bad of Ess. He shouldn't have done that."

Jik and Kel were silent.

"What about that girl? Ess wanted us to tie her up but it was just a joke really. He called her the enemy."

"You made it very easy for Samuel, didn't you?" Jik said. "He didn't have to work very hard to get you to go along with what he wanted."

The man looked a bit uncomfortable.

"He made things exciting," he protested. "It was just a bit of fun."

"Just a bit of fun," Jik repeated.

He stood up and led the man across to where Marheh lay on the floor. She was very still and the side of her face that could be seen was pale against her dark hair. Jik thought she had probably entered the discipline of the soul to join with Nemle and Sul in singing them protection and to find comfort in their harmony.

The burn stood out, livid, angry.

"Do you think she thought it was fun?"

"Oh shit!"

He opened and shut his mouth a couple of times then added "Did Poppy do that?"

Jik's silence was response enough.

"Poppy's my sister," he said apologising. "She thought Ess was great. Well, we both did really, but she's more adventurous. My name's Miles but Ess used to call me Milly, to tease you know, because sometimes I wasn't so keen."

He looked at his feet, at Marheh and then at Jik.

"Could I... a doctor... or ... or something to help her?"

"Not a doctor," Jik said slowly, studying Miles' face. "But perhaps you could take her in your motor to where she can be helped."

Miles seemed quite enthusiastic about this suggestion, though whether helping was his main motivation or simply a desire to get rid of the evidence Jik was not certain. Kel would go with them while Jik remained to watch over Poppy and Samuel.

"What about him?"

Miles indicated Hud's body, but Jik shook his head. There must be some formalities associated with his death. Jik was not ready to make any decisions about that yet. He did not know enough although he knew the important thing, Marheh was not responsible.

Kel and Miles went off to bring round the car while Jik crouched beside Marheh to ease her back into herself. She wanted to try to walk though she was obviously in a great deal of pain.

"There's nothing the matter with my legs," she insisted, pushing herself to her feet where she stood swaying a little until Jik took hold of her to steady her. Her tunic slid down to cover the burn and she bit back a cry of pain.

"I'm alright."

She stood, holding onto Jik and looking around the room at Samuel, at Poppy and finally at Hud.

"Is he...?"

Jik nodded.

She was silent for a few moments.

"Poor Hud," she said at last. "I think he saved me really. That must have been the moment when Samuel turned away from me. That gave me my chance."

She turned her face into Jik's broad, comfortable chest and he held her gently until they saw the car pass the window when he guided her out into the hall and through the open front door.

There was no way she was going to be comfortable in the car, but she perched on the edge of the seat and leaned forward to rest her folded arms on the back of the seat in front. She was glad to be in a position to hide her face from Kel's sharp eyes. When she was settled he slid in beside her. The front seats were occupied by Miles and the chauffeur, who she thought might have been the man who had admitted her to the Manor that morning.

"Will you bring Sul back with you?" Jik asked. "I think we need his advice about Hud."

Kel nodded as the door closed and the car moved slowly away.

For Marheh the ride was an endurance test, but it was taking her to Nemle and *Day Bringer* and she was able to contain the pain by thinking of them. The chauffeur knew where to take them since he had taken Samuel and Hud to the boats only the day before.

Kel wondered about him as he drove them smoothly along. He seemed to be impervious to any kind of mental communication yet he was not Yareblis. Obviously Samuel had not been able to influence him. Although he did as Miles requested, it was as an employee not because he was influenced by mind control. It would be interesting to discover more Kel thought, though now was not the time.

The journey was soon over. Kel could not help comparing this smooth, rapid passage with the morning's long and difficult journey.

"This is where I waited yesterday," the chauffeur said, pulling up in a small lay-by beside the lane.

Kel nodded. He could just see *Storm Cloud*'s prow beyond the high hedge.

"Why would you stop here?" Miles said, puzzled.

"Didn't ask," the chauffeur said. "This is what Ess wanted."

"This is as close as we can get in the motor," Kel said.

Marheh lifted a grey, exhausted face and tried to push herself upright. Kel leapt out to support her, calling Miles to her other side. She wanted to protest, but the two men gave her no chance. Kel wanted Miles under his eye as well as wanting the support for her. They almost carried her the short distance to the water road.

Nemle sensed their coming and stepped off *Day Bringer* to meet them. Miles gasped as she appeared on the path as if from nowhere. She had so many questions, but knew this was not the time for answers. She held out her arms to Marheh.

"I'll take care of her now," she said, steadying herself as Marheh sagged against her.

"We're going back," Kel said. "And Jik wants Sul to come with us. Will you be alright?"

Nemle nodded. "Go quickly and come back safe."

She helped Marheh onto *Day Bringer* and down the steps into her cabin, scolding and encouraging almost in the same breath.

Kel gathered up Sul and went back with Miles to the Manor while Nemle cared for Marheh, helping her to undress, tending the burn on her back and putting her to bed. She was horrified at Marheh's obvious exhaustion and appalled by the burn. Treatment would need all her skill and all Marheh's courage and she would probably bear the scar for life.

Before she would let her sleep Nemle made sperit and fed it to her a sip at a time. Then she drew the covers up as far as the burn, touched her cheek gently and settled herself beside her on the floor.

At the Manor Jik spent the time of Kel's absence sitting in the chair opposite Poppy and trying to clarify the situation for himself. There was no indication that there was anyone else in the house although he realised that the silence surrounding him did not necessarily mean that he was alone. He needed to know more and his only source of information at the moment seemed to be Poppy. Was it better to release her from Marheh's command so he could question her or should he wait until Kel and Miles returned? And what of Hud? Marheh thought he had saved her, provided the distraction that gave her an opening to attack Samuel. How had Samuel become so strong? He was even younger than Marheh. Of course if he had no conscience about how he practised or on whom then he could develop his ability more easily than any Silberay.

He decided in the end to leave any action involving Poppy or Samuel until Kel returned with Sul. It would be safer to wait, but it was difficult not to be impatient. He spent a few moments crouched beside Hud's body straightening his limbs and closing his eyes, grieving for the man he had once been. Then he deliberately set himself to sit quietly on the threshold of the discipline of the soul, not losing himself in the music, but holding himself poised and ready, aware of the dark emptiness that emanated from Samuel and trickling a little of his light into the place only to see it apparently subsumed.

Kel and Sul arrived just over an hour later with Miles and the chauffeur. Sul entered the room first and paused in the doorway with the others behind him. Jik saw him scan the room and take in Samuel's frozen stance and Hud's still form, then their eyes met in quiet acknowledgement. Jik stood as Sul made his slow way across the room. The others kept back as Jik and Sul spoke together then all gathered around the small table where Poppy was still sitting motionless and unseeing.

Miles touched her anxiously.

"How did she get like this? I know she hurt your friend but…"

He looked from Jik to Sul and then back to his sister.

"She wouldn't have meant to."

"I can release her," Jik said. "As I did you, but there are bigger issues involved."

Miles looked uncomfortable.

"We followed Samuel. He thought of things to do and we all did them."

"Without thinking yourself?" Sul asked.

"It was just fun," Miles protested. "He made things exciting. We didn't need to think about it."

As Miles talked they learned something of the situation at the Manor. Samuel had come nearly six years ago as the adopted son of the new gardener and his wife. At first he had been quiet and kept to himself but it was not many months before he had become friendly with Miles, flattering him and encouraging him to amuse himself in destructive ways.

"He seemed a lot older than his years and things happened around him," Miles said. "Nothing ever happened here before, nothing interesting. I was supposed to be learning about the estate, but that's just boring and I don't have to work really, neither of us do. Poppy was bored too. Samuel can do anything with anyone."

It was all Samuel. He was clever and amusing and could do all kinds of things with people, and he got better and better at it. It was harmless. People were frightened a bit or embarrassed a bit, but they mostly deserved it. Then Samuel had told Miles and Poppy about this person he'd met who belonged to some cult or other. They had stopped him from doing what he wanted and tried to make him into one of them. The one he talked about was pretty gullible and believed Samuel when he said he wanted to join them.

"It was him," Miles said, gesturing towards Hud.

The three Silberay listened with increasing sadness as Miles told them how Samuel had toyed with Hud, flattering him and pretending to look up to him. He had persuaded Miles and Poppy to invite him for long visits to the Manor where he had enjoyed the luxury their wealth could provide. Samuel could make him perform for them it seemed. He would tell Miles and Poppy what he planned and they would laugh together as Hud carried out the moves intended to mock him.

Miles and Poppy had an absent father who preferred to travel the world rather than remain at the Manor. Their mother went with him usually, but she had died on one of the trips when they were still at school. There were a few servants still, but they had their own quarters and stayed out of sight.

Several had left, Miles explained.

"Servants are so conservative," he said. "They disapproved of us."

Sul, who had known Hud better than the others, could see how he had been tempted. He would have seen himself as a leader, a wise councillor with three devoted acolytes and in the end even the Silberay had believed his image of himself, appointing him to teach Silberay law and allowing him to take an apprentice. Samuel could have easily persuaded the Apprentice Master that he was a suitable candidate. Not only had he lived on *Storm Cloud* but he had also spent time at the Harbour. It seemed he had been cultivating Hud ever since.

It was a long story and when they had heard it the three Silberay realised that whatever action they finally decided to take Samuel could not be released to develop his power any further.

"I think perhaps it must still be between him and Marheh," Sul said.

Jik made a movement of protest.

"Not Marheh alone of course. He was targeting all the Silberay through her. But it began with her and she must decide the end."

"Hasn't she been through enough?"

Sul nodded.

"More than enough, but through implies an ending. She has not yet reached the ending."

"The discipline of the mind has the potential to be a powerful weapon if practised assiduously, but its purpose is purely self-defence. As an apprentice you may practise engaging and communicating with your mentor. After a strenuous session you may feel weary or even a little disoriented. Your mentor will understand this."

The Silberay Apprentice: a handbook

Chapter Seventeen

On *Day Bringer*, Marheh soon slept, exhausted by her battle with Samuel and the pain of her burn. Nemle watched beside her for a time, but when she was confident that Marheh's sleep was easy and natural she went back to the galley and began to prepare food for them all. She had no idea when they would return but she knew they would need to eat some time soon. So much had happened since she discovered Marheh missing that morning it was hard to believe the day was barely half over.

She mixed the dough for a loaf and put it to rise then prepared a big pot of vegetables. Soup or stew, it wouldn't really matter, she thought, as long as it was filling and tasty.

When the loaf was finally in the oven she washed up and went to check on Marheh. She was still lying on her stomach where she had been put but she was no longer sleeping. Her eyes flicked towards Nemle as she entered and it was clear that she was in pain. Nemle went to sit on the bottom step where Marheh could see her without moving her head.

"Do you want to tell me about it?"

Marheh did not answer immediately and Nemle placed one hand over hers and patted it gently.

"Are you angry?" Marheh said at last in a husky little voice.

"I'll be angry later."

Marheh attempted a smile, but it was not very successful.

"I was stupid to go on my own."

"Yes."

"I thought I could make it be over."

"Really?"

Marheh did not answer. Nemle would not let her get away with prevaricating even now and she did not want to look any further into her motives.

"Could you manage something to eat?" Nemle asked at length.

Marheh nodded slightly and closed her eyes as Nemle stood up to leave.

She was not away long. She returned with a bowl of porridge sweetened with honey and insisted on feeding her a few spoonfuls before she would let her try for herself.

"Hud is dead," Marheh said when she had surrendered the bowl again. "I was struggling so hard to defend myself then something distracted Samuel and he... he turned away for a moment."

Nemle focused on preparing another spoonful and slid it into her mouth as she paused.

"He saved me Nemle." Marheh choked a little. "I hated him and he saved me."

Nemle concentrated on feeding Marheh porridge, not wanting to betray her shock at this news. When the bowl was empty she put it on the floor and let herself slump for a minute.

"He had nearly forgotten how to be Silberay," she said. "But not quite... we can remember that."

They were both quiet for several minutes then Nemle pushed herself to her feet.

"I'll need to replace the dressing. It's better if it doesn't dry out, but it will hurt."

It did, and Marheh bit her pillow and endured while Nemle spread comfrey ointment thickly over the burn and covered it with damp gauze. Then she guided her into the discipline of the soul for respite from pain, for remembrance of Hud and for protection for the others.

The three at the Manor were still working out how best to resolve the various issues Marheh's confrontation with Samuel had raised. Jik was strongly of the opinion that as well as dealing with Samuel and Hud, Miles and Poppy would need support and guidance.

"Miles certainly had a Yareblis control in place and I imagine Poppy does too," he said. "They can't just be released from it and left to fend for themselves. They seem to have no personal values to guide them."

Sul agreed.

"It's a pity the Manor is so far from the water road. Kel would be a good friend for them both." Sul nodded towards the table by the window where Kel was sitting listening to Miles. "It's too long a journey for him to make regularly though."

Jik looked thoughtful.

"It's quite easy by motor," he suggested.

The end of Hud's life needed some kind of formal acknowledgement and recognition and this was beginning to seem urgent. Silberay were cremated when they died and their ashes returned to the water road. There was always a time of remembrance at the Gatherings, but Silberay usually died quietly at the Harbour and there was not much precedent for this kind of death. Sul suggested that Miles and Poppy might be helped to initiate the civil formalities necessary to register the death.

The still, frozen figure of Samuel brooded over the activities in the sitting room and this too was becoming increasingly difficult to ignore. The Silberay knew that this was their business and that he must be removed from the Manor and dealt with before Miles and Poppy had any chance of reclaiming their lives and making any positive change.

All this takes so much time and energy, Jik thought, drawing Miles and Kel away to give Sul room to release Poppy. Decisive action isn't really enough to solve the problem. He smiled at the two younger men and began to explain to Miles what Sul was doing.

Ten minutes later he was outlining to them all that needed to be done for

Hud. Poppy however could not keep her eyes off Samuel. She seemed to have very little interest in Hud's death and when Miles went off with Kel to telephone the appropriate authorities she stood in front of Samuel staring at him.

"Boo!" she said suddenly and giggled. Then, before Jik could prevent her, she gave him a push.

He seemed to crumple as if whatever had been holding his knees, hips and spine in a standing position had been jolted out of alignment. Jik caught him and lowered him to the floor. Poppy laughed. Sul began to remonstrate with her in his quiet voice. Miles and Kel came back to report that a doctor was on his way and would be with them in twenty minutes.

Jik, looking around, saw that Samuel's presence would raise too many questions in an official mind. He needed to be out of the way and the best place for him would be the water road. He and Kel would stay to support Miles and Poppy, the motor would take Sul and Samuel to the boats. Sul and Nemle were strong enough and wise enough to guide Marheh's dealings with Samuel and were best left to do so uninterrupted. So it was arranged and Jik breathed a sigh of relief when he had watched the car through the gates feeling confident that he and Kel could deal with what remained.

Once at the boats Sul used his mind to guide Samuel onto *Storm Cloud* and into Kel's cabin. He placed him on Kel's bunk and stood for a few minutes establishing control and remembering the difficult, angry teenager he and Kel had tried to care for. They had failed, worse than failed really because their actions had given Samuel the knowledge he needed to infiltrate the Silberay. He sighed a little. They had done what seemed right at the time. The boy had been hard to love and no doubt that was where their failure lay, but given the choice again they would take the same action driven by the same hope that they could make a difference.

He made his way along to *Day Bringer* knowing Nemle would be anxious to hear what was happening and feeling the need to discuss with her what he had found

He and Jik had thought there might be a need to reinforce the control on Samuel's mind, but Sul found there was very little left to be controlled. It seemed Marheh had all but destroyed him. He had spread himself very thinly, placing controls all over the place as well as poisoning Daniel. It was as if, at his defeat, these controls had all come ricocheting back to add to the havoc Marheh had wrought. But there was something more that he did not understand.

His knock roused them from the discipline where they had been trying to sing light. They had both found it a struggle, Marheh because pain kept breaking through, Nemle because she was holding and supporting Marheh's faltering song. Nemle welcomed him in, guiding him through Marheh's cabin, pausing a moment beside Marheh to suggest she try to sleep then going with him into the saloon.

Marheh, left alone, lay obediently with closed eyes for a while, but the dull, throbbing pain in her back would not release her to sleep and her mind too was suffering the effects of her battle with Samuel. She whimpered a little and castigated herself for a coward. She wanted to shout and kick something. At other times, when she felt this way she could run off the trapped, angry mood, but not this time. She wanted the toilet too and though the sensible thing would be to call for Nemle to help her she was not feeling sensible.

There's nothing wrong with my legs, she told herself as she had told Jik earlier and forced herself out of bed.

Dressing seemed impossible, even putting on her slippers too difficult so she set off, naked, barefooted through the engine room to the bathroom, trusting that Nemle would have shut the door across the entrance to the galley. It was a slow, painful journey.

As she had hoped, the door seemed closed, but Nemle had left it ajar so she could hear if Marheh needed her and as she reached it she heard Sul say her name, heard Nemle exclaim and begin a protest. Then there was silence and she heard Nemle's footsteps coming towards the door as if she had become aware of her presence.

She called a warning as Nemle's head came round the door.

"Oh Marheh!"

"I'm alright. I can manage."

"You don't look as if you can manage," Nemle said, but she left her alone to do what she needed to and make her way back to bed.

Fifteen minutes later when she again lay sprawled face down on her bunk Nemle came through to check on her, to make sure the dressing was still in place, to cover her carefully and to scold a little.

"Silly child, why didn't you call me to help you?" she finished.

"I'm not a child."

"No," Nemle said, studying her gravely. "No, I know."

She turned and went then and Marheh tightened her fingers into fists and pushed at the mattress. She hated the way she was feeling. She wanted to call Nemle back and apologise. She wanted to scream and cry and make the world feel bad because she did. She wanted... she didn't know what she wanted, that was part of the problem.

And they were talking about her, Nemle and Sul, discussing her. How dare they! Listing her faults no doubt. At least she had pushed them into action even if it had been foolish to go alone. Samuel had been so strong, much stronger than she was despite all her practice. Her mind, still weary and bruised, flinched away from the memory of the moment when defeat seemed inevitable, but she forced herself to consider it, to replay the struggle. There was something nagging at her. It was almost as if Samuel had drawn on something else, something she half recognised.

What had he said, he would take what he wanted from her mind and join it to his. Would it have worked, she wondered, or would her mind have been destroyed? He wouldn't have wanted the part of her mind that tried to live up to the Silberay promise, would that bit have just shrivelled and died or would it have continued to fight him?

Would it work for her? What if she tried to join Samuel's mind to hers? It didn't matter how much she practised with Nemle she would never learn to do the things he had done because they were wrong, but with his mind joined to hers she wouldn't need to, she would have the benefit of his practice.

She moved restlessly then caught her breath at the pain it caused. It wasn't fair. She didn't deserve to hurt so much.

When Nemle came again to check on her she was crying, slow, unhappy tears, part pain, part frustration and self pity. Nemle sat down beside her on the bottom step wondering whether she should be bracing or sympathetic. It was hard, the bottom step and she was tired. She closed her eyes. What would help Marheh best? How would she respond to Sul's suggestion that she had not yet finished with Samuel?

An anxious voice saying her name roused her from her thoughts and she saw that she had accidentally helped Marheh best by doing nothing and giving her someone beside herself to think about.

"Are you alright?" Marheh was asking her.

"Just a bit tired. It's been an anxious day."

"I'm sorry Nemle."

Nemle smiled at her then reached in her pocket for a handkerchief and blew her nose. For a moment or two she had thought she might cry.

Marheh propped herself up on her elbows.

"I'm sorry Nemle," she said again, her voice stronger this time.

She sniffed and rubbed the heel of her hand over her wet cheeks. "I was feeling sorry for myself."

Nemle gave a wry smile.

"It doesn't help much though, does it?"

She levered herself off the step and stood up.

"Food is the answer. I know I'm hungry."

"Can I come out?"

"If you feel up to it, but you must promise to go back to bed for a proper sleep after."

She helped her into her nightdress and slippers and followed her out to the saloon where Sul was resting in the armchair. He smiled a greeting as Marheh came past and eased herself into her seat at the table, wincing a little as the movement made the pain flare. Nemle buttered them all a thick slice of new bread and ladled her vegetable stew into bowls. Marheh discovered she was very hungry and found that the food helped her to regain her equilibrium.

"I think I must have been a little bit mad," she said as Nemle refilled her bowl. "I wasn't thinking straight at all." She hesitated. "I even contemplated taking Samuel's mind into mine. He said that was what he planned to do with me."

"Your mind is still recovering," Nemle said. "It is always a dangerous time. Best not to think too much. Sleep and the discipline of the soul are the way to healing."

"Do you think it would be possible?" Marheh continued, unable to let the idea go. "Remember when we took the water dimension from SP. What if I'd tried to keep it then and use it?"

She faltered and her eyes widened.

"SP," she said, and then again. "SP."

Nemle looked at her, concerned. She remembered SP, of course she did. He had been the school principal of the Yareblis training school where Samuel had been the head boy. After he had tried to destroy Marheh they had managed to remove the water dimension from his mind so he could no longer threaten them. It had been a new technique and one which few Silberay could perform even now, six years later.

"What about SP?" she said. "We disabled him. He can no longer see the water road let alone use the discipline of the mind."

Marheh breathed out slowly and carefully and shook her head as if she was ridding herself of something.

"It couldn't be that," she said, more to herself than to Sul and Nemle.

Nemle looked at her sharply then reached across to take her bowl.

"Back to bed with you," she said, and no one mentioned the unresolved issue of Samuel.

At the Manor the doctor had been and gone and set in motion the procedure for dealing with Hud's body. Miles summoned a servant and ordered food for the four of them. Jik watched and listened as they sat around the table. Both Miles and Poppy seemed to have attached themselves to Kel and were telling him about themselves and their lives.

It seemed to Jik that they had been allowed to do more or less what they liked without anyone to take much interest in them since their mother died. School had provided some degree of discipline while they were there but the years since had been devoted to the pursuit of entertainment and under Samuel's reign entertainment had become increasingly outrageous to the point where the village had turned its back and few of the servants stayed for long.

Then the gardener and his wife who had adopted Samuel and tried for a time to shape his values died.

They had been holidaying with Samuel at a small village on the coast. One day they had gone for a walk and not come back. Later their bodies had been found by a man fishing from the rocks. The cause of their deaths had never been clarified although their injuries were consistent with a fall from the cliffs above. Samuel had chosen to walk in a different direction that day.

"So of course he came back here and lived with us," Poppy said.

Jik watched her pretty, animated face framed by a shining cap of straight fair hair and wondered whether she would remember what she had done to Marheh.

"He made things so much fun," she continued. "Exciting."

"But you were hurting people," Kel said.

She pouted.

"Only a little bit and they were the enemy." She looked at him as if willing him to understand. "It was a game. Them against us."

"But what if the other people didn't want to play your game?" Kel asked.

Poppy did not really seem to understand the import of his question, but Miles looked a bit uncomfortable.

"We didn't really give them any choice," he said.

Jik looked from one to the other. It would not be easy or quick to help these two turn their lives around. He wondered whether Poppy needed to be confronted with Marheh's injury. He would wait a little longer and see if she or Miles remembered. He thought perhaps he should also try to find

223

out whether Samuel had acted alone.

The meal over he asked Miles to show him the rest of the Manor. Poppy wanted to come too and so they all accompanied Miles through the house.

It looked a bit tired and unkempt Jik thought, as if no one much cared, but obviously it had been very grand once.

The ground floor had a library and a big formal entertaining area Miles called the ballroom, as well as the sitting room and the dining room they had already seen. A separate door led to the kitchen and servants' wing. Upstairs were another small sitting room and several bedrooms all opening off a kind of long gallery that looked over the staircase. Jik asked to see Hud's room, wondering whether it might hold a clue to the man's thinking, but at first glance it held little of interest.

"Perhaps you will allow us to pack his possessions," Jik said. "We can return them to his people."

"You might as well," Poppy said. "We don't want them."

She wandered around opening drawers and tossing things onto the bed.

"He didn't have much."

Kel folded the few garments deftly and packed them into the soft bag Jik found in the wardrobe.

"Just this," Miles said, holding up a large, ornately bound book. "He seemed to think this was important."

Jik and Kel looked at each other then Jik took the book of Silberay law away from Miles and placed it firmly on top of the folded garments.

"It is not very important really," he said. "But it ought to go back where it came from."

He insisted on seeing Samuel's accommodation next, hoping he might find some indication of Yareblis influence, but there was nothing obvious. Perhaps he had acted alone, building on his early Yareblis schooling.

"So it is only you two who live here?" he asked. "No one else?"

"We still have a few servants," Miles answered.

"And Aunt Philly," Poppy added. "But she's gone strange these last few years."

Again Jik and Kel exchanged glances.

"How is she strange?" Jik asked.

Poppy shrugged.

"Doesn't speak, doesn't move, doesn't eat unless someone shows her how. She has an old woman who looks after her."

"May we meet her?" Jik asked.

"Jik might be able to help her," Kel said.

"Or Marheh."

"You have such weird names," Poppy said. "And who's Marheh?"

Miles turned away abruptly then swung back. "Is she...?"

Jik nodded.

"Why would she want to help anyone associated with us?"

"Perhaps you will have the opportunity to ask her yourself."

"Ask who what?" Poppy broke in impatiently. "What are you talking about?"

"Don't pretend you don't remember." Miles turned on her. "You did it. You hurt her."

There was silence for a moment as Poppy assimilated his words.

"The enemy was here," she said. "We tied her up."

"And you burnt her with the poker," Miles said when she seemed to have finished speaking.

"Ess wanted me to."

"You burnt her with the poker!"

Miles raised his voice, shouting at her as if to awaken some small understanding of what she had done.

"So?" Poppy challenged him.

"She wasn't an enemy. She was a girl like you."

"Ess said she was the enemy."

"Samuel thought she was the enemy," Jik said, speaking firmly to get their attention. "He made her his enemy because once she had acted in a way that could have changed his life. She was never your enemy, or his, but he forced her to defend herself."

Poppy tossed her head and looked unconvinced, but Jik thought she was considering his words none the less.

"Now, what about Aunt Philly?" he continued. "Where does she fit?"

"She's really Aunt Phyllis," Miles said. "She came to live here after we finished school. She's our father's sister."

"She was the enemy too," Poppy added.

"I don't think she approved of Ess," Miles said. "But she got sick pretty soon after she came here and we don't see her now."

"I'd like to visit her," Jik said.

Miles led the way up the stairs to the next level, the former nursery on one side and Aunt Phyllis' apartments on the other. He knocked and a tall, almost gaunt elderly woman opened the door.

"Mr Miles," she said. "Miss Phyllis seems a little brighter today."

"You always say that," Poppy said.

The woman looked disapprovingly at Poppy and then surveyed each of the Silberay. Her face softened a little and Jik realised that she had recognised their uniform.

"Can you help her?" She was speaking directly to Jik.

"I think so," Jik said. "Already I imagine the control will be weakening."

The woman nodded.

"So that's it," she said. "Has he gone?"

"We have him and will take care of him."

She opened the door wider to invite them to follow her into a small sitting room. It was a peaceful place, softly lit from a bay window, warmed by a small fire, furnished in quiet colours and enhanced by flowers, three vases placed around the room where its occupant could see them without moving.

Aunt Phyllis sat in a big wing chair. Her hands were folded in her lap, her ankles neatly crossed. She seemed as peaceful as the room.

Jik went towards her, knelt before her and spoke silently to the pain in her eyes.

It was twilight when Nemle again went to check on Marheh. She and Sul had spent what was left of the afternoon resting on their respective boats. Nemle guessed that Sul had been spending time with the discipline of the soul as she had, but her own efforts had been distracted by concern for Marheh and in particular by the desire to spare her from further dealings with Samuel. She stood for a moment looking down at her sleeping apprentice. My daughter, she thought, feeling love for her fill the shadowy space and wrap itself like an extra blanket around the quiet figure in the bunk.

She continued through the back cabin and up to the back deck where she paused again. Around her the light was fading, colours softening then disappearing as evening fell and the world took on a sombre hue. The others won't be back now, she thought, and began to consider whether there were things she should be attending to, checking the fire on *Autumn Wind* perhaps, making sure Sul had everything he needed, offering help with Samuel.

It all came back to Samuel really. She stepped onto the bank and walked along to *Storm Cloud*. She had protested when Sul said that Marheh must complete what she had begun, but really there was no alternative that would not destroy him as if he had never been. Knocking briskly to announce her presence she made her way on board *Storm Cloud* pausing as she entered the back cabin to look at Samuel, another still, shadowy figure on a bunk.

Sul offered her his armchair as she entered the saloon, but she waved him back and sat instead at the table.

"I'm sorry I was angry," she said. "I didn't want to accept it, that Marheh..." She put her head in her hands for a moment then looked up again. "But not tonight."

"No, not tonight," Sul said, and she felt his sympathy.

"Kel has communicated with me," he continued. "His skills are developing and I understand something positive has happened at the Manor but they won't be back tonight."

"Something positive," Nemle repeated, thinking Marheh would have been able to communicate a fuller picture.

"You know Marheh is exceptional," Sul added, reading her thought.

"She is, isn't she." Nemle spoke quickly then flushed a little at the realisation of how proud she was of Marheh's talent. "You must come and share our supper," she said.

Marheh joined them again, still in nightdress and slippers, a bit brighter after her sleep, at least in her mind, although the burn continued to trouble her. She wanted to know what was happening at the Manor and Sul filled her in as best he could without mentioning Samuel.

"Miles and Poppy," she said, taking time over each name. "But what about Samuel?"

"Samuel is in Kel's cabin on *Storm Cloud*," Sul told her. "He needed to be removed from the Manor so rebuilding could begin."

"What will happen to him?"

Nemle moved uneasily then stood up.

"Can I get you some more to eat?" she asked them both. "Another slice of bread, cheese?"

Marheh shook her head.

"What is it you're not telling me?" she demanded.

"The best that could happen would be to uncover his soul," Nemle said.

Marheh looked at her plate.

"I don't care what's best, I just want him to be stopped."

"He is stopped," Sul said. "You have stopped him."

"That's alright then," she said.

Nemle slid a mug of sperit onto the table in front of her.

"Drink this up," she said. "Then off to bed with you."

Marheh opened her mouth to argue then closed it again. They were keeping something from her, she knew, but let them. She didn't have energy to argue.

Going to bed involved another painful session with Nemle and the comfrey ointment, but it was over at last and she was dosed with chamomile tea to help her sleep and left in the familiar comfort of her bunk. As she closed her eyes her mind drifted back to the question of Samuel, but she slept before she could come to grips with it.

At the Manor they slept too.

Jik and Kel had been given beds, one in Samuel's room, one in Hud's. Jik had gently entered Aunt Phyllis' mind and lifted the control Samuel had placed there. She emerged slowly from her long imprisonment. She was very weary, but managed to speak a few words to her attendant who was transformed by joy. Miles and Poppy seemed taken aback to find her recovering, but they were obviously fond of her and Jik found it a good omen for the future.

Golden light in early dawn
Grows to make a perfect day,
Waking stillness holds the morn
Gently, gently come what may.
    Arise now
    Strong and free
    Become who you were meant to be.
Silver light of evening sky
Softly, sweetly eases pain
In healing sleep the night goes by
Till day and work return again.
    Arise now
    Strong and free
    Become who you were meant to be.

Songs of the Silberay

Chapter Eighteen

The morning dawned blue and bright. Marheh felt a little spark of optimism as the sunlight poured through her cabin window. Samuel was stopped. She had stopped him. Sul had said so. She was aware of a dull ache across her lower back but her mind was no longer aching and the fear she had not really acknowledged had lifted. Only now when it was gone did she realise how much she had been affected by it. Experimentally she eased herself onto her side and felt the ache sharpen. Nemle had explained that a bad burn like this was vulnerable to infection and the painful treatment she was being given was necessary for prevention as well as healing.

She would like to get dressed, but thought Nemle would probably veto the idea for today. Sighing a little she rolled back onto her stomach and fitted her cheek into the still warm depression in the pillow. Samuel was on *Storm Cloud*, just next door. The thought made her uneasy even though Sul had said he was stopped. What was it they were not telling her last night? She closed her eyes and tried to recapture the pleasure she had felt on awakening, but it was gone.

A few minutes later she eased herself carefully out of bed and went slowly along to the bathroom.

Nemle was already up and busy in the galley. She greeted Marheh with a smile and a light touch on her cheek then handed her a mug of sperit.

"I hoped you might sleep a bit longer," she said.

Marheh took her drink and moved across to the table in silence. She watched the steam rising from the mug, breathed the spicy, fruity aroma.

"What is it you're not telling me?" she asked at last.

Nemle did not answer.

"Has something happened to Jik or Kel?"

It was a sudden frightening thought, but Nemle reassured her quickly.

"You have to tell me Nemle." Her voice rose.

"Yes, I can see that I must," Nemle said, bringing a mug of her own and sitting down opposite her.

"It's something to do with Samuel isn't it?"

Nemle nodded and began to explain, choosing her words carefully.

"Samuel is defeated," she said. "His mind is destroyed as yours would have been if he had been able to take it. As he is we could take him to Haven Cottage and over a few months he will fade and die. Then it will be as if he had never existed."

"You can't expect me to be sorry about that," Marheh said as she paused. "It was him or me."

Nemle nodded.

"You did what you had to to survive. Now you could perhaps be generous enough to disinter the spark of Samuel's soul that he buried and give him that much of survival."

Marheh stared at Nemle trying to take in what she was saying then she turned away.

"No!" she said, her voice was sharp and high.

She stared out the window at the shining strip of water, the field of green, sparkling dew-laden.

"No!" she said again and the harshness in her voice surprised even her.

Nemle reached out to touch the hand that had clenched itself into a fist.

"It's alright," she said.

Marheh gave her a stony glare and pushed off her hand impatiently.

"I'm going back to bed," she announced, getting herself awkwardly out from her seat and trying to present a blank, unconcerned face.

Nemle watched her go. It was a lot to ask, but she had sown the seed and she had faith in Marheh. She finished her drink letting her thought drift and then began to plan for the day.

Back in her cabin Marheh was still holding herself rigid. How dare they even think of asking her. Well now Sul and Nemle would have more faults to catalogue. She dropped down onto her bunk and pulled her pillow over her head. The bright day's promise seemed like a mockery now. At first she grumbled and sulked in the darkness then gradually became aware that she was battling with her "don't want tos". It wasn't fair, why should she be asked to do more? She didn't care if he had buried his soul, it was his choice, nothing to do with her.

Then Nemle came with her basin, cloth and jar of ointment.

"I'm sorry daughter," she said. "I know you don't want me just now but I need to change the dressing."

Marheh pushed away the pillow and looked up at Nemle's concerned loving face.

"It's alright," she said on a sigh. "I know."

Nemle knelt beside her and put the basin on the floor.

"I don't want to Nemle."

Nemle began to roll up her nightdress and she shifted a little to release it.

"I don't want to."

Gently and carefully Nemle eased away the old dressing. Marheh gripped the pillow with her teeth.

"This is his fault, all this," she said when she could speak again. "Why should I do anything for him?"

Nemle looked intently at the burn on Marheh's back then moistened her cloth.

When the pain was ended, the fresh dressing in place, the nightdress decorously adjusted she said it again.

"Why should I do anything for him?"

Nemle pulled a blanket over her and sat beside her.

"I can't help wondering," she said at last. "Whether you and he are not a little bit alike. What might he have become if he'd had a home and loving parents? What might you have been, brought up as he was?"

There was a long silence then.

Marheh wanted to protest Nemle's words but deep down she could acknowledge they held some truth. She knew how much her life had been influenced by her family and their belief in the values of the Silberay.

"Even if you are right," she said at last. "I don't think I can."

"Why not?"

"Because... because I would have to love him and I don't want to."

"Why not?" Nemle said again after another moment of quiet.

Marheh did not want to answer. She had barely acknowledged even to herself how much the shame of her beating was poisoning her life. Nemle was insistent, seeing something of what she would not express.

"Obey me daughter."

Marheh's eyes widened in surprise at Nemle's tone then she blushed, deeper and darker until she felt as if she had been dipped in boiling water. She closed her eyes but could not rid herself of the image that haunted her – herself, strung up, half-naked, before all the Silberay, waiting to be punished.

"Answer me daughter," Nemle said, forcing herself to speak firmly, though she thought now that she already knew what she would say.

Marheh struggled to get a word out, any word. In the end the word shame shouted itself into the little cabin just ahead of a storm of weeping.

"I can forgive everything else," she said when the storm was passed. "But not that. I did nothing wrong. He controlled those people, but I still feel ashamed because of what they did to me."

Nemle sat quietly beside her, holding her hand. There was no need to say anything more. The words had been spoken. Marheh was Silberay. She would do what she had to. She waited until Marheh's breathing showed that she slept then moved back to the saloon to take up her mortar and pestle and begin preparing a new batch of comfrey ointment.

Jik and Kel also woke feeling optimistic. Jik especially was looking forward to returning to the water road. It was years since he had spent a night away from *Autumn Wind* and he felt as if he was missing a part of himself. The discovery and recovery of Aunt Phyllis had been an unexpected bonus. He went down to breakfast and was surprised and pleased when she joined him.

"I would not wait for my niece and nephew."

Her voice came from the doorway as he was studying the array of breakfast offerings and wondering whether he could help himself.

"My recollection is that they are not early risers."

Jik turned to smile at her. She walked slowly into the dining room supporting herself with a well polished walking stick. Jik drew out a chair for her.

"What may I get for you?" he asked.

When he had supplied her needs he filled a bowl with porridge for himself and sat down opposite. Looking at her he realised now that she was probably about his own age although her physical weakness made her seem older.

"You took your time coming," she said.

"You knew then?"

She nodded.

"I've always been able to see the water road to some degree. It made me different though and my parents and my brother did not want to know. After my brother married I moved away to a home of my own. It was close to the water road and I began to know the Silberay who passed."

"I'm sorry we let you down," Jik said.

"You're here now."

She paused to butter a piece of toast. Jik saw that even this needed concentration and an effort of control.

"No doubt my strength will return as I use what I have," she said. "Has he gone?"

Jik nodded.

"Gone for good, but these two will need you."

"That's why I came back when their mother died, but I have not been much use to them so far."

Jik looked at her gravely and thought how courageous she was.

"You didn't give up or give in," he said. "That will count."

Kel entered then with Miles close behind. They had barely sat down when Poppy appeared. She alone seemed unaffected by the bright morning and barely glanced at the others before pouring a cup of tea and seating herself.

"Back to boredom," she announced loudly.

Jik sighed a little. It was not going to be quite as straightforward as he had hoped.

After breakfast he found himself at a loose end. He longed to be back home on *Autumn Wind* but was reluctant to leave while the situation at the Manor seemed so unstable. It was no wonder Miles and Poppy were bored, he thought. They never needed to do a thing for themselves and seemed to have no interests and no concept of public service. He went outside to walk in the garden, hoping the exercise might prompt ideas. Here too there was evidence of neglect. Although the grass had been mown the garden beds were overgrown and plants had gone to seed.

He strolled along the gravel paths, noticing that weeds had begun to sprout here too. Though he enjoyed the morning sunshine he could not help thinking how much more he would have enjoyed it from the deck of *Autumn Wind*. He was anxious too for Marheh. Nemle and Sul would care for her, he knew, but in some ways he understood her better even than Nemle because he had seen her grow up. He had been a big factor in her decision to become apprenticed to the Silberay. He had recognised her latent talent, but saw now that talent brought its own problems, not least in the development of the maturity to use it wisely.

But Marheh was not his problem just now. He made an effort to return his thoughts to Miles and Poppy. They were his problem and one for which he could find no easy solution. He wondered who else they had injured at Samuel's behest and whether they could be encouraged to take responsibility for their actions and even perhaps attempt some restitution. Should Poppy and Marheh meet? Would that be asking too much of Marheh? Miles seemed to have a conscience though it was well hidden.

He found that he had walked all around the extensive garden without achieving any real plan. He was just making for a conveniently placed seat when the chauffeur emerged from the stables and came towards him. He waited, wondering about the man, and greeted him in his usual easy manner as he came nearer.

"You seem to be making rather a lot of decisions about the place," the man said. "What's going on?"

"I can see you must be wondering," Jik replied. "But surely you must have wondered before this."

"That Ess?" The man shrugged. "Knew better than to try his tricks with me. I do my work and keep out of the way."

"But now you're asking questions," Jik pointed out.

"Yes well…"

He kicked a little at a tufty weed in the path. Jik waited.

"Those two kids, Miles and Poppy, they weren't so bad before he got to them. Poppy was a cracking rider, but he couldn't ride so she gave it up."

Jik strolled towards the seat, the chauffeur walking beside him.

"Are there still horses she could ride?"

"Her two favourites are still here, but she doesn't come near them now. I give them a bit of attention when I can."

The two men sat and surveyed the Manor.

"The boy you call Ess will not be back," Jik said at last. "Miles and Poppy will need help to reclaim their lives though."

The man sat up straighter, turned to Jik.

"That's the best bit of news I've had in quite a while. How did you manage it?"

"I didn't really. I'm just here to pick up the pieces."

Another silence as Jik thought of Marheh as he had last seen her, grey with fatigue, struggling to conceal that she was in pain.

"I let a girl into the house this morning?" The man made it a question.

"Did you?"

"A dark girl, in trousers."

"Yes. My niece. She fought with him."

"Right," the man said, having spent some minutes assimilating this. "And she was the one I took away again yesterday.

Jik nodded.

"Miss Poppy will need something to interest her and it had better be the horses." He stood up. "I'll see what can be done."

Jik looked after him as he headed back towards the stables. People were often surprising, he thought, pleased to find another supporter in this unexpected guise. He stood up and made his way back inside, assessing his plans for the day and wondering whether he could fit in a visit to *Autumn Wind*.

Marheh drifted out of sleep, lying for sometime in a halfway place where she was held lightly in a loving embrace. Inevitably though, thoughts of Samuel pushed into her peacefulness. Nemle and Sul were asking too much of her. She couldn't make herself care about him and she would have to care to be able to do what they wanted. But she was Silberay wasn't she, even if she felt herself a failure as an apprentice. Her thoughts went round and round but this time she was not fighting against them and they seemed to be leading her somewhere.

Abruptly she pushed back the covers wincing a little as the burn reacted to her movement. She thrust her feet into slippers and grabbed her shawl. A few moments later Nemle looked up from her work to see Marheh's feet, her slim, bony ankles, the hem of a plain white nightdress moving past the window towards *Storm Cloud*.

She put down her tools with an exclamation of surprise.

"Leave her be," she admonished herself. "She is old enough to make her own decisions."

So she waited, unable to return to work or to keep from anxious wondering.

After perhaps half an hour she could wait no longer. She made her way out of *Day Bringer* and along to *Storm Cloud*. She knocked lightly on the roof and entered the back cabin without waiting for a response. Marheh was standing looking at Samuel where he lay on the bunk.

"From the first moment we met, he made me uneasy," she said quietly without taking her eyes off him. "He knew what he was doing too. He was pleased when I was punished for standing up for Trodkali and you know how he struck me with SP's walking stick."

Nemle stood on the bottom step looking first at Samuel then back at Marheh.

"He looks harmless now, even peaceful... just nothing really." She paused but still did not look at Nemle. "I'd all but forgotten him, but he hadn't forgotten me. I thought I was helping him then but he perceived that as injury. Six years of planning, acting, working for revenge. It seems incomprehensible really."

She stopped again and this time looked directly at Nemle.

"And you and Sul expect me to unearth what is left of his soul."

"Yes," Nemle said dropping the word into the stillness, unaccented, expressionless, just the sound, like a single drumbeat and like the drumbeat it seemed to linger in the small cabin carried on the air.

It was a long time before she moved and then it was as if some essential life force had leaked away.

"I can't Nemle," she said, her voice flat and expressionless.

Then she turned and left.

She looked not just weary but defeated. Nemle bit back a cry of concern and hovered uncertainly in the small space not sure whether to go after her. She chose in the end to return to *Day Bringer* via the well deck and her own cabin. She would have liked to visit with Sul and have him share her concern but understood that Marheh would find this a betrayal.

Marheh felt *Day Bringer* respond to Nemle's return, noticed she had taken the more difficult route and made a face. Obviously she was to be left alone to contemplate her misdeeds. Well it was no good. She couldn't do it. She knew the theory. If there was even a tiny grain of goodness that had been Samuel's buried soul then it could be added to the sum of good in the world and he would live through that grain though his mind and body would die. She knew the theory, but she couldn't find it in herself to care or even to believe there was anything to find if she did care.

She stood in the centre of her cabin. The little space that had once seemed to fit her like the shell fit the snail now seemed like a prison. Maybe she would have to leave the Silberay only that was what Samuel had desired. She swayed a little and fell to her knees beside her bunk. If only she didn't hurt so much perhaps she would be able to think better. Nothing Samuel could do would force her from the water road, nothing. She crawled onto her bunk and lay face down. Sul had told her Samuel was defeated, but here he was again, still tormenting her. How could she possibly love him enough to uncover his soul?

When Jik arrived she woke, cold, hurting and a little disoriented. He stood on the bottom step looking down at her. His head nearly touched the ceiling, his broad shoulders seemed as wide as the doorway and his warmth filled the cabin.

"Jik!"

"You look like six pennyworth of God help us," he said. "What's the matter, Nemle been beating you?"

She struggled out of the bunk and into his embrace. He held her close for a

239

few moments then put her away from him.

"Where's Marheh the great?" he said, giving her a little shake.

"Who's she?"

"As bad as that is it? Have you eaten today?"

"Not really."

"No wonder you look like something that's been left out in the rain."

Marheh managed a smile at that and allowed him to turn her around and propel her towards the galley.

"I was only thinking you must be getting hungry," Nemle said.

Her smile welcomed them both.

"Will you join us?"

Jik shook his head. "I had a big breakfast and a bigger lunch and I can't stay long, but I'd love some sperit. They don't know about sperit at the Manor."

Marheh watched for a minute as Nemle got up and began to ladle stew into bowls. Then she gave a little sigh and tried to wriggle out of Jik's firm hands to go back to her cabin.

"Food first," he said, guiding her to the table. "And don't you want to hear what's been happening at the Manor?"

She glared at him.

"Stop humouring me. You're treating me like a child."

He raised his eyebrows and looked at her with affectionate reproach. She continued to glare, angry and sore, then drooped suddenly.

"And I'm behaving like one I know, but I can't do it."

"Well if you can't, you can't," he said. "Whatever 'it' is. No need to starve yourself, or get in a pet about it."

Nemle laughed.

"I haven't heard that expression for years."

She handed him a mug of sperit.

"My grandmother used to say it when I was a small boy fretting over some imagined wrong. No need to get in a pet, she'd say comfortably and you could see at once she was right."

"My Great Grandmother?" Marheh asked, interested in spite of herself.

"One of them," Jik said.

Nemle handed Marheh a bowl of stew and a big slice of buttered bread.

"It must have been nice to have a grandmother, I never knew mine" she said and went back to the galley for her own food.

When she was settled at the table opposite Marheh Jik perched on the folding stool between them and began to tell them about his day at the Manor, about Miles, Poppy and Aunt Phyllis and about his talk with Jonathan the chauffeur. Marheh listened and ate her stew and felt better.

After about twenty minutes Jik put down his mug and stood up to go.

"Things are working out better than I expected," he said. "But it will be a couple more days before I can come back to *Autumn Wind*. Having the motor is a great help. Jonathan says he is happy to drive any time. I've asked if he will take Samuel to Haven Cottage."

"When?" Marheh asked abruptly, thrust back to her dilemma.

"Two or three days I think."

Jik appeared not to notice the change in her manner.

"It will be at least that long before we can arrange the ceremony for Hud and the motor can't be spared for long until that's over."

He looked from one to the other.

"Can you manage Samuel for that long? I know it's a lot to expect."

"I'm sure we can," Nemle said, careful not to look at Marheh. "Sul's been doing it all up to now, but we ought to help."

"I'll be off then."

He kissed Nemle and waited while Marheh got up for a hug.

"Thanks for the sperit. I hope to be back to sleep tomorrow night, but anyway I'll come and visit."

When he had gone Nemle and Marheh sat in silence for some time. Then

Marheh looked at Nemle and saw that there was not condemnation only loving concern. She wriggled uncomfortably.

"Don't look at me like that."

"It's hard not to when I know you're hurting."

Marheh rehearsed a couple of responses in her head but they sounded childish and ungrateful so she said nothing.

"Why don't I change the dressing then you can have a wash and put on a clean nightdress. I'll brush your hair for you if you like."

Another difficult silence then Marheh said abruptly. "You're too nice to me. It just makes me worse."

Nemle laughed. "I'll wallop you if you prefer, but changing the dressing will be quite enough to bear I think."

Marheh's brown eyes studied Nemle's face for a few moments then she drained the last of her sperit and stood up.

"Let's get it over with then," she said.

The next couple of days were not easy. Nemle felt as if she was treading on egg shells she was being so careful in her dealings with Marheh who knew she was being humoured and resented it. She longed to be able to walk off her mood and work out her muddled thoughts instead of feeling confined and cosseted. She wanted to hit someone or something and caught herself on the edge of snapping at Nemle. The burn still needed dressing night and morning, but it was not as painful as it had been and she was able at least to dress.

She couldn't prevent her thoughts returning again and again to Samuel. Not just the expectation Nemle and Sul had of her but the actual battle and the sense that she had that Samuel had drawn on strength beyond himself.

At last she brought herself to speak of it to Nemle.

"Samuel spent some time at the Harbour after he left Kel and Sul, didn't he?" she said, carefully examining the plate she was washing so as not to look at Nemle.

"Close to three months I think," Nemle said, wondering what was coming.

"You remember how we left the part of SP's mind that could see the water road there for safe keeping?"

"Yes."

"I think Samuel found it and took it into himself. That's why he could do all that stuff – the poison in Daniel, the illusion of my hands – that's why he thought he could do it with me."

Nemle stood in silence, tea towel forgotten, thinking about what she had said.

"You think Samuel was drawing on SP's ability?" she asked at last, turning Marheh towards her to look into her face.

"Yes," she said. "Yes I do."

She swept the remaining dishes into the sink heedless of the possibility of breakages.

"Now you can go and tell Sul I'm crazy as well as disobedient."

She dropped in the dish mop after the dishes and turned as if to go but Nemle was in her way, holding her firmly.

"Not crazy and certainly not disobedient and I don't discuss you with Sul."

Marheh stared at her fiercely for a moment then slumped wearily.

"I know that really," she said. "Oh Nemle – what's the matter with me?"

Nemle held her and did not answer.

Kel and Jik both visited in the motor during the waiting and this lightened the atmosphere a little.

It was during Kel's second visit that Marheh went with him to *Storm Cloud* at a time when Sul was with Samuel. He was controlling the movements of Samuel's hand and mouth as he drank from a cup of sperit. He looked tired and Marheh felt another stab of guilt knowing this was something she could do. She turned away quickly, but the image of the fair young man and his weary carer would not be put aside.

When Kel had gone she walked a little way along the path beside the water road until she was out of sight of the boats then she sat down on the grass and looked out over the fields. What Sul was doing was the kind of thing she had helped with at Haven Cottage. She was quite capable of helping with Samuel. It wouldn't be for long. He would be taken away in a few days. She need never see him or think of him again. She had defeated him. Why didn't she feel triumphant? Nemle and Sul had spoiled any triumph she might have felt. They were asking the impossible. Samuel didn't deserve any consideration from her and she wasn't a bit like him whatever Nemle said.

She bit her lip and sighed, closed her eyes for a moment and pictured the home she had not seen for three years. Her parents had been proud of her decision to become apprenticed to the Silberay though it meant she would seldom see them in the future. The active pursuit of goodness and beauty had seemed like a shining jewel, beckoning, full of promise when she had chosen it, but it was a chimera, a child's dream of chivalry and romance.

She stood up and began to walk back to *Day Bringer*. She would leave the water road, she decided. The reality would never be equal to her dream. In the meantime, she supposed, she had better offer to help with Samuel. She could do that much even if she couldn't do what they really wanted. But when she made her offer Nemle smiled and thanked her and refused it.

"Sul and I can manage. It's not for long. I know how difficult it would be for you." She said, and perversely Marheh resented this consideration.

The next day Kel had come with Jonathan in the motor to take them all to Market Mondborough to attend the short ceremony for Hud. Jik had arranged it, a simplified version of the crossing ceremony that would take place at the Harbour next Gathering.

The undertaker had provided them with a space, a small, plain room, but quiet. The unadorned wooden coffin that held Hud's body rested on a low table and the five Silberay stood around it. Marheh stood between Jik and Kel, Nemle and Sul stood opposite. Nemle looked old, tired and sad. Marheh remembered anew that she was seventy six and the events of the last few weeks had taken their toll. Normally she always seemed to Marheh to be ageless.

The two mentors placed their hands on the coffin, palms down and waited a minute in silence. Then Nemle began to sing, introducing the refrain of a Silberay death song. One by one the others joined her until they were all singing softly. As the refrain began again Sul spoke over the music.

"Hud, you wanted to be wise, now you have left folly behind."

Marheh, still singing quietly, thought how carefully truthful Sul's words had been. Both Nemle and Jik spoke in turn out of their knowledge of him. Kel simply said goodbye. Then it was Marheh's turn. The song pulsed gently beneath her thoughts like a quiet engine moving her along. She knew it would be enough for the ceremony if she simply said goodbye as Kel had done, but it did not seem enough for her. The refrain continued as she tried to put thought into words. Sorrow, forgiveness and gratitude, how could she express these? At last she spoke, short, difficult sentences.

"I'm sorry we clashed. I won't remember the hurt. I'm grateful for my life. Goodbye Hud."

The song continued and she joined it again feeling as if some hardness had eased within her so that it was only right and natural when this song of voice and heart lifted them together into the soul song.

They did not spend long there, but long enough for her to understand that Hud's song, unpractised, undeveloped though it was, added to the richness of their harmony and, when they left again it did not leave with them.

The motor took Sul and Nemle back to the boats, but she chose to walk with Jik and Kel. Walking always seemed to oil thought and she was very quiet as they went through the town and down the long lane to the water road. She did not even notice that Jik and Kel had tempered their pace to hers, something she would normally have resented. Jik and Kel would sleep on their boats tonight and tomorrow the motor would come for Samuel.

When they arrived back at the boats they found that Nemle and Sul had prepared a special meal for them all on *Day Bringer*. Their time together was nearly at an end. Once Samuel had been safely deposited at Haven Cottage they would separate. *Day Bringer* would continue on while *Storm Cloud* and *Autumn Wind* would go back and resume their assigned routes. Marheh thought how generous they had been, dropping everything to support her and Nemle and see she was protected and vindicated. But it was all wasted, because she was going to leave the water road, wasn't she?

She thought of the choice she had dedicated herself to when she became apprenticed, she thought back over the good times, the times when she had felt uplifted and confirmed in the life she had chosen.

The meal was over, but no one wanted to leave. Nemle brought out cheese and chocolates and her own elderberry wine. The old ones reminisced. She and Kel listened and questioned. This was her life. She couldn't leave it.

She excused herself and made her way quietly through to her cabin. *Day Bringer* was already moving in the water as the others changed position or went to replenish a glass. They wouldn't notice if she left. The curtains were drawn against the evening dark. They wouldn't see her go past.

Quickly and quietly she boarded *Storm Cloud* and went into the back cabin. The curtains were not drawn and the window made a lighter patch of grey but the bunk was shadowy and dark. She reached towards the place where she would have kept her candle and found Kel's with matches beside. Carefully she lit the candle. Flickering shadows played around her. She moved it, placed it where it softly illuminated the still figure on the bunk. Then she studied the blank, youthful face.

Was Nemle right when she had suggested they might be alike underneath? Was there any buried soul for her to find if she allowed herself to look?

Once before she had searched for a Yareblis soul. She knew she would have to enter Samuel's damaged mind and from there sing her own soul song, but that would only be the beginning and even for this she would need to banish every feeling except compassion for the starved, neglected soul that was the essence of Samuel.

She lowered herself to the floor to sit cross-legged beside the bunk. Deliberately she acknowledged the pain in her back then put it aside. She felt a moment of fear as she began to approach Samuel's mind even though she knew he could no longer harm her. There was scarcely any resistance as she entered, a tiny fluttering pulse beat for a moment somewhere within the desolation then was still. She allowed her mind to spread into his then began to seek her portal to the soul song.

For a time her candle flame flickered and spluttered and refused her entry, but she persisted and at last knew she was singing.

Singing into nothing.

The golden light that accompanied her song disappeared into a vacuum and was lost almost at the moment of production. The song flowed out of her until she felt herself emptied of all light, all warmth, all hope. Still she kept singing, no longer light but tears, bitter, sorrowing tears for something lost, imprisoned, denied existence.

Was it herself, buried there where the tears gathered?

Something was buried, drawing her tears to itself. The singing hurt now as if the song was wrenched from her note by note, tear by tear, but she could not stop for where her tears gathered, nothing began to seem like something, a cloudy darkness that softened as she poured herself out. Almost hidden in the cloud was a tiny spark.

There was joy in the discovery and light amongst her tears and the light and the tears mingled to nourish and uncover the spark.

After that, she told Nemle later, after that it was just like polishing a piece of long neglected brass. Hard rubbing, dirty hands, but something to show at the end of it.

Initially the others did not realise Marheh had left them. It was Jik who first expressed concern, but Nemle shook her head when he suggested looking for her.

"Not yet," she said. "She has a hard decision she needs to make."

She longed to go to her, or at least to enter the discipline of the soul and sing with her, but she knew she must not, that she must give Marheh the chance to choose what she would do and to act alone.

An hour, more than an hour went past. It seemed an eternity to Nemle as she waited and the others, despite their cheerful conviviality could not really distract her from thoughts of Marheh. Rigorously she had kept herself away from even a hint of mental probing or from the soul song, but at last she could bear it no longer.

"She will be with Samuel," she said to Jik. "If she has done the work we asked of her she will be exhausted."

Jik nodded and departed.

When he pushed open the door to *Storm Cloud*'s back cabin Kel's candle flickered and went out, but the moment of light had shown him Marheh, slumped on the cabin floor. Carefully he descended, crouched beside her, lifted her in his arms. She made a little sound between a snort and a sigh and he realised that she was sleeping. As he carried her to *Day Bringer* she opened her eyes and muttered his name, but did not really emerge from the place where she was. He laid her on her bunk, knelt to remove her boots then drew a blanket over her and went to report to Nemle.

Next morning at dawn, Nemle was wakened by a strange sound on *Day Bringer*'s roof. Too rhythmic and heavy to be the slap of duck's webbed feet, she could not imagine what it might be. Bleary-eyed, more curious than anxious, she struggled out of bed and opened the door into the well deck. There on the roof was Marheh, dancing to the wakening sun. The slap of her bare feet provided the rhythm for her movement, her arms reached out to embrace the world, her face was intent, uplifted.

After the first moment of surprise Nemle knew this was not something she should be watching. She went back to bed, rather reluctantly, closed her eyes and at length fell asleep again as the sounds of Marheh's celebration beat into the fabric of *Day Bringer*'s being.

ABOUT THE AUTHOR

Rosalind, like many Australians, loves to travel. She fell in love with the canals of England during her first visit there and this has remained a life-long passion. She spent nearly three years living and traveling aboard a 37ft narrowboat and this experience has informed her writing so that although the stories are fantasy the boating experience is authentic.

When not writing she enjoys walking her dog, practicing her violin, painting watercolours, choral singing, reading and of course traveling.

Marheh can be contacted at Marheh@gmail.com